Praise for other Elna Holst Books

Lucas

"There was an excellent balance of romance, passion, drama and humor. It was engaging from start to finish and I completely fell in love with the book and will re-read it many times." — LezReviewBooks.com

"This is 249 pages of beautiful writing. [Lucas]'s structure and form are opulently crafted. Its text is written so elegantly, it nearly sings... This is a book for people who love to read, especially those who love the classics." — The Lesbian Book Blog

"This is a wonderful book (with plenty of steaminess) written with exceptional art and craft." — Best Lesfic Reviews

"The writing is strictly phenomenal... If you are a fan of historical fiction, *Pride and Prejudice*, or just a good love story, then *Lucas* will not disappoint you." — The Lesbian 52

"I was on the edge of my seat for a good 50% of the book." — Kissing Backwards: Lesbian Literature Reviews

In the Palm

"This story got me in the palm of its hand... it's got everything in one well-written package: adventure, mystery, and romance." — LezReviewBooks.com

"Castaway with a companion and better ending." — Goodreads reviewer

"Who doesn't like a book that makes you laugh out loud one moment and then burst into tears the next?" — Goodreads reviewer

"I loved how dark the beginning of the book was, how vivid and painful the imagery got, how intense the MC's situation is." — Amazon reviewer

For the space of a breath or two, that wolf had entranced her, mesmerised her, made her believe—the impossible. And that was all it took.

Nothing about this wolf was as it should be.

Pyotra Nikolayevna Kulakova lives in a small Russian settlement in the northern Siberian taiga, where the polar night lasts for a good month out of the year and the temperature rarely reaches above freezing point. Pyotra's days, too, seem congealed and unchanging, laden with grief, until her baby brother's close encounter with a tundra wolf upends the lives of the three members of the Kulakov family in one fell swoop.

Pyotra and the Wolf is a queer retelling of Sergei Prokofiev's symphonic fairy tale, structurally influenced by matryoshka dolls and memory castles. This is a story of darkness and light, love and loss, beast and human. Whichever way the spinning kopek falls.

PYOTRA AND THE WOLF

Elna Holst

A NineStar Press Publication

www.ninestarpress.com

Pyotra and the Wolf

Printed in the USA

ISBN: 978-1-64890-194-2

First Edition, January, 2021

Also available in eBook, ISBN: 978-1-64890-193-5

WARNING:

This book contains sexually explicit content, which may only be suitable for mature readers. Depictions of graphic violence.

For my little duck

"The forest had found a tongue, and the hounds were burning as with fire."

> —Russian proverb / Lev Tolstoy, *Childhood* (1852, transl. by C.J. Hogarth)

"And, still but little reassured, mine eyes

Saw Beatrice turned round towards the monster,

That is one person only in two natures."

> —Dante Alighieri, *The Divine Comedy* (1320, transl. by Longfellow, 1867)

Part One

Prologue

On the day that was to change the lives of the three remaining members of the Kulakov family forever, it was night. Pyotra Nikolayevna Kulakova lived with her grandfather and younger brother outside a minuscule Russian settlement in the northern Siberian snow forest, where the polar night lasts for a good month out of the year. According to the unsmiling face of the clock on the wall on Boris Ilyich's *izba*, however, it was in the early hours of the morning that Pyotra pushed her weight against the door, caught between the dread of the freezing cold without and staying trapped inside, unable to procure sustenance for the two men under her care.

Her brother, it might be argued, was too young to be called a man, and her *dedushka* was worn and grey, an old curmudgeon who had lost his eyesight, if not his wits. Pyotra loved them dearly, desperately, with the parentless child's determination to cling to what has been left her. Boris, in turn, doted upon his grandchildren: Pyotra, the twenty-two-year-old, and Sergei, nearly twelve. Not that he ever told them as much. It was not his way.

Pyotra sighed as the door refused to budge. A metre of snow had fallen while they slept. "Come help me, duckling, if you want to see the sun again."

Sergei made a noise through his nose. He sat by the fireplace, fiddling with his tackle, oiling his rod, making sure the lines were not tangled. It was a new favourite pastime of his. Lately, he had taken it into his head that he was to be the future provider of the family. Pyotra assumed it was a notion he had picked up at the village school. Their father had never been much of a provider; he had made sure he had his vodka, and that was that. Sergei was too young to remember.

"There won't be any sun for another week or so," he replied, holding his rod up for inspection. "And stop calling me 'duck.'"

Pyotra hid a smile. She was by no means ready to let go of her private memory of Sergei taking his first waddling steps towards her, as their mother, Serafima, gasped, "Look, look who's walking. My little duck!"

It was all that Serafima Anatoliyevna had left her offspring; that and her grey-blue eyes, her peculiar-coloured curls, and her steely resolve to survive, to thrive, even in the most austere and unforgiving corner of the world.

Except, she hadn't. She had walked out into the Arctic night, only to be brought back by a search party a few days later. Parts of her, at least. Bones, hair, ravaged flesh, the gold wedding band by which she had been identified. *Attacked by a pack of wolves* was the universal verdict. Their father could not cope, it was likewise said; he drowned his sorrows in liquid comfort and went down with it.

And then they were three.

Pyotra Nikolayevna had never been able to forgive her parents for dying. But she could not give up on their little duck, bright-eyed and pink-faced, holding his chubby arms out to her as if she was the centre and epitome of existence.

His arms were not that chubby any more, but still.

At the table, Boris moved uneasily, his unseeing eyes directed towards the unflinching darkness of their one grimy window to the outside world.

"Let it be, Pyotrushka," he burred, winding his fingers through his beard. "There's an ill wind blowing. It smells like...wolf."

Pyotra clicked her tongue. Shaking her head at her grandfather would be a waste of energy better employed in breaking out of the snowed-in log cabin. "For pity's sake, Ded. This isn't the nineteenth century, nor even the twentieth. The weather holds no omens to be deciphered. If you smell something off, it's probably Sergei."

"*Ey*!" Her brother looked up at her for the first time, adorably affronted.

Pyotra winked at him and turned to give the door another mighty shove. It cracked open a centimetre or two, a small avalanche of fresh snow tumbling in through the opening.

"Bring me the spade and the bucket, duck," she called over her shoulder to Sergei, her tone of voice forestalling opposition.

As she started shovelling, clearing a passage out at less than a snail's pace across a rugged cliff, Pyotra Kulakova sighed anew. This was going to be one long day, irrespective of the lack of sunlight.

*

It was past noon before Pyotra and Sergei—who eventually grew bored with his own resistance—had managed to come as far as to the communal road leading down to the village, which had been cleared by the local snow removal team. Pyotra took one look at Sergei's blanched face and sent him back to fill up the samovar for Boris, while she proceeded down to the one shop within an eighty-kilometre radius.

"I will be back in a couple of hours," she told him, pinching some warmth into his cheeks. "Don't do anything stupid, please."

"I'm not the stupid one." Sergei stuck out his tongue and batted her hands away. "That hurts!"

"Not as much as frostbite, let me tell you. Or better yet, let Dedushka tell you. That'll keep you both occupied."

With a rude sign—another new trick they had that eminent educational institution to thank for—Sergei ran back to the alluring warmth of the hearth. Watching him go, Pyotra felt a sting of loneliness. Of loneliness, but also of the constant worry that came over her whenever she had to leave him, leave them both. Since her father's earthly remains had been lowered into the ground to join her mother's, two years after their first, gut-wrenching loss, Pyotra Nikolayevna had lived with a droning terror at the back of her mind, which she hadn't any better name for than Things Could Happen. The namelessness of it only served to magnify her dread.

Shaking herself, Pyotra straightened her headband torch, hiked her empty rucksack higher onto her shoulders, and set off.

*

Mariya Petrovna Leonova's shop lay in a squat, rectangular building encased in corrugated iron, the word магазин painted in red along its side. Mashka was no artist, but she got her message across.

Business had been good to her over the years; she could easily have invested in a new sign, less motley shelves, and a sturdier floor inside. But being Mashka, she had invested in her twin passions: Persian cats and budgerigars. How she kept them alive in the relentlessness of the Siberian deep-freeze—fifteen or so cats and twice as many budgies—was a mystery that no one in the village had solved yet. She kept herself to herself, did Mashka Petrovna. Although, unmarried and unbothered, she had always had a good eye to Boris Kulakov.

"And how is your grandfather?" the shop owner par excellence called out as soon as Pyotra entered.

Pyotra paused to kick the excess snow off her boots. It was Mashka's standard mode of greeting, picking up as if they had been interrupted in their last conversation for a few minutes, when in reality it was a matter of weeks, sometimes an entire month.

Apart from her own two legs, Pyotra had no means of transportation, but she had a strong enough back that she could carry several weeks' worth of provisions for the two-hour hike. Conveniently, as they would otherwise have had to rely on Mashka's delivery service, which entailed having to deal with Mashka's toothy-grinned nephew Dmitri, whizzing around on his snowmobile. Pyotra had tried that when Boris had been down with pneumonia and she had been reluctant to leave the house for four hours in one go. Never again.

"Boris is Boris, Mashka," she replied. She was at times tempted to add he sent his love. Her grandfather would do no such thing, however.

"The widow Tsvetayeva has gone and got herself married again, to a man fifteen years her junior. I tell you, what is the world coming to?" Mashka put her knuckles to her hips, head tipped back in disgust.

"Love is love," Pyotra turned her back on the *magazin* owner, busying herself with picking through Mashka's scant supply of tinned vegetables. Peas and carrots. Carrots. More peas.

"It's unseemly is what it is," Mashka continued, unperturbed. She sniffed in disapproval. "She never had a decent bone in her body, that one. Did I tell you she was after your ded in our youth?"

"You may have mentioned it." Pyotra sniggered soundlessly among the sacks of flour. She hefted one into her trolley, followed by three jars of pickled beetroots. Sergei needed his vitamins.

"Lucky he already had his eyes set on your grandmother. She was a saint of a woman. How she could have had a son like—" Mashka broke off, wisely. However much Pyotra Kulakova privately resented her father, she did not suffer others to speak ill of him. He had been unwell, a sickness of the soul, of the mind. Of the heart, if Pyotra were to be honest. She could understand, even if she could not pardon.

"I have something for that brother of yours." Animated by the idea of a possible upsell, Mashka rose to her toes—no mean feat for a woman in her seventies—and picked a green box covered with a lid of transparent plastic from a shelf behind the counter. The sharp points of the fishing hooks inside each compartment glittered under the fluorescent light. "Special delivery from Arkhangelsk," Mashka crooned, sweeping her gnarled fingers over the box as if she were performing a conjuring trick. "Prime steel."

Pyotra shook her head, not deigning to look closer at the offering. Mashka Petrovna knew the weak spots of all her customers. "It's not his birthday for a few months yet. We couldn't afford it."

Mashka tsked. "These beauties pay for themselves. You'll have fish on the table every day, guaranteed. Between us, I'll give you a good price. You could pay in instalments. Just don't tell anyone—apart from Boris, of course. You tell your grandfather everything, I know. You're a good girl, Pyotra."

"We can't afford it," Pyotra reiterated, fixing her gaze on a faded poster to Mashka's right. It showed a man in grey overalls admiring the exaggerated bulge of his bicep, and above him, radiant as the sun: an orange. Her mouth watered. "We'll have some frozen orange juice."

Mashka peeked up at her, a canny expression in her watery eyes. "Three cartons for the price of two?"

Pyotra gave a brief nod, feeling hooked, lined, and sinkered. It was the one luxury item she fell for, same deal every time.

*

She wished she could have bought those hooks for Sergei. Mashka would probably have been as good as her word and given her a fair price, if only to keep herself in the imaginary good books of Boris Ilyich. But Pyotra didn't like to encourage him—Sergei, that was—in this newfound pursuit of his. He would freeze his digits off if he kept out at all hours. And he wasn't as strong as he liked to think; what if the fish dragged him down through the hole in the ice, pulling him into the frigid water, and Pyotra wasn't there to help? She couldn't be there all the time. There were things she needed to do. And what if Boris couldn't hear him; what if Sergei's lungs were too shocked from the cold to scream, and—

Pyotra pushed a fist into her chest, trying to knock her wildly beating heart into adopting a more sedate rhythm. The rucksack felt like so much lead on her shoulders. The light from her torch skittered along the glacial road.

"He's not allowed to go out on his own," she reminded herself out loud. "He wouldn't."

The firs surrounding her on her homeward stretch stood mute, unwilling to echo her reassurances back at her. Their silence seemed a contradiction in its own right: *Wouldn't he, Pyotra Kulakova? Don't you know your little duck?*

A howl tore up the preternatural quiet, and Pyotra was running—never mind the weight on her back, the distance left to cover—because she knew, in her bones she knew the answers to those questions. She did know Sergei. He would.

As she turned the corner onto what they called their 'meadow,' a clearing with a small pond and a larch bending over it, Pyotra Nikolayevna Kulakova's worst nightmares seemed to have come true in one fell swoop: the tail and hindquarters of a huge, menacing beast were sticking out of a hole in the ice—the hole she herself had assisted Sergei in drilling two days ago, and which, with the stubbornness of the almost twelve-year-old, he would have been able to reopen himself, given enough time. Say, three hours or so. While Pyotra—

The front of the wolf resurfaced, and in its maw: Sergei.

Pyotra let her rucksack thud onto the tightly packed snow and drew out her father's rifle, long in disuse, but—

she prayed to the saints, the angels, Baba Yaga, anyone within hearing range—still loaded.

The dripping wolf was dragging the lax body of her brother onto the ice, sniffing him, fangs exposed.

Pyotra cocked her rifle.

The head of the wolf snapped up.

Chapter One

They stared at each other, Pyotra and the wolf. The rifle shook in her hands. She had only rarely used it to shoot at another living, breathing being, irrespective of what malevolent creature of the night had skirted the sideboards of their diminutive abode. It wasn't that she was against the killing of animals; she ate the game the local hunters peddled from door to door, and after what had happened to Serafima...

But there was something strange about this wolf. As she gazed deep into its black eyes—*Black eyes*, she would think to herself later, *are wolves even supposed to have black eyes?*—she could swear she saw a spark of intelligence there, something not merely of canine cunning, but of cognisance.

The wolf angled its head and lifted one paw in what came eerily close to a human gesture of supplication. As Pyotra's finger eased from the trigger, it backed off, slowly, still keeping her rooted to where she was standing with those indomitable eyes.

It would soon be out of the reach of her torchlight.

Pyotra lowered the rifle, straining her eyes to catch a last glimpse of the beast as it turned and scampered away: it had a white ring around its tail.

And then it was gone.

With a harrowing cry, Pyotra Nikolayevna brought herself back to reality, rushing up to Sergei's lifeless body, so still—too still—on the ice. She blew air between his bluish lips, massaged his chest, ranting and raving like a madwoman until finally, miraculously, the boy gasped and she turned him on his side, letting him hurl up the stinging water that had got into his lungs, his stomach, and she knew not where.

All she knew was that he was alive, if only just: her brother, Sergei. Her duck.

She scooped him into her arms as though he weighed no more than a snowflake in his soaked-through clothes, and that was when she registered it: the torn skin, the deep, blood-filled marks around his neck where the wolf's teeth had sunk in.

Pyotra Nikolayevna Kulakova's mind went red.

*

"This is a bad idea, Pyotrushka." Boris sat on a stool by Sergei's cot, holding his small hand between both of his, his head rotated in Pyotra's direction.

She stopped and studied the deep furrows across his forehead, the lines of cares past and present down his liver-spotted cheeks.

She had called Mashka the night before, after they had made sure Sergei wasn't in any imminent danger. He looked shivery and drawn. He didn't speak to Pyotra. He didn't have to. She could see the haunted look of contrition in his eyes.

Dima would be up with the local nurse-cum-midwife in less than an hour to examine his wounds. Pyotra planned to be gone before then. She didn't need the airhead Dima's input on her scheme, and she didn't need the nurse to tell her Sergei's wounds weren't life-threatening.

She had arrived in the nick of time. What if she hadn't? What then?

You didn't let a wolf that had acquired a taste for human blood run loose.

How could she have been so stupid? What had possessed her? *A wolf with human eyes.* Sergei—any of the children in the settlement—would never be safe as long as that man-biting beast was free to roam the land.

Pyotra remembered how the pack suspected of mauling her mother had been hunted down and extinguished, one after the other. She'd had this demon within shooting range. She had failed her brother. She had failed the village as a whole.

Well, she wouldn't fail twice.

"Take care of Sergei, Dedushka. And take care of yourself, please. No going outside unless it's an emergency. Don't let him out of earshot, you hear? I'll be back before long."

"Pyotra, there are real huntsmen out there. Let them take care of this business. That wolf will be tracked and killed soon enough. This is madness; it's not your responsibility." His voice had risen from his usual timbre, making him sound like a raspy bassoon. Pyotra had made up her mind, however. She tightened the straps of her rucksack, revelling in the weight of the newly oiled and reloaded rifle at her side.

"You're wrong, Ded," she answered softly, as she pulled open the door to step outside. "This is my wolf."

*

And that was how Pyotra Nikolayevna, less than twelve hours after her baby brother had been plucked out of the pond by a wild wolf, found herself in the northern Siberian taiga, alone with her gun and her thoughts.

She cringed at her dramatic exit. The truth was, she couldn't rightly say why she felt it incumbent upon her to track down the animal—except that it had tricked her.

For one fleeting moment, that wolf had made her believe in things that did not exist; it had made her feel that it was, essentially, a benevolent spirit, appearing out of nowhere to preserve Sergei in his hour of need.

A wolf! Pyotra shook her head as she trudged through the untrodden snow—or nearly untrodden. By the light of her LED torch, she could make out the prints of swift paws, heading in a north-easterly direction. Heading, she realised, with a sinking feeling in her guts, towards the tundra.

Benevolent spirits did not leave tracks. And they certainly did not leave the imprints of their vicious fangs on the necks of defenceless children. With her fur-lined mitten, Pyotra swiped at her treacherous eyes. She had made a complete fool of herself.

Tomorrow, when the hunting team saw fit to go out, these tracks could be snowed over. The trail would be cold, but to them it wouldn't matter; they would chance upon some unlucky beast or other, a convenient scapegoat, while the real perpetrator—the wolf with the white ring around its tail—would have long since made its escape.

They would scoff at her protestations: a wolf with a ring around its tail? Did it by any chance have a horn on its forehead, too, little bat wings all along its back? Trust women!

If they had done their job, this wouldn't be happening again.

And if she hadn't insisted on going off for groceries herself...

Pyotra gripped the strap of her father's rifle tighter. She would hunt down this wolf, and she would exact her revenge: for Sergei, for Sima, for everything.

Who knew but that the beast itself had crept up on her brother and scared him so that he had ended up in the water? Never in all her life had she heard about a wolf rescuing a human from drowning out of the goodness of its animal heart.

A thud to her right had Pyotra close to jumping out of her own skin. She crouched down, fumbling for her rifle, her ears ringing in the sudden quiet. As she waited, Pyotra cocked her weapon, not daring to hope her prey would be whimsical enough to come running into the circle of light before her. The 'real huntsmen' had night-vision scopes, or there would be little doing for them the greater part of the year. Pyotra had no such luxuries. She carried arms strictly for her own protection, the instinct ingrained in her from her father, her father's father, back to the days of Ivan the Terrible. Boris had only relinquished his own antiquated piece once his eyes were so clouded over he couldn't tell friend from foe.

Nothing happened.

Pyotra was on the point of standing up when a fur-covered something darted out in front of her, and she pulled the trigger, reflexively, the recoil buffeting her shoulder with enough force to make her cry out loud from the stab of pain.

Blinking away her tears, she scrambled to her feet, hobbling to where the something had fallen to the ground. A clean, instant kill, she noted hazily. Beginner's luck.

Blood had seeped onto the snow where the hare lay, its white fur speckled with it. Pyotra bowed her head in remorse. There was nothing for it. Scrunching up her nose, she lifted the carcass and slipped it into her leather satchel. If she had killed it, she might as well eat it. It was the least she could do.

*

During the last years of his life, before what had befallen his wife, Nikolay Borisovich had regularly taken his daughter out hunting. It was frowned upon—by her teacher, most of all—but Kolya had given up waiting for a son, and what was more: he genuinely seemed to appreciate being in the company of his gauche, prickly, never-fitting-in daughter. She basked in his attention, lapped it up—of course she did. Which just made his desertion of her, of them, of *himself*, all the more painful.

Remembering this was like picking at an old scab; Pyotra Nikolayevna was shocked by the freshness, the palpitating soreness of the wound beneath.

She hadn't been out in the vast wilderness of the snow forest since the last time Kolya had taken her, over ten years ago. By that time he had had a son, finally, and then...

Pyotra made a noise in her throat, and bit savagely into her cheek. The taste of copper and iron filled her mouth. She had a wandering mind, not fit for a hunter. Not fit for—

She took a deep, staggering breath and forced her attention outwards, towards her surroundings. She was hemmed in by looming conifers on all sides, seducing her into a false sense of security. She had lost and picked up the trail of the wolf more times than she cared to dwell on, within the space of a few hours.

At this point, Pyotra wasn't entirely sure she was tracking the right beast. What if she came upon another wolf? Did she have the bloody-mindedness to shoot to kill, indiscriminately?

She hadn't even managed to do that with the one she was after.

In fact, whenever she had tried to close her eyes, after she and Boris had administered first aid to Sergei, after they had stripped him of his wet, sleety attire and covered him in knitwear and fells, ensconcing him with hot water bottles, after Boris had planted himself heavily on the little stool by the boy's side and told Pyotra in a gruff voice she, too, needed her rest— After all this, when she lay in her narrow bed and endeavoured to do as she was bid, the only thing she could see were those black eyes, those almond-shaped slivers of a starry night, gazing deep, deep into her own.

For the space of a breath or two, that wolf had entranced her, mesmerised her, made her believe—the impossible. And that was all it took.

Nothing about this wolf was as it should be. But that didn't make it any less of a threat. If anything, that made it all the more dangerous.

It had cost her a night's sleep, and it was beginning to take its toll. Pyotra yawned into her arm, covertly, as though some snowy owl might see and tell on her. Her pace had dropped, little by little. She was struggling to keep her eyes open, let alone put one foot in front of the other, sinking into the snow with each step. She needed to pitch her tent and get into her sleeping bag, or she would fall asleep where she was, quietly freezing to death beneath the deceptive blanket of canopy and stars.

She couldn't do that to Sergei or Boris. It wouldn't be fair. She wasn't her parents.

Surely, the wolf, too, must stop to rest?

Pyotra didn't know. She didn't even know whether she cared at the moment. The bitter cold of the world around her had etched itself onto the skin of her face, nipping at it; a few hours more without relief and she would have permanent frostbite. And, after all, she couldn't avenge herself upon Nature itself.

Shining her torch around as far as it would reach, Pyotra checked her compass and made sure she knew in what direction to start off again in the morning. A frozen-over stream twinkled to her left: a ghostly still of what, during the milder months, must be a babbling brook. Now it was voiceless, powerless.

For some reason, this chilled her to the marrow of her bones; but she decided to set up camp by the side of it, regardless, in awkward solidarity with what it once was, what it must be—would be—again.

Once her tent was up, Pyotra crawled inside, being careful to bring her rucksack and rifle. The hare, however, she couldn't stomach as a bedfellow, and in any case, it made more sense to leave it outside in the natural freezer. She dug a hole for it in the snow and covered it up, satchel and all.

Turning off her torch, she groped her way inside her sleeping bag through the thick, impenetrable darkness; Pyotra was struck by the thought that this would be all the same to Boris. She couldn't say why, but somehow it comforted her. Her ded, in this very moment, would be watching blindly—but with his big, surprisingly gentle hands—over her brother, his ears pricked for intruders, his nose filled with the scents of home: the smoky smell of the dwindling fire, the disinfectant the nurse had, no doubt, applied to Sergei's neck, the clean cotton sheets and the mustier fragrance of the heavy wool blankets.

Pyotra put her own hands flat to the sides of her face to warm herself, as best she could.

"I will be back, Dedushka. I promise."

Her voice was as thin as spider's silk.

Chapter Two

The human pointed the barrel of a gun at her. It was wavering, unsteady, but close enough that it didn't matter; if it took the shot it would hit her. How could she have been so careless?

All for the sake of a moment's pity, for the sake of one blustering human cub, who had caught her attention with his antics, his utter disregard for his own safety, his visible, infectious excitement when something pulled at his hook.

The fish had caught him, and he had caught her. That was ever the irony of the hunt.

Yet here she was, alive to tell the tale, and so was the cub—or would be, she hoped. Not that she was out of the woods. The other, bigger—but not very—human still held that gun raised.

Why didn't it shoot?

Volk stared at it, puzzling over the riddle. She stared at it until she was just about cross-eyed; she wasn't used to meeting a human gaze. She hadn't done so for...a very long time. Many, many moons.

Volk was not in the habit of keeping track of time. It was, after all, a ridiculously human pursuit.

What she did know was they didn't have time for this, or she would have sacrificed herself for nothing, she and the cub both lying dead on the ice.

Don't shoot. Her wolf tongue could not form the words. She brought up her paw, instinctively, and to her astonishment she—she didn't hear it or see it or smell it, exactly, but—she *sensed* a shift in the human. Could it be that it understood?

Volk was not about to wait around to find out the answer.

She backed far enough away that the bigger human couldn't possibly consider her an immediate threat. Once she was sure it wouldn't be able to fire that gun at her about-tail, she whipped around and shot off, the latent boost of adrenaline making her paws fly across the icy snow crust, barely touching the ground. Her body was run through with minute tremors: the thrill of the hunt, for once from the receiving end.

Not that she expected the bigger human to follow her. If it cared for its cub, it had more pressing concerns. But her animal instinct was to fly, fly, and so she flew, in a rush, into the heart of the forest, into her own realm.

Oh, she had been pursued by humans before; she had heard the whistle of bullets about her ears, smelled them coming, their acrid scent announcing their presence long before they came into view. They were laughable hunters, but deadly, for all that; she had witnessed first-hand what those firearms could do.

Not this one, though. This one had taken her unawares, crept up on her—but then, she might have known not even humans would be stupid enough to leave their cubs completely unattended.

Could it be the cub's mother? It hadn't smelled like it. It had smelled...nice.

Volk yipped, narrowly missing the bole of an old pine. She circled around upon herself and stopped, panting. Her sides ached as though she were about to split in two. From deep inside, she felt the bubble of laughter rising up; she had faced the muzzle of a gun; she had looked Death in the eyes, and it had smelled *nice*.

She shook herself, gnawed at an itch on her front leg.

Doty old wolves doth easy prey make, someone had told her once. It came to her like a susurration through pine needles.

Volk couldn't think. It had been too long; she had run too far; the past was an opaque box, welded shut. One time she had been...

But now, she was Volk, and that was enough.

She wished the human's scent would leave her nostrils. She wished she could shake it off, scratch it away like an annoying louse. Volk ran her whole treacherous snout deep into the snow, welcoming the sharp sting, the instant, insensate numbness. She growled, deep in her throat, taking pleasure in the vibrations spreading into her breastbone.

Then she heard a click, a tick, and—not waiting to see whether it was the cocking of a gun, the clink of ice against ice, or some bird of prey, opening and shutting its beak as it tried to fathom her behaviour—she picked up her tail and ran.

*

She hadn't planned it, but she felt it in her limbs, little by little, the direction she was taking. It was the direction she always took when overwhelmed or disoriented, lost or troubled. Volk was heading to the tundra, her true home.

She had a place there, little more than a cave, where she spent what passed for summer in the barren environment she inhabited. With the returning light came her inevitable change: the loathsome weakness, the frail frame.

She would need to prepare for it; she had left it too long already. Her wolf mind was a dreamer's, a nomad's, a constant traveller's floating together of this and that, there and here.

Perhaps that was why she had strayed so close, insensibly close, to that human dwelling. Or maybe it was not the wolf in her at all, but something else. No matter which, it had nearly cost Volk her life.

The hairs along her spine bristled. She was too close to the change; there was a heaviness in her bones, tingling up and down her legs; she was *thinking*.

Recollections were forming themselves into random, entrancing patterns in her mind, like flecks of dust, splashes of colour jarring the near monochrome of her quiet night-time existence.

Volk was afraid to stop, afraid to rest. Dimly, subconsciously, she was afraid if she slept, she would wake from her wolven dream.

But practically, she needed to eat. It had been too long; her strength and her speed were dwindling. If she didn't stop to hunt, soon enough she would not be able to.

Cursed be that human cub! Cursed be the weakness lurking in the depths of her wolf heart. Cursed be the bigger human, whose alluring scent—impossibly— reached her like a distant siren call, a breath of warmth upon the wind.

Volk skidded to a halt, raised her head, and sniffed. No, she *did* smell it.

What was happening to her?

She sat back on her haunches and licked at her sore paws. She shifted her ears, trying to catch some telltale sound, some telltale *something*. Then, for the second time in the space of a human night and day, from one heartbeat to another, she acted contrary to every tenet, every rhyme and reason that usually guided her along her path. She doubled back upon herself. She retraced her steps, and a current of something indefinable surged through her. She trembled with it. She could have barked with sudden, quixotic glee.

Chapter Three

Pyotra woke from a dream of Sergei's grubby little mitts reaching for her. He was always two years old in her dreams, the age he had been when Serafima was killed. His mouth blew bubbles through smetana; canned beetroots stained his fingers a lurid, purplish red. "Po'ta!" he called her, with a strange urgency to his infant voice, as though the twelve-year-old were trying to break through. He wiped at the smetana on his cheeks, smearing it out into his downy hair. She would need to bathe him now. Why did he always have to be such a nuisance?

As her eyelids fluttered open, the impression faded away; Pyotra felt ashamed of herself, but also bloated, puffy-faced. She had been weeping in her sleep. Her lips were dry and brittle.

It took her a moment to remember where she was, and why. She didn't have time for this. She had a wolf to catch, a wolf which was moving further and further away from her, increasing the distance between them, slipping out of her reach.

Bracing herself against the uneven floor of the tent, Pyotra sat up and zipped down her sleeping bag, hissing at the cold air that touched her as she put on her multiple layers in preparation for venturing outside. She needed to skin and cook that hare, then be on her way, quick as she could.

Pyotra gripped her rifle, which had lain by her through the night, ready for she knew not what, and opened the door flap of her tent.

As she turned on her LED light, she let out a moan—of fright, of shock, of dismay, of all of the above and none of them. Curious, she took off her mitten and hunkered down, running a gloved finger along the flurry of paw prints outside her makeshift shelter.

They were fresh.

Well, of course they were, or she would have noticed them when she had pitched her tent in the first place.

But it didn't make sense: Why had she not woken up? Why had the wolf—for there could be no doubt this was *her* wolf, its particular tracks having imprinted themselves on her mind—not clawed its way through the weave and... It must have smelled her, a living, breathing, easy prey. She shuddered and pressed the gun to her, as though it were a talisman that could ward off the enemy by its mere proximity. The wolf knew she was armed.

Pyotra blinked, and couldn't help smiling at herself. *The wolf knew she was armed...* What would be her next hare-brained idea? If the wolf was such a shrewd creature, why didn't she try a verbal negotiation? *Dear wolf, if you will only promise not to come after me and mine, I won't be obliged to shoot you. Think about it. It's a win-win solution.*

Shaking her head, Pyotra decided not to waste energy on trying to come to grips with wolf psychology and instead bless her lucky star that she had fresh tracks to follow—that somehow, for some reason, the wolf had veered off course. Perhaps it had needed to eat, which reminded her...

She cursed under her breath as she turned to find the snow dug up, right where she had deposited the hare. She crept forward to examine the hole and her forehead creased, her breath coming out in a puff.

The poor frozen remains had been torn in two by jagged teeth, the head and breast carried off or devoured, for all she knew, half a metre from where she had been resting her own head at the time. But the hindlimbs and hindquarters were still there.

The wolf had left her the rump, the downy white tail raised in alert: frozen stiff and unyielding.

*

Bemused and unsettled, Pyotra did what she always had done in times of doubt and distress: she focused squarely on practical matters. She prepared and fried the half of the hare left her, scraping off the pelt and placing it back in her satchel.

True, it was only part of a skin, but she was sure she could find some use for it. She could mend the lining of Boris's spring cap, for example.

Unless she had a complete wolf hide to carry back with her. A shiver ran down her spine and she saw it again, standing before her, its paw raised, its grey fur silvery in the moonlight. Its black-as-coal eyes...

Huffing, Pyotra knocked back the last of the *chay* and stood. She didn't really want that blasted wolf's skin, but it was definitely getting under hers.

*

Once she had packed up her things, Pyotra felt more level-headed, setting off in the direction she had taken out with her compass the night before. The wolf had, for some inscrutable reason, turned back and found her, hot on its trail.

Thinking about it, she guessed she could understand why it would have preferred eating the hare rather than going to the trouble of tearing up her tent to get at Pyotra. But why, for the love of the Holy Virgin, had it left the rump?

Wolves were opportunistic, lazy, wily—and a host of other epithets she had heard people use, relegating them more or less to the role of Satan in fur—but dainty eaters?

Never. A wolf, any wolf, but especially one that was on the run, or had been, should be perfectly able to eat an entire hare in one sitting. Even if this were not the case, why would it leave the choicest bit?

The conundrum of it was giving her a headache. Her nose was insensible with cold. Pyotra pulled one of her scarves up higher about her face. She had strapped on her snowshoes, but she felt as heavy as if she were wading knee-deep through the unrelenting white. It was the wind; she was moving against it, leaning into it, with all her might. The boughs of the firs around her danced and twirled. Any moment, one of them might snap and fall across her path, or with her luck, why not directly on top of her?

It was not a good time to be out in the woods. She hoped her grandfather wasn't beside himself with worry. She hoped he focused on Sergei, on putting on a brave face for the sake of his youngest grandchild.

Poor Ded, he'd had his share of loss and then some. First their grandmother, Anna, whom neither she nor Sergei had ever met; she had been something of the local beauty, it was said, though in a place with barely a hundred souls... Then his eyesight had gone, his daughter-in-law, his son, in quick succession—really, it was too much, even for a Siberian to bear. Pyotra smiled a little, despite the hard wind, her heavy step, her miserable frame of mind. Her grandfather was fretful, surly, superstitious, at the best of times. Yet he was all they had in the world, and they—his wayward granddaughter, his topsy-turvy grandson—were everything to him. Unlike Kolya, Boris Ilyich had never found the children to be an insufficient reason to live.

That wasn't fair. Pyotra knew this, in her heart of hearts, but... She had appreciated her ded's gesture when, after her father's funeral, he had returned with them to his izba in the woods, and before their very eyes, taken his three bottles of spirits from out of the pantry and poured them to the angels, as he called it. They had smelled the sharp and mellow fumes of rum, brandy, and vodka for days afterwards. Not once, in all the years that had passed since, had Boris asked her to restock.

Pyotra wiggled her shoulders to adjust the load of her rucksack, drew her hip belt tighter, and turned her head from left to right, scanning the tracks ahead. The wind was blowing fly snow across the wolf's path, obscuring it; but the tracks were deep and easy to make out, their direction clear and straight for north-northeast. The beast's internal compass was infallible, but...

Pyotra scratched her head through her layers of hats and scarves. Something bothered her about this, though she could not for the life of her pinpoint her unease. Why would the wolf be treading so heavily? Was it injured? Was that why it had gone scavenger hunting right at Pyotra's doorstep, as it were, rather than trying to catch live prey? Was that why it hadn't managed more than half a hare, before being overcome with fatigue, choosing to withdraw to lick its wounds rather than finish off its meal?

Chewing on the inside of her cheek, Pyotra hitched her mittened thumbs under her shoulder straps. This wolf was an enigma. She couldn't make sense of it.

*

She stopped earlier this time to preserve her much-needed store of energy, wise from the night before. For whatever reason, the wolf's pace had slackened; Pyotra felt as if she could almost sense it, glimpse the ringed tail in the periphery of her vision. It was all nonsense, but be that as it may, she would rather not sleep as soundly as she had done when it made its raid on her camp. She must have been sleeping like a log.

She told herself that it was simply not to send the lingering wolf into a fleeing panic that she had chosen not to try to shoot another hare. She had her store of freeze-dried food, but, if she were to be honest with herself, that wouldn't last her long if she didn't add game along the way.

The simple fact was, loath as she was to admit it, shooting the hare had spooked her. She wasn't sure if she had the heart for it, which, considering her current mission, was problematic, to say the least.

When she had been out in the forest with Kolya as a ten-year-old, life and death had been largely abstract concepts to her; she had been more concerned with winning her father's approval. She had wanted him to take her seriously, not dismiss her as a little girl, which, ironically, was exactly the thinking of a little girl.

Now, at twenty-two, the taking of a life had hit her with stark force; from one second to the next, she had turned an armful of life into something abject and unpleasant—into so much meat. True, it was only a dumb animal. But its abruptly lifeless, marble-like eyes had been eloquent.

The thought of having to fire the rifle anew sickened her. Pyotra could only cross herself—an inherited nervous tic, a warding-off of evil, although she couldn't rightly say how—and hope it would pass.

After she had set up her tent and had a light supper of sugary chay and dry reindeer meat, Pyotra pondered where she was and if, when the time came for it, she would be able to find her way back.

She should have taken her bearings more regularly. She should have left signs for herself: broken-off twigs, some kind of formations in the snow. As it was, the persistent gale was erasing her tracks behind her, as if she had never been there at all. The way the schoolmistress down in the village had wiped the letters волк from the blackboard, chalk dust spreading through the air, before Pyotra had had a chance to copy them out.

She hadn't been a brilliant student, by any standards. She had been distracted, grief-stricken— winded, as though she had received a physical blow, making it hard enough to breathe, let alone think, write— much too early in life.

But mostly, she had been consumed with anger. An anger eating away at her, never voiced but left festering like a neglected wound.

Only briefly, in her teens, had Tatyana brought her out of herself: lovely, kind, and much too clever Tatyana Ivanovna, who had gone off to university in St Petersburg. St Petersburg! It might as well have been the moon.

At first, Tatya had sent her postcards with vistas of the Baltic Coast, the Nevsky Prospekt, the Petersburg Hermitage. When she sent one with the statue of Catherine the Great on the front, and a mention of Finnish Irma on the back, Pyotra had stopped responding to them, stopped pretending another life was waiting for her, in the far-off former capital by the Baltic Sea. After a while, the one-sided correspondence ceased.

Pyotra hoped Tatyana Ivanovna was happy. Truly, she did.

She doused the flame of her cook set and gathered up her spread. Thinking about Tatya served no other purpose than to make her maudlin, restless, in equal parts. She should know better by now. This was the life that had chosen her; this was where she was meant to be, with her little duckling, her blind grandfather, her wo—

Grimacing at herself, Pyotra zipped open the tent and crawled inside. Her *wolf*, indeed!

She fell asleep without another thought and slept heartily, dreamlessly. She slept as though she hadn't seen a bed in years.

When she woke her mind was a blissful blank, until she recalled herself: She was out in the boreal forest, alone and, frankly, lost in the dark. She was on the hunt.

Pulling on her clothes, she stifled a yawn. How was it that when one slept really well, one somehow got into it, one's body craving more and more?

Pyotra rubbed the residual sand out of her eyes, clicked on her torch, and peeked her head out of the domed tent. She sucked in her breath, swallowing down a yelp.

Like the night before, there were paw prints in abundance. Serpentine loops from where she had been sitting with her tea, to the tent, to where—Pyotra blushed—she had relieved herself.

Yet this wasn't what made the hairs on her neck stand on end. No, it was the fact that at the very spot where her tent opened, a bloody half of a carcass lay. The rump end of a recently caught hare.

Chapter Four

Volk had not meant to steal the human's kill. It was embarrassing, unbecoming to her; she wasn't a thief. She was pragmatic, she had to concede; there were winters when, in dire straits, she had been forced to loot the rubbish heaps at the back of human abodes. Every so often, a winter came when food was scarce, the woods swept clean of any likely quarry. Volk was a survivor. She did what she had to do. But she wasn't a rampant thief.

It was the heady aroma of the human. It did things to her head.

As she closed in upon it, the scent became so thick in the air she could taste it. It made her limbs tremble with exhilaration, her mouth water, her rear end take on a life of its own.

To go this close to its camp was a particular species of insanity; the human was armed and ready, waiting for her. It made no sense to seek it out, except that—it fired up her senses.

Volk halted in front of the thin barrier it had spun around itself, and inhaled open-mouthed, her tongue tingling.

It had come after her. What would possess it to do such a thing? It had that rifle, yes, but really... Volk would not have lived as long as she had in the northern Siberian taiga if she didn't know how to lead the odd huntsman astray. When they came in packs it was more difficult, a challenge even, but Volk had yet to meet her human match.

She blew out air through her nose and scraped at the frozen layer of snow in front of the tent. It had been an unconscious act, at first, but soon she was digging purposefully. The hare she unearthed was all but frozen through; it must have been hours since it had received its lethal blow.

A tendril of saliva dribbled from Volk's jaws onto its snowy coat. She snatched it up, and with her paws pressing down on it, she tore the carcass in two. It seemed a good joke to her: Why should not they, hunter and hunted, share a meal to strengthen their limbs for the journey ahead?

The human stirred inside its shelter, and Volk danced away as if it had taken a pot-shot at her. She grabbed the upper half of the hare by the nape of its neck, like a pup, and slid away into the woods.

Boldly close to the human's camp, Volk settled down to eat. It was the best meat she'd had for a long while; it fairly melted in her mouth, tasting succulent, gamey, yet laced with an indefinable sweetness.

All through her feast, Volk imagined the human's hands on it. She imagined the human coming out in the morning to find its part of the plump hare: the best part. At least Volk could say that much in her defence.

She laid her head on the hare's remaining fur and drowsed, sated.

*

It was not until she woke up, with a low growl ready in her throat, that she saw how unreasonable her actions were. She was a predator, not a carrion crow. Her behaviour had been base, demeaning; she couldn't reckon with it. And what would be the human's reaction? Anger, fear, or perhaps a combination of the two?

Would it scorn what it might perceive as her leftovers?

Humans were a haughty species. In all likelihood, it would redouble its efforts to catch up with her.

Volk felt a pull at the corners of her mouth, her chin lifting. It caught her off guard; she hadn't felt that pull since... She shook herself, rose to her feet, and picked up her trail, placing her paws down carefully, determinedly, turning every so often to make sure her prints stood out, bluish-black in the white.

After a while, when she was sure the human was up and on its way after her, she circled round to come downwind of it and catch its scent. It was struggling, wearied, she could tell. Would it give up the chase?

Somehow, Volk doubted it. She doubted it very much, and the doubt filled her, once more, with inexplicable zest.

*

Volk crouched, almost flattened against the ground between the sapling firs, her neck stiff from lying in wait. The frigid bite of the snow hurt the pads of her paws; the tiny whiskers along her nose vibrated.

Cocking her ears, she listened to the minute sounds of the glacial forest: the groan and crackle of ice, the tops of the trees rustling gently, voles moving deep beneath the top layer of snow. She wasn't interested in them; they were a mouthful, at the most, and hardly worth the effort expended in pursuit. Besides, she didn't think her human would appreciate a measly vole as a peace offering. She had seen cats bringing mice to the doors of men, with nothing but a swipe of a broomstick by way of thanks.

Not that this deterred the felines. Volk had given up any pretence of understanding those creatures a long time ago.

She shifted uneasily, in an effort to clear away these unwelcome distractions and focus her attention. The stars shone overhead: too many for wolf or human to count. It was getting late. But she knew—

In a flurry of motion, Volk was on her feet, bounding through the air with deadly precision. The hare's brown eyes rolled in its skull; it leapt aside, stomping the ground, but it was a millisecond too late. As her teeth closed on it,

Volk could feel its careening pulse beating up into her mouth. She shook it, sinking her fangs deeper. A swift kill was her trademark. She didn't get off on fear.

When she was certain the last remnant of life had ebbed away, she let the lean body fall between her front paws. She panted with nervous energy, her limbs quivering with the residual rush. Volk threw her head back and let out a howl before she could stop herself. The sound echoed between the boles of the giant firs; she was drunk, the sharp tang of blood in her mouth, the kill at her feet hot and tender.

Ravenous, she tore into it, tendons snapping, bones crunching. She fed as the beast she was, with gluttonous abandon, without diffidence or shame; she was Volk, a wolf of the Siberian tundra, a creature of fur and flesh and bones, running noiselessly through the polar night, her heart beating in tandem with her swift paws across the snow.

Except the change was coming. The dull ache had started, the one that whispered words through her mind, a foreign language that was becoming increasingly familiar, that told her: *soon, soon.*

Disgusted, Volk threw back her head again, but this time her weak howl sounded close to a moan.

She snapped up the end of her repast and set off to find the human. *Her* human. A strange thrill rippled through her as she padded her way, sure-footed, through the familiar terrain.

Chapter Five

Pyotra ate the hare. She ate it, and smacked her lips as she did; it was juicy, lean, deeply satisfactory. She had fried it with a sprinkling of sage as a Sunday treat. Pyotra liked it better than her own kill, which was hypocritical. But it wasn't so much that she hadn't been the one to spill the blood this time, as that it had been...well, a gift. Ridiculous!

She was not used to gifts. Obviously she wasn't, if she could interpret half a dead hare left outside her tent by a stray wolf as a gift. A *gift*.

A warning, more like: this is what will happen to you if you insist on pestering me with your presence in these woods.

Although this was merely a 180-degree flip in attributing human traits to animals; it was men, not beasts of the wild, who put up Beware signs, who lined their wheat fields with the corpses of rooks and crows. Wolves marked their territory with urine, she supposed, but that was the beginning and end of the similarities.

They did not signpost idle threats. And they certainly did not come bearing gifts.

Nothing about this wolf was as it should be.

Pyotra hoisted her rucksack onto her knee and worked her arm through the loop of the shoulder strap. She was staring hard at the paw prints surrounding her, imagining the sensitive pads of those paws. Would the wolf's charcoal eyes close in pleasure if she stroked them with her finger? she wondered. Could wolves be ticklish, like Sergei had been as a babe?

Mother of God, but she was losing it. She had heard people could become unhinged when isolated from human society for too long—cabin fever, or something like it, irrespective of whether or not a cabin was involved.

Pyotra hadn't seen a cabin since she left home. There were hunters' huts strewn about the southwestern taiga, she knew, but that was in the diametrically opposite direction from where they were heading. To be frank, she was grateful for this; the southwestern forests were where the majority of wolves were found, running in close-knit packs, swooping down on their prey in a terrifying—stupefying—swarm of teeth and claws.

Pyotra's throat tightened. It took her a few moments to make out the wolf's exit prints in the whirlwind of activity that had been its movements outside her sleeping quarters. Despite this, she was fairly certain it was just the one wolf. Sergei's assailant—unlike Sima Anatoliyevna's—did not appear to belong to any group.

It was a lone wolf.

Pyotra stumbled over her own feet as it hit her—why had she not considered this before? It was pure, dumb luck; even with her father's rifle and the heavy load of extra ammunition she carried, it was doubtful she could have withstood the onslaught of a pack.

Picking her way ahead through the dark, Pyotra tried to summon forth what she had been taught about lone wolves. She wished she could have looked it up, gone down to the tiny library behind the school where she and Tatyana had used to meet—in that other life that had been hers for such a brief period of time, a mere hiccup, a wink of an eye—and pulled out the tattered tomes on the regional flora and fauna.

Back when Kolya was alive, she had been reading in them during lunch breaks, eager to seem more knowledgeable than her tender years would have suggested. Pyotra squinted, pushing against the layers of memory like she would push a sore tooth with her tongue. *The lone wolf is...usually female...expelled from a pack, or straying of their own accord...stronger and more aggressive...dangerous, but a less efficient hunter, subsisting on smaller prey or carrion.*

Pyotra spun around, clutching her gun. She thought she had heard something, but there was nothing: only the branches of an old spruce dancing in the wind, scattering a miniature snowfall around itself. The crystals glistened innocuously in the beam of her headband torch.

She had been speaking out loud, she realised, probably spooking herself as the woods warped and echoed her own voice back at her.

"Carrion," she repeated to the offending spruce, but it didn't answer back. Not this time.

Pyotra pulled her scarf over her nose and mouth. "The lone wolf is typically female," she told herself, putting one snowshoe in front of the other. For some reason, it made her smile.

*

She should be scared out of her wits. But Pyotra Nikolayevna Kulakova felt nothing so much as a vague sense of excitement where she lay in her sleeping bag, listening to the unmistakable sound of an animal on the other side of her frail wall against the night.

More than anything, she was surprised. The wolf had never woken her before now. She had been out in the forest for little over a week, and she was reasonably sure that by this time tomorrow they would have reached the tundra. A nonsensical, childish part of her had been looking forward to it; despite its relative nearness, Pyotra had only ever seen that great, barren landscape in explorers' snapshots, on maps in semi-outdated atlases.

Kolya had promised to take her when she was older. Now she was, but he—wasn't.

Loud snuffling followed by a low growl alerted her to the wolf's immediate presence, less than half a metre from her head. Pyotra sat up, her heartbeat painful against her ribcage.

Slowly, agonisingly, she began unzipping herself from her sleeping bag, section by section, endeavouring to make as little noise as was humanly possible.

It wasn't quiet enough, not by a long shot. The growl intensified, and she could hear scratching, digging. She pulled on her fleece top and grabbed her rifle. It was icy cold in her bare hands, and the thought of what she might use it for sickened her, but...

The weave was beginning to tear. Another first, and somehow it disappointed her. Pyotra pushed her feet into her boots, and with the barrel of the gun jutting out before her, she opened up her door flap and peered out.

The beast was momentarily blinded by the sharp jab of her LEDs. It lasted only a second or two, and then it came for her: a great leap; a huge, shaggy body; bared, vicious-looking incisors.

Only a second or two, but it was time enough for Pyotra to spot the difference: no white ring around the tail. No silver-tinted guard hairs. No unfathomable, tarry eyes.

This wolf's eyes were yellow as bright brass ten-kopek coins.

It wasn't her wolf.

Pyotra had time to come to this conclusion, but she hadn't cocked her rifle; she was fumbling, shaking, a keening sound like a hiss passing over her lips. She was going to die out here. Like her mother, she would be torn to pieces, and just as pointlessly. How would Sergei ever forgive her? How would Boris?

A shot rang out, knocking her flat on her bum; she had managed to fire, and she was so close it should have been all right, but she'd missed, she'd *missed*—she could have laughed wildly at the ludicrousness of it: Pyotra, misfortune's favourite.

Claws slashed her left cheek, blindsiding her with real, physical pain. Instinctively, she lashed out with the useless gun, like a battering ram, throwing her attacker off-kilter.

Pyotra was yelling now, a crazed, fear-riddled scream that resounded through the silent surroundings. She readied her rifle anew.

Then, as she was rising to her feet, warm blood streaming from the cuts on her face and down her neck, a grey fury came hurtling out of nowhere, descending on the groggy intruder like the Archangel of Vengeance. They both roared.

Pyotra clapped her hands over her mouth, the gun sliding onto the snow at her feet.

It had come. Out of the woods, out of the night: the wolf she was tracking, the wolf who had kept her well fed and paced throughout their trek, who had— The wolf she had left her safe, uneventful life behind to pursue.

To shoot. Pyotra knelt and picked up Kolya's rifle, her stomach clenching as she pointed it at the tussling wolves. Her wolf had the stranger by the scruff of its neck, and the brute was none too happy about it, bucking ferociously, and there was no way—no way at all—Pyotra could be certain of hitting the one or the other.

And it shouldn't have mattered.

But it did.

The yellow-eyed wolf snarled; with a dodge and roll, too swift for Pyotra's head or eyes to make sense of from where she stood beholding the spectacle over her trembling barrel, it had thrown off the silver-grey who landed, with a sickening thud, sprawled on the ground.

Yellow-eye yelped victoriously, dancing on its feet, and then a report sounded and it slumped, in profound surprise, onto its haunches, crumpling into a heap on the snow. Its throat gurgled. A fan of blood oozed from its slackened jaws.

Pyotra dropped the rifle as though it had fired itself. She was breathing in sobs and gulps, a drawn-out moan issuing from between her frozen lips, reverberating through her, as she stumbled towards White-ring-around-its-tail. The lone wolf. The she-wolf. *Her* wolf.

It didn't move.

Pyotra sank to her knees, her vision blurred, the naked fingers of her left hand raking through the fur on the wolf's neck. It was the first time she touched it, and the hairs there were so soft, almost like baby hair, some distant part of her noted. She closed her eyes and willed there to be a pulse; she wasn't too educated when it came to the pulse points of wolf anatomy, but surely any creature—any *living* creature, that was—would have a pulse at the neck.

"Don't be dead," she heard herself say. Her heart throbbed in her throat.

The wolf sighed.

Pyotra's eyes flew open; for a disorienting moment, it was as if no time had elapsed since she had last gazed into those deep, unnaturally dark eyes, as Sergei's unconscious body lay between them on the ice of the pond.

The wolf shifted beneath her hand, its fine hairs tickling her palm. Pyotra allowed herself to exhale, tiny sparks crackling at the edges of her field of vision. She felt woozy.

Gingerly, the wolf rose to its feet, a yowl escaping as it placed weight on its right front leg.

"You're hurt!" Pyotra dove for the damaged limb, as though she could heal it with nothing but her bare hands, but the beast stopped her, buffeting her away with its warm nose.

"I could help..." The words died on her lips as she sat back, coming to her senses. She was speaking to a dumb brute.

The wolf limped over to the motionless shape of its yellow-eyed opponent. It bent its head to sniff at it, snorting and blowing out air through its nose.

When it seemed satisfied the other wolf was well and truly disposed of, it looked back at her, and Pyotra could have sworn on Mashka Petrovna's enticing advertisement poster that it was attempting to *smile* at her.

She smiled back. The wolf hesitated; its head to one side, its eyelids blinking slowly. The end of its tail curled in upon itself.

Pyotra held out her bare hand. It was growing white from the bite of the cold air; in another minute or two, she would have to cover it up if she meant to keep it. The wolf rumbled out a warning.

But then, as she didn't move, it padded up to her, pressing its nose into the exposed flat of her hand.

Its tail quivered. The hair on its crest seemed to rise.

A whimper reached Pyotra's ears, and she couldn't for the life of her say whether it was she or the beast who was responsible for it.

Her face warmed, just as the wolf tore its snout away, scuttling backwards, and—confusingly—there was fear in its eyes as it turned on its heels and ran.

"Wait!" Pyotra pulled on her glove, her hand still moist with the wolf's warm breath. "Don't go— I— "

I wanted to talk to you.

Chapter Six

Volk caught the scent of the other wolf in the nick of time.

She recognised it dimly: another loner like her, yet nothing like her at all. This wolf would not think twice of partaking of a weakened prey served up to it on a silver platter. It wouldn't *think*. It had no morals—why should it? All creatures were alike, all were either eater or eaten, under the wide expanse of the all-consuming night.

Volk would have thought nothing of it herself, if she weren't so perilously close to the change.

In some ways, this wolf would be doing her a favour; she should have either killed or shaken off the human long before now. She certainly should not have kept feeding it, slowing down her pace for it; kept close to its campsite; watched over it as it slept. She shouldn't have paid nightly visits to where it rested, skirting its cocoon like a bitch in heat—like a—

The growl of the other wolf reached her as a jagged rip in the fabric of the still forest. A haze of wrath descended upon her, making her heart pound in furore, as though it would claw its way out of her and storm to where it was needed, whether the rest of her was ready to follow or not.

Volk's jaw clicked. She was too weak, this close to the change; she would be no match in fang-to-fang combat for a wolf in its prime. A *proper* wolf.

She would have to rely on the element of surprise.

Despite every fibre of her being willing her to throw caution to the wind, she fell back on the patience of the predator. She made a wide berth around the area where the campsite was, moving soundlessly to get downwind of her rival. Not that Volk wanted to eat the—but it was *her* human. She felt queasy at the mere suggestion of another wolf touching a hair on its head.

Her skin was too tight around her throat and chest. The likely outcome of this encounter was not in her favour. Maybe she would keep the other occupied for a while. Perhaps it would give the human a minimal chance of escape.

The human was resourceful. She had to trust to its powers of reason.

A shot sounded, and Volk broke into a run. As she leapt out from the sheltering firs, all she registered was the tawny pelt, the flashing claws of the wolf, and the smell of fresh blood permeating the air. Her mind melted into a red-hot stream of rage.

Volk hurled herself at the offender, smashing into her with a roar that tore out of her throat like a war cry.

She was too big for Volk, all muscles and tendons and a winter girth that was nothing short of impressive. But she was slow, Volk noted as she buried her fangs in the intruder's neck; Tawny-legs was used to relying on her brute strength to save the day.

In all likelihood, it would, this time too.

Already, Volk's own strength was dwindling. She had come so close, so close to reaching the tundra and her dwelling there. And she had intended—*she had intended to take the human with her*.

She had intended—

She deserved to die.

Pain exploded through her as Tawny-legs threw her off, and all went black.

*

Volk came to herself as if from a pleasant dream, or into one; she couldn't be sure, but she felt as if something—someone—was touching her.

A light, steadfast circling on her neck sent thrills down her spine. Her paws twitched. She opened her eyes, and—impossibly—the human was hovering over her, its mouth moving softly, a curl of hair feathering across the scratches on its blood-stained cheek.

For a moment, Volk simply lay there, as the human continued to grope her neck. It was possible it meant to have her hide off her back. Volk didn't know that she minded overmuch. There were, undoubtedly, worse ends.

The human turned its gaze from her neck to her eyes and... Volk lost herself, found herself, lost herself again.

The hidden self within seemed to push against the dullness of her lupine brain, but she had forgotten something—*they* had forgotten something. As she drew a breath deep into her nostrils, savouring the human's by now familiar, yet ever tantalising scent, she identified the something like a dip into icy water: the presence of another wolf.

She wanted to spring up, but she dared not; the pulsating throb in her right front leg did not bode well. Instead, she raised herself slowly, cautiously; but she couldn't help protesting at the pain.

The human cried out. Its eyes widened, hands reaching out; its stance alone betrayed its worry on her account.

How lovely it was—how distracting. Its firearm lay in the snow, forgotten. Volk felt a surge of something within, something complicated, tangled, impossible for a mere wolf to unravel.

Veering away from it, she went up to Tawny-leg's prostrate form. She had met this other solitary before; but she suspected that Tawny, unlike herself, had once belonged to a pack, grown up among others of its kind.

They hadn't been on the best of terms. Volk's scent teased and provoked the larger bitch—confused her. For the most part, they kept out of each other's way. It was the smell of the weary human that had lured Tawny-legs off her beaten track, and Volk—couldn't blame her. They were predators. And the human, rifle or no rifle, was a babe in the woods.

Volk smelled the acrid remnants of gunpowder on the dead wolf's pelt; she found the entrance wound of the bullet.

For all its physical weakness, the human could obviously take care of itself. Volk looked over at it again; it seemed she couldn't stop doing so. After a moment, the human held out its hand, so pale with cold it was all but invisible against the backdrop of snow and ice.

Not stopping to consider what she did, Volk hobbled over to it, pushing her nose against it, inhaling greedily. It was a heady form of torture, a sweet, scent-filled feast, and for the second time within the space of a few moments, Volk felt the stir and push, the tightening of her skin, the whispering.

The human made a little noise, somewhere between a cub's and a lover's. A...what?

The piercing comprehension knocked the wind out of Volk. She was shifting. She would change within the next day or two, at the most, though it was too early. But somehow, something within her had responded to— It didn't matter, the whys and wherefores. What was important was that the human could not be allowed to see, to understand, or all, all would be lost.

Besides, she was too far from safety: a good two days and nights, even at her best pace. With the human in tow, maybe five.

It was all wrong.

Volk wrested her muzzle from the light, tender grip of the human's hand and backed off, spikes of pain shooting through her wounded leg.

With a sore leg: six.

She had permitted herself to dream, near subconsciously, recklessly—and she would pay the price for such foolhardiness as she froze to death in the Siberian winter, a naked, pitiful excuse for a creature.

Volk did the only thing she could do, although it was a lost cause, an unattainable end: she spun on her tail and fled.

Behind her, the voice of the human echoed, and for the first time she heard it clearly, as though a veil had been lifted. It said: "Wait!"

Chapter Seven

It was too late to turn around. This was the mantra that kept Pyotra going, for hours on end, after she had breakfasted in the company of a dead wolf.

She could have skinned it and gone back home. No one would have been the wiser. Boris, even had he had his eyesight, would not have seen the original wolf, and Sergei had been unconscious when he was dragged out of his watery predicament.

But the wolf had saved her duck.

That was not how the story was supposed to go, but she could not turn the proverbial blind eye to it any longer. It was what had happened.

The wolf with the white ring around its tail had rescued her brother from drowning, for no apparent reason, no conceivable benefit to itself. And tonight, it had saved her—and she had tried to save it right back, only... Only it was wounded. How could a wild animal protect itself, how could it hunt for food, with a broken leg?

As Pyotra sat with her scanty meal, brooding over the outline of the fallen Yellow-eye in the shadows, she concluded that by saving her, the wolf she had been pursuing had signed its own death warrant. It broke her heart.

It had preserved her brother's life, and she had hounded it to the brink of destruction for its trouble. The intensity of the guilt she felt made her rock in place, as though her chest would literally split open, the mess within spilling out.

At last, she finished up her chay and packed up, leaving the vulpine carcass behind. She had made her mind up. *Her* wolf would not end up like that, a feast for the scavengers of the coniferous forest. Not if Pyotra Kulakova could help it.

*

As Pyotra had expected, the wounded wolf's tracks were not hard to follow. It had taken off in a frenzy, flying across the snow and away from her, but the inevitable drawback of having only the three good legs to sprint on had taken its toll.

Although she was two hours behind, she was gaining on it. Pyotra was glad and vexed to see it. A plan had started to form in her mind.

She could not expect a wild animal to trust her; that was asking too much, she knew, even of such a strange specimen as this wolf had turned out to be. She wondered idly if it had been raised by humans; it happened, she had heard, though for the most part not in northern Siberia. She could think of no other explanation for its behaviour. It fit. Sort of.

She needed to trap it. Preferably without shooting it, as that would defeat her purpose.

Stopping for a breather, Pyotra checked that she had her old reindeer-skin lasso at the bottom of her rucksack. It was a curiosity, really; Kolya had purchased it for her from a passing Nenets tradesman. She hadn't used it since she was a girl, but she had been quite adept with it, once; she had used to entertain herself by catching the fat ponies Plenyanikov kept in a paddock behind his house, until he had complained to her grandfather and Boris had taken the lasso away.

He had returned it to her years later, when he judged she had grown out of the habit. She had kept it in her rucksack ever since. Pyotra wasn't sure if she could trap a still-standing sapling with it, let alone a swift-moving wolf. But it was the only course of action left her.

For the umpteenth time, she hauled her compass out of her breast pocket. Yes, they were heading straight for the tundra, which was both alarming and—just maybe—a good thing. It would be unknown territory to her, like stepping onto the surface of an unfamiliar planet; but no trees would be in the way as she threw her lasso. There would be nowhere—she hoped—for the wolf to hide.

Every pore in Pyotra's face ached with exposure. Her LED light swung to and fro, illuminating the path ahead of her, which would have been no path at all if it weren't for those distinct paw prints: the perfect rounded ones, and, every so often, the smudge and stumble of the fourth.

"Poor *lyubov*," she crooned, her eyes prickling. "Baby, we need to rest."

The woods were silent, but something stirred to her left and, unthinking, in the flow of the moment, Pyotra lifted her rifle and fired. She had seen only that it was something smaller, more delicate than a wolf.

As she shone her torch at it, she found it was another hare, twitching but felled to the ground. What were the odds?

She was beginning to think she must have a knack for this hunting business after all.

Her heart shrank with pity as she came up to the thing. It wasn't quite dead; the globe of its shiny, nut-brown eye peered up at her and blinked.

"I'm sorry," Pyotra whispered, kneeling and tugging off her mittens. She transferred the hare onto her lap and, as swiftly and mercifully as she could, broke its neck.

Pressing it to herself like a limp toy, she started to cry, and she had so much to cry about she feared she would never be done: Sima, torn to pieces like a rag doll; Kolya, drowned in the flood of his own misery; Boris and Sergei, helpless and waiting for her; Tatyana Ivanovna... Herself and the wolf.

"I got you food," she blubbered, holding the mutilated hare out to the surrounding darkness. "Please. Please take it."

She dropped the carcass back onto the snow where it had fallen. She couldn't stand to look at it. Some animal or other would snatch it up.

Scrubbing at her face, Pyotra turned away and prepared to set up camp.

*

In her dream, it was summer. There was barely any snow, and school was out for the term. She was waiting for Tatya behind Plenyanikov's barn, her hands balled into restless fists; she wished she had her lasso, anything, to keep them occupied. She lifted her face and angled her head back to catch the sun, closing her eyes, and—as so often in dreams—out of nowhere, Tatyana was there. Her warm lips skimmed Pyotra's ear as she whispered her name. Pyotra's instant exultation was of an intensity that bordered on, toppled over into, pain.

"Pyotra, Pyotra," Tatyana lilted, her hand sneaking under Pyotra's shirt, caressing the plane of her stomach. The edges of her nails grazed the underside of a loose breast. "Whatever will I do with you?"

Pyotra couldn't reply. She only just managed to suck in a ragged breath, but it didn't matter: Tatya's lips had already left her ear. They travelled down the taut line of her neck, planting kiss after kiss that bloomed, unfurled across her sensitive skin.

Tatya's thumb stroked the contours of the nether part of Pyotra's ribcage, and Pyotra's fists opened to the sun. As Tatyana Ivanovna's lips came up to meet her own, she thought her world couldn't possibly burn brighter.

And then it did.

With a gasp, Pyotra sat up, her tousled hair swishing against the inside weave of the tent, her chest damp with perspiration. It took her a moment or two to surmise that she wasn't sixteen any more; she was twenty-two; it wasn't summer, but dark winter. She was alone in a domed tent in the boreal forest at the lip of the tundra, and Tatyana Ivanovna was far, far away in the southwest, in St Petersburg with Finnish Irma.

She buried her face in her hands, taking a deep breath to try to steady her rattled nerves, her soaring pulse. How had her life come to this? What was she doing? If this was a belated act of teenage rebellion, why wasn't she on her way to the nearest major city, to board an airplane, to go to St Petersburg, to... Why had Pyotra run in the opposite direction, into the wild, hot on the heels of a feral and ferocious beast? What was she trying to prove?

At this, however, she righted herself, a sense of direction returning to her. This was no time for self-recriminations or moping over things that belonged to the past. There was a creature out there that had risked its life for her, that was in mortal peril because of her, and every minute she squandered might spell the difference between life and death. She didn't have time for Tatya. Not today.

Squirming out of her sleeping bag, Pyotra knuckled the dream out of her eyes and dried herself off with her travel-sized towel. She pulled on her fleece and trousers, grimacing as she moved the buckle of her belt in a notch. One and a half weeks of constant wandering and subsisting on a spare diet of meat and tea would do that. She changed her socks and pressed her feet into her boots.

It had been moronic of her to leave her kill from the night before out in the open.

"You must learn to keep a check on your emotions, Pyotrushka," she quoted under her breath, her mind's eye seeing Boris in his seat at the kitchen table, his fingers rapping the tabletop, his face turned in upon itself. She huffed. "Step one: stop thinking so much."

Switching on her torch, she popped her head out of the tent.

And there, right in front of her, like a gruesome but unmistakable love letter—making her laugh out loud with the surprise, the relief—was the rump end of the hare she had shot, tidily delivered, dusted with shimmering snow, and surrounded by lupine prints.

*

Her wolf was alive. It was alive and it was close—but moving steadily towards the tundra. What did it want out there? Pyotra shook her head as she put one snowshoe in front of the other, sweeping over the wolf's tracks with her own. Surely there was more quarry to be found in the taiga?

She had read about tundra wolves: the wolves of the great plains and steppes. *Canis lupus* was an incredibly versatile species.

Pyotra had always held a deep-seated aversion to them, because of Sima, and because of what they could do to the odd sheep or cattle, when circumstances drove them too near to human habitations.

Her wolf was different. It was unpredictable. It was gentle when it should be fierce, and yet, when it had taken on that yellow-eyed fiend, it had seemed like a thing possessed.

Pyotra could but too well remember the agony she felt as she searched for its pulse, not knowing whether it was still with her or not. As though they had become unspoken companions, their relationship transmuted somewhere along the way, without her noticing it, acknowledging it, until then.

Had the wolf known? she wondered, before smiling at herself. Soon she would be at a point where she expected the poor brute to start answering her questions, preferably in Russian, please.

Pyotra's thumb pressed against the tight coil of her lasso. She was carrying it in hand, practising as she went along; she had caught branches, curling roots, the protruding tip of a largish rock.

It was nothing compared to a moving target, but her aim was improving, the dexterity returning, little by little, to her out-of-practice fingers. She had whooped when she caught the rock a few hours ago, pulling the rope taut and angling up to it as if it had been one of Plenyanikov's ponies. She had stroked its pretend muzzle as she eased the loops of her rope off its craggy neck, hushed and soothed it as if it were a live catch.

There had been a time, a year or so after Kolya had passed, in her early teens, when she had dreamt of running away to join the reindeer herders, flitting across the tundra in one of their wooden sleds, cooped up with their beautiful, black-eyed children in their distinctive fur coats.

The vision had always made her think of Sergei, and she had recognised that she couldn't do it; she couldn't go through with it, in the end.

For that matter, twenty-two-year-old Pyotra thought ruefully, the people of the tundra would more likely than not have found her laughably inept. What use had they for a little ruddy-faced Russian matryoshka? They were a nation unto themselves, the last of the nomads, fighting for their right to remain essentially out of step with the century into which they were born.

Well, she would get to see it at last: the tundra. Her wolf was hellbent on reaching it, and whither it went, along came Pyotra, its self-appointed hangman turned protector. She could have wished they had been further along in the season, that there would be at least the hope of, the mere sliver of daylight to see it by. Her headband torch only reached so far; she would not be able to appreciate the full expanse of the tundra, the emptiness of it.

Pyotra grunted, turned right past a gathering of spruces, and walked right into the dancing sky.

Chapter Eight

She had never seen anything like it.

Oh, Pyotra had caught the occasional glimpse of the Northern Lights before. She had spent twenty-two years—a lifetime, albeit a short one—in one of the darkest corners of the Nenets Autonomous Okrug. But this: the sky stretching out unbroken around her, the flickering of green and purple fire so close it reflected off the endless flat of snow... Never, never.

Her heart squeezed tight like a fist; her mind contracted to a glowing pinpoint of *now, this*. She was kneeling in the cold white, her arms extended; if the aurora borealis had, in that moment, swooped down one of its electric green tendrils to pick her up, carry her off the face of the earth, Pyotra Nikolayevna would not have been able to muster more than a mild, watered-down shade of surprise. She would have welcomed it.

"Oh, oh," she mumbled, moaned, and the night sky twinkled and shone down at her, teasing her for her inane hankering after the polar day. Who needed sunlight, that commonplace gaudiness, when Night put on all her splendour, dressed herself in her finest, to guide one through her realm?

Tears slipped down Pyotra's cheeks, chilling her as they froze in the north-westerly wind. Her throat burned with held-back sobs. She felt as though she had been hollering at the top of her lungs—but she hadn't, couldn't. Disoriented, she turned her head in time to see a shape of grey fur slinking away. It could not hide its awkward limp, nor its onward path out onto the lit-up plain.

"Wait. Wait for me," Pyotra croaked out, and she could have sworn she saw the wolf's ears twitching, its pace slackening, almost imperceptibly. It had to be a trick of the light.

*

The aurora lasted all night. Pyotra had a timepiece passed down from her elusive grandmother—the saint, she had come to think of her, as that was the general consensus among the old people of the village, and like a saint, Pyotra only knew her *babushka* from a faded photograph placed on the mantlepiece, right next to the gold-plated icon of Saint Eudoxia. Every so often, as she struggled through the drifts of snow, Pyotra thumbed open the heavy, engraved lid of Anna's watch to check how the hours elapsed.

On the tundra, the snow was blue at night, haunted by the moss and lavender ghosts of the borealis lights. The awe that had gripped Pyotra as she stepped out into the ethereal show—like stepping into the midnight mass of some stained-glass-windowed cathedral, except there were no voices humming, no sound to break up the surfeit of the visual feast—had left her wearied, wrung-out, oddly empty.

She wanted to stop and rest, but she couldn't. There were no trees to shelter her from the whip of the wind. But more to the point: the wolf showed no sign of stopping. It ran as though its life depended on it; yet with each tread it must be growing weaker.

If Pyotra could only make it listen, make it understand—

"You'll die if you keep this up!" she shouted, exasperated, a little after three o'clock. This time the beast gave no evidence of having heard her. The fleetness of its feet made her think of an epic poem, droning on and on and on. *The Odyssey.* A *bylina.* Her eyelids drooped as they had done in school whenever the teacher lectured upon the topic. Tatya had been the avid pupil. Not she.

Pyotra appreciated stories. What she didn't appreciate were erudite pontifications upon them. She preferred a more active stance.

But at five in the morning, most of her action had seeped out of her.

"To hell with this." She halted abruptly, easing her rucksack off her aching hips and shoulders almost in one movement. "I'm having a break, you hear? You do as you please; see if I care."

She was shouting at the tracks ahead of her more than at the wolf itself. An ice fog had come on, accompanied by a snowfall that didn't bode well for the journey ahead. Pyotra knew she was taking an ill-advised risk; by the time she was ready to continue, the tracks of the wolf might not be visible. She had taken out the direction, though, and as far as she could judge, the animal seemed to be travelling in a straight line, north by northwest.

For all she knew, the pig-headed beast might be willing to fall prey to overexertion rather than accept help from a human hand.

"It doesn't understand you," Pyotra reminded herself, as she rooted around for her cook set, her sugar, her bag of chay. It wasn't enough, but she hoped it would give her a teeny boost of energy. What she really needed was a five-course meal and a bed of eiderdown. The side of her mouth quirked.

"I think you do understand me," she continued her one-sided conversation, lighting the flame with matches from out of one of her innumerable front pockets. "I think you just don't *want* to listen to reason, is what I think."

Pyotra sat back, huddling into the hood of her jacket. The light from her LEDs did precious little for her in this weather; but to turn them off and sit in darkness, a blind person in a snowy desert, was a less-than-palatable option. It felt like a giving in, letting go—and despite everything, she was not ready to do that.

"I won't find my way back on my own," she told the aluminium pot as she lifted it off the stove and poured hot water over the tea leaves in her wooden cup.

What exactly was she hoping for? That the wolf would show her the way home to Boris and Sergei, in gratitude for her having 'saved its life'? This wasn't a fairy story. And even if it were, no tale had ever told her she could rely on the generosity of wolves, the eaters of grandmothers and lambs and piglets, the trickers of blue-eyed girls in carmine riding hoods.

But she had a debt to pay and she would pay it. In the end, that was all there was to it.

The tea leaves in her cup swirled and formed into a pattern as she raised it to her lips. Startled, she lowered it again to study it closer. She had thought the outline looked distinctly wolven, but now the silhouette was vaguer, more—more human, for lack of a better descriptor.

Something stirred at the corner of her eye. Pyotra Nikolayevna Kulakova let her cup fall onto the snow and reached for her rope.

Chapter Nine

The human had stopped. Volk sensed it almost in the heartbeat it happened, as though an invisible string between her and her pursuer had snapped. This was her chance to get away.

She had never expected to come this far; she wouldn't have, if the—the female human, the woman, she knew now—hadn't started after her, continuing her single-minded chase, supplying Volk with fresh meat and plenty of rest. Volk had stayed close to the woman's tent at night, though she doubted other wolves would be as brazen as Tawny-legs; most wolves, after all, had learnt to be wary of humans. It had simply been a comfort to her, lying there, a swift leap or two away, sniffing the air for that sweet, intoxicating scent as she drifted off into a healing sleep.

It was almost like being part of a pack, gradually accommodating the other into one's life, adapting one's habits and needs to suit theirs. And in return—

Volk snorted, thrust up her head, and made an about-tail. She couldn't do it. She couldn't leave her behind. Not now.

A blizzard was coming, and even if the human had proved she was not devoid of survival strategies, she was a stranger to the tundra.

Volk had no time left for breaks. Her muzzle twitched in annoyance, her upper lip curling back into a snarl. They were a bloody useless species, humanity, as far as she was concerned. They—

Volk sat back on her haunches, blinking in surprise, as the noose tightened around her neck.

"Gotcha!" The woman held the rope in a steady, confident grip, dark spots blooming on her cheeks, tufts of matted hair visible under her hat and hood.

The brightness of her torch stung Volk's eyes. Volk tugged at the snare holding her, desperate to back away.

"Don't," the woman said, and there was a pleading note to her voice that Volk would have picked up on, even had she not comprehended the actual words. But she did. "You'll strangle yourself. Please, I'm not your enemy."

Volk ducked her head. *Oh, but she was.*

"I just want to take a look at your leg."

She wondered if the woman had started to become aware that Volk could parse what she said. No, it wasn't possible; it was outside of human ken. For the most part, at any rate. But then, humans chattered away at animals all the time, those they considered their personal belongings as well as those who ran free. Volk had seen a man talking to an owl once. She had heard a little girl singing to a deaf and dumb pool of water.

Volk growled softly. She had to act her part. Though what they needed was to run for shelter, now, at once, hours ago. How could she get her message across?

The woman had sunk to her knees, crawling closer on all fours. It would have been sweet, endearing almost, if it hadn't been for the tight grip she kept on that rope in her front paw. Hand. Hands, they were called.

A whine escaped Volk, animal instinct at war with her hourly increase in abstract thinking. The fine hairs on her nose trembled.

She had every reason to fear this encounter, and yet she had turned and run straight into it, because it would be a pity, such a pity...

We are both of us going to die out here.

Ever so slowly, the woman extended her mittened hand towards Volk's wounded leg. Volk bit back a bark. The change would heal it, but she couldn't tell the human that. Not even were she human herself did she know how she would begin to explain it.

And she wasn't. She wasn't this or that. She wasn't either/or. She was—

"I am going to touch you, okay?"

Volk huffed. She bucked her head. Then she did the only thing she could think of doing, and it seemed so simple, so evident a thing to do, she mentally bit herself for not coming up with it sooner.

She raised her eyes to meet the human's, and she shook her head, exaggeratedly, willing her to understand.

The woman's jaw dropped. She tumbled back upon her backside in the snow. Volk felt the creature inside her snigger; her heart swelled a little. *Cute*, that was the word she was searching for.

"Did you—did you just shake your head no?"

Volk nodded emphatically. *Yes.*

The woman held her head between her hands, as if she had to physically hold it in place on her neck or it would drift off like a hot-air balloon into the cloud-obstructed sky.

"Can you understand me?" The question was barely more than a whisper, as though she were afraid to ask.

Volk nodded curtly. She tried to remind herself that this was the only way forward, but it pained her, gave her a sick feeling to admit it.

"But how?"

Volk tipped her head to the side. She stood up, motioning for the woman to do the same, tugging at the rope that was still twisted around her arm. A leash could work both ways.

The wind had picked up. Snow and hail whipped Volk's face, biting through her fur. The human had no such protection. She needed shelter. *They* needed shelter. Could Volk dig a hole large enough for the both of them, with just the one good paw, and try to convince— No, it was out of the question.

Suddenly, an image of the other night in the taiga came to her, and she yipped, straining at the rope to reach the place where—yes, the human's rucksack, half-hidden in the snow but there it was, and in it was the thing they needed, the very thing. How slow-witted she was!

Volk turned her head to appraise her partner-in-tow. A memory of fluffy dogs with heterochromatic eyes drifted through her consciousness; huskies running alongside the reindeer herders across the plains. Her mouth twisted in a disdainful sneer, but they had no time to lose. She whined at the human like she had heard those domesticated canines do and scratched at the rucksack with her paw.

"You...you want something in my bag?" The woman looked dazed, but she crouched obediently by Volk's side, without a trace of wariness.

Volk nuzzled the human's cheek and gave it a broad lick.

The woman laughed, a low, pleasing sound in her throat that made Volk's tail shiver, her ears prick.

"Mother of God, but it's freezing," the human said conversationally, wiping her cheek with the one hand as her other undid the clasps on her rucksack. "It's like a storm..."

Her voice hitched, and Volk whined again, buffeting the woman's arm with her nose. The human looked straight into her eyes. "You want me to put up the tent?"

Volk nodded vigorously, not minding in the least if she looked like a cartoon character, a caricature of the Big Bad Wolf. *Yes, yes, yes.*

The woman slapped her forehead, shaking her head as she pulled the near-magical shelter out of its cover. "You're right. You're so right. This is insane; you should be in a circus or something. You're cleverer than I am."

Volk closed her eyes briefly and decided she hadn't heard that. They were doing too well.

There was nothing Volk could do to help the human assemble their makeshift cave, but she was fast once she got started, Volk noted with approval. Pitching a tent in an oncoming blizzard was a challenge to the most experienced of nomads, but *her* human did not lose her head. She went about her task almost blithely, and—may the Saints forgive her—Volk wagged her tail in encouragement, dancing around the perimeter, surreptitiously checking the security of the poles.

The woman forsook her mittens to finish up, and Volk felt that squeezing inside her again as she watched her exposed hands darken with the cold. As often as she could without being in the way, she went up and blew her warm breath over them.

"I'm okay. We'll be okay." The woman's teeth were clenched. Her words were barely audible over the howling gale.

"There," she said at last, and there it was: their one slim chance of survival. The tent wobbled, hail drumming at the weave, but it remained standing. "We better get inside."

Volk nodded, her nose twitching. Yes, it was their one hope. If she began digging herself a bivouac now, she would be digging her own shallow grave in the snow. And yet, to share quarters with a human...

"Come on, little wolf." Somehow, the woman was already inside, spreading out her mat and sleeping bag, and something bright and fuzzy beside it: for...her?

Volk lowered her head, sniffing at the material as she took one reluctant step after another until all of her was inside the cramped space. The woman zipped closed the opening.

The scent filling Volk's nostrils was overpowering, an explosion of olfactory delight that shook her, dizzied her.

Volk opened her eyes to the sound of the human's giggling, and to her dismay she saw that she had rolled herself into the fuzzy stuff, grunting like a boar who had found a pool of dung.

"You like it, eh?" The woman spoke mildly; a tentative smile flickered across her lips as she shrugged out of her wet anorak and placed it over her rucksack at the foot end of her mat. "It's just my old towel, I'm afraid, and used too. I wish I had something better to offer you, something warmer, but..."

Volk had shaken her head, just once. The woman inclined hers.

"I'm going to turn off my torch. You promise not to eat me up in the dark?"

Volk snorted, turning her scruff on the minx. And then she went quiet, barely breathing, as cold human fingers knitted into her pelt.

Chapter Ten

She woke with her arm thrown over the wolf. Her nose was buried in the soft fur at the nape of its neck.

Pyotra stiffened, her breath catching, and the beast moved, opening its sharp-toothed maw in a groaning, guttural yawn.

This was reality. She was lying in her tent on the tundra, snuggled up close to a feral wolf. It hadn't been a dream, though it should have been; this was wrong on so many levels Pyotra felt her brain might implode from the strain of making any kind of sense of it.

She clicked on her torch.

The wolf turned, its strange black eyes winking at her. Its expression was utterly unreadable—it was a wolf, for crying out loud! Its expression was that of a wolf, pure and simple.

Except nothing of this was either pure or simple.

Pyotra withdrew her arm, which lay slung across the animal's back. Her face warmed, as though she had inadvertently invaded a stranger's personal space. She licked her lips, dry and cracked from the constant cold.

"Do you... Can you still understand me?" Her face flushed even more; she felt like a fool as the dark eyes stared back at her.

Then, reluctantly, the wolf bobbed its head.

Pyotra didn't know if this made the situation better or worse. Did it prove she hadn't been hallucinating from exposure during the blizzard, or did it confirm she was still hallucinating?

"This is unreal," she told the wolf, and it laid its chin on its front paws, looking askance at her.

"Do you think the storm has passed?" It was a dumb question; it was so quiet one could have heard the proverbial pin drop.

The wolf peered over its shoulder towards the zipped-up door flap of the tent.

"You're right." Pyotra sat up, worming her way out of her sleeping bag. "We should get out of here."

*

Something was different. Pyotra couldn't say what, but as she opened the flap of the tent to peek out, it came to her. It wasn't just that there was no wind, no driving snow; something had happened to the darkness. It was...less. And what was more, it was lessening by the second, the polar night sky fading to a washed-out grey.

"Hey, it's—"

The wolf shot past her like a silver bullet.

Pyotra had no time to think; pure reflex made her grab the rope that ran alongside of it. *How rude of me*, she thought hazily, even as she wound the lasso around her elbow. How had she not thought to take it off the poor beast?

The last coil unlooped, and Pyotra was pulled out through the opening, sliding forwards in a spray of snow, her woollen undergarments wet through in a matter of moments.

"Stop, stop!" she cried, spitting like a cat as snow muffled her. The reasonable thing to do would be to let go of the damned rope, but... She didn't.

At last, they came to a halt, the wolf growling and panting, frantic as it tried to attack the offending rope with its teeth, the white of its eyes showing.

Pyotra was shaking where she lay, curbed by the sudden cold and exertion, but she pushed up on one arm and...

And her world spun off its axis.

*

The wolf collapsed, twitching in the feeble half-light of the year's first dawn. Its legs scrabbled over the ice-crusted snow like those of a dog dreaming of running. But the wolf seemed to be in agony, moaning with pain as its eyes rolled back in its head, its body wreaked by spasms. Was it having a seizure? Did wolves have epileptic fits?

A boy in her class—Vanka, his name had been—had been diagnosed with EP after having a grand mal right in the classroom, on a dusty, dreary afternoon in March. One moment, Vanka had been sitting quietly at his desk in the back of class; the next, he had been writhing in convulsions on the rough-hewn plank board floor. When it was over, he'd had splinters in his face and arms, and he had hurt his tongue so badly a chunk of it had come off and he couldn't speak properly for weeks afterwards.

The family had relocated to Syktyvkar about six months later. They wanted to live within calling distance of a hospital.

Pyotra couldn't blame them. She, too, had been spooked, and she hadn't even known Vanka all that well. No one had seemed to. He had always been a taciturn, introverted child.

There was a not inconsiderable risk the wolf would lash out at her—scratch or bite or worse—but Pyotra had to do something, anything.

The line between them had gone slack; Pyotra let go of the rope as she stood, her legs trembling.

The wolf didn't react. If anything, the paroxysms increased. Pyotra made a strangled, only half-human noise in her throat and rushed up to the flailing heap of fur and bones. She put her hands on its chest and flank, trying to steady it through sheer physical pressure; but what she felt made her yowl and withdraw involuntarily.

The palms of her hands had pinkened from the brief contact. The wolf was burning up, its body the temperature of the hot plate that passed for a stove back in Boris's cabin.

Blood roared in Pyotra's ears, and for a second she worried she was going to pass out, making herself doubly useless, but then—

With a harrowing howl, the wolf stretched out every movable limb at once, its paws curling in a way Pyotra didn't think she had ever seen an animal's paws curl before, and she trained her eyes on them, focused all of her precarious hold on consciousness on them, as they turned—impossibly—into human fists.

Her vision blurred. The white-and-grey world around her swam and faded into a pinpoint, a buzz, and finally, nothing at all.

*

She was back in the tent. Pyotra couldn't recall how she had got there, her mind fuzzy and vague, barely able to register her surroundings. But something—some*one*— shifted beside her: a faint sound reached her ears, as of bones creaking.

The wolf. The bitter tang of blood filled Pyotra's mouth as she turned her head, not wanting to, but unable not to.

A person was lying next to her. A human, olive-skinned but pale and shivering, wrapped ineffectually in Pyotra's yellow towel and nothing else.

Pyotra swallowed and looked into a round face framed by untidy black hair, lips thinned to a line as if the person—*she*—was biting down on them.

"It's you."

It was an observation, not a question. It was a letting go...of reason, of what had constituted her grasp on reality until then. Of sanity itself, in some ways.

The wolf's dusky eyes met hers, and for the first time they made sense to Pyotra. The woman's lips parted slightly as if to speak, then closed again. She didn't nod. No need.

"You speak Russian, don't you?"

The woman raised her eyebrows, and Pyotra felt like an idiot: If *the wolf* had understood Russian, why wouldn't the woman the wolf had turned into?

The woman the wolf had turned into... Pyotra pinched herself, striving to regain her presence of mind, to fight off the buzzing gnats of unconsciousness threatening to overtake her ears. She inhaled deeply.

"I think you need this better than I do." Pyotra opened her sleeping bag, confused for a moment to find herself in her underwear, a sock on one foot, a streak of wet down the central part of her torso, before she remembered: the wolf had dragged her across the icy snow. The wolf had tried to flee.

She wrapped the insulated bag around the shuddering form of the stranger beside her. The dark eyes widened a little. Pyotra nodded encouragingly, cajoling her to put her feet into the end of the bag, lift herself up so that Pyotra could slide the bottom of the bag under her. She zipped her up and the woman, at last, let out a sigh.

"*Spasiba*." Her voice was rough and hesitant, unsure of itself. Pyotra glanced at her furtively.

"Will you—" She bit the inside of her cheek, wondering how best to phrase herself. "—will you stay...like this, now?"

The woman moved her head. Pyotra wasn't sure what she was doing, what she was trying to communicate, until she heard her neck creak, followed by a light gasp of relief.

"*Da*." The stranger blinked slowly. She was falling asleep, Pyotra realised. "I am...old wolf."

"Oh." This told Pyotra absolutely nothing. There was a world of questions she needed answers to. But she would have to be patient, it seemed, because the—the wolf woman had gone to sleep, unceremoniously, right there in her tent, and Pyotra didn't have the heart to wake her. Whoever—whatever—she was.

*

"Only youngsters change with the phases of the moon."

The woman sniffed the stale black bread Pyotra had found at the bottom of her rucksack. She didn't seem convinced it was edible.

If she thought about it, Pyotra couldn't hold it against her; but she felt piqued, all the same. She hadn't wanted to leave the stranger unguarded while she slept what appeared to be the sleep of the dead. Besides, she doubted she had the skills necessary to find and shoot game on the tundra. This was the best she had to offer.

"If you dip it in your tea, it'll soften."

The woman lifted those maddeningly expressive eyebrows again. They were seated outside the tent, lighted only by Pyotra's headband torch. The sun had set again within the hour. It was a start, however.

"It was the sunlight that incited your change, wasn't it?"

The stranger nodded unwillingly. She raised their shared cup of chay to her lips and blew on it, the steam curling away into the dark.

Pyotra's spare clothes didn't exactly fit the wolf woman; she was sturdier built, but shorter by half a head or so. Despite this, she managed to exude a confident ease in her borrowed threads that Pyotra found disconcerting.

"I'm Pyotra," she burst out, only now remembering they'd had no formal introduction. "What should I call you?"

For a split second, the woman looked taken aback. Her gaze travelled out across the snowy plain, and Pyotra wondered if she still had a predator's night vision. Her eyes, after all, hadn't changed.

"Volk," she answered finally, decisively. She put the cup down in the space between them, not meeting Pyotra's eyes.

"That's not really a... Well, it's not a woman's name, at any rate."

It was too much to take in, all of it, or she would have stopped herself before the offensive statement was out of her mouth; but there it was. She felt unreasonably hurt that this—*Volk*—would not give her a proper name to call her by. Who ever heard of a woman named Wolf?

"It's what I am." The soft, close-to-whispered reply did more to chastise Pyotra than if Volk had shown any sign of anger.

"I'm sorry," Pyotra muttered, grabbing the cup and being careful not to turn it from where Volk had put her lips to it, moments ago. It was a dubious gesture, but the only one she could think of. "I...thank you for saving my life, Volk. And my brother's life. I shouldn't have come after you."

Volk shrugged. "It's what people do."

This time, there was a distinct edge to the wolf woman's voice, but Pyotra didn't think it was directed at her personally. She took a sip of chay, her skin prickling as she felt Volk watching her.

"So he is not your cub then?"

Her brows knit together as she looked back up, before she understood what Volk was referring to.

"Oh, you mean Sergei! No, he's not my...cub. How old do you think I am?"

Volk rubbed at her nose. "I'm glad he survived. I thought, since you came after me, he didn't."

Pyotra lowered her gaze. How could she explain that she was no better than all those other *people* this strange creature scorned; that she had bought into the whole 'ye shall not suffer an animal who has tasted human blood to live'?

"You bit him. I mean, you broke his skin. I'm sorry, he and Ded, they're all I have, I—"

Volk had risen of a sudden, hulking over her. Her eyes were as wild as when she—as when the wolf had been— "You're lying!"

Pyotra gawked up at her, and for a moment all she could see was the wolf, the ferocious beast barely contained within the confines of human flesh.

This—this being could snap her neck as easily as if it were nothing but a stray twig on the ground of the boreal forest. For all Pyotra knew, Volk might be planning to; she knew, after all. *Pyotra knew.*

The oboroten' was supposed to be a fairy tale, a harmless fantasy, a whisper escaped from a lunatic asylum. It wasn't supposed to be *real.*

"Please." Without thinking, Pyotra had raised her arms to shield herself from the expected blow. "Please, Volk, I won't tell a soul, I promise!"

Volk snarled, her hands fisting, and something stirred in Pyotra. She would never be able to say why it was, how she could have known, but she extended her hand and touched one of those balled-up fists, feeling the minute vibrations, the heat that it should have been impossible for any living thing to endure.

"Don't." She pushed her thumb in between the wolf woman's fingers, even though they were scalding her. "Stay."

Volk snarled again and crumpled to the ground.

Chapter Eleven

A white face swam before her, wraithlike against the backdrop of the starry night. Volk couldn't focus her eyes; her skin itched, close to breaking, as if a thousand needles threatened to pierce through it. She wanted to howl in pain, in grief and agony, but the moonlit face moved closer, iridescent, carrying with it a scent that made her dulled senses sit up and take notice.

Pyotra.

Volk opened her mouth slightly.

"Volk!" A cool, smooth palm cupped her cheek. "Please, talk to me."

Her eyes were a greyish blue. Volk hadn't noticed before. As a wolf, her perception of colour was dulled. The eyes looked worried, wide and wet.

"Fine." Volk pushed her throat and tongue into some semblance of cooperation. "Good."

Pyotra gasped. "Oh, thank heaven!"

Volk sat up. She had been lying on the ground, in the snow. She had been...*shifting*. Or almost. Volk wriggled her fingers, felt the sides of her neck and jaws.

Something had happened; something had provoked her beyond what the wolf was prepared to deal with in this vulnerable skin.

"The cub." Volk shook her head, straining to clear her muddled thoughts. "Did you say... Did I... Was he bleeding?"

Fear flashed through those icy grey-blues. The human—Pyotra—huddled together, making herself small. "It was nothing. You saved him. Please..."

I won't tell a soul. That was what she had said.

"I'm not going to hurt you. I am not concerned—" Volk clicked her tongue in frustration. How had everything become so entangled? If she had left the cub to his fate, that would have been the end of it. Perhaps it would have been preferable to— "You have to tell me the truth. You don't have to be afraid of me, Pyotra, but I—I have to know."

"Why?" Pyotra sat back on her heels, staring at Volk with those haunted eyes. She chewed at a piece of loose skin by her thumbnail. Her hands must be freezing, exposed to the Arctic night for so long.

"You should put on your mittens." It came out gruffer than she had intended. It seemed to be physically impossible for her to interact with this oddly provocative female without intimidating her.

In her lupine form, she'd had a plan for her. Volk had meant to—

"He had wounds on his neck from where your teeth had pricked his skin. They weren't life-threatening. If I had known what you... I wouldn't have come after you. It's just that I have some issues with wolves."

Volk's head was spinning again, but she would not give in to it; she had done enough, enough, and then some. She trained her mind and her senses on the woman in front of her, shamelessly using her proximity, her allure, to ground herself.

When she was somewhat composed, she saw that Pyotra had put on her mittens. Her cheeks were glowing red, her soft lips parted, and Volk felt a buzz in her ears, in her belly, which had nothing whatsoever to do with turning.

"We have to go."

"What?"

"The cub—your brother— I— He should not be alone for his first change. I'm sorry. I'm sorrier than you will ever know, but please believe me when I say I did not mean for this, any of this, to happen."

Pyotra ogled her, incomprehension writ large across her sharp-angled features. Even through the many layers of her attire, Volk could see her chest rising and falling jerkily with the rapidity of her breathing. "What are you saying? I won't let you—"

Volk neither moved nor spoke. She felt too tired for this, too tired for anything, everything. Life as a wolf was infinitely simpler. A curse on the returning light.

She stood where she was, watching the human spin around and run towards the tent. They had moved away from it, Volk realised; she couldn't say how it had happened. She had lost her wherewithal, as usual around this...Pyotra. It didn't matter which skin she was currently inhabiting.

Galina had warned her about staying alone for too long.

Volk blinked as Pyotra returned, cradling her rifle, the barrel trembling as she pointed it at her.

She snorted, and the last bit of colour drained from the human's face.

"I won't let you hurt him. I don't care who or what you are."

She looked lovely on the opposite end of a lethal weapon. It was the way she had looked the first time Volk had set eyes on her. Volk let out a regretful breath. If only she had shot her then.

"Shoot me if you will, Pyotra. It won't make any difference to Sergei. He is still going to turn into a wolf by the next full moon." Volk lifted her eyes to the sky. "Three weeks from now."

Pyotra cried out, desperate in her consternation and fury, and Volk recognised that cry: the roar of the mother wolf. She ducked instinctively, but too late; a burning pain tore through her right shoulder. Volk—the wolf—flung herself at the shooter, toppling them both to the ground. She bared her teeth, growling, ready to sink them into the exposed flesh of the woman's neck, to drain her, to fill her up with—

Volk yowled as Pyotra's mittened hand braced against the fresh gunshot wound to her shoulder. Pain sliced through her like a white-hot rod, a foretaste of the innermost circle of hell. Through the haze, she saw her blood staining the wool, saw the pinched look of worry on the madwoman's face, and even though she was close to throwing up the scant contents of her stomach—even though she had just been well and truly shot at!—she threw back her head and laughed.

Volk laughed until salt water ran down her cheeks, until the stars trembled and blurred, usurping her field of vision. The smoking barrel of the rifle poked her in the guts, wedged between them, and by all rights, by all reason, she should be dead, dead, four times over, her bones picked clean by scavengers, the queer secret of her existence buried soundly under layers upon layers of falling snow.

Pyotra jostled Volk, struggling to emerge from underneath her.

"I better dress that wound," she said, and Volk continued to laugh.

Chapter Twelve

Pyotra hadn't meant to shoot the wolf woman. Not for real—not when Volk so patently trusted her not to. And besides, Volk, irrespective of her name and her superhuman abilities, was a *person*. She didn't go around murdering people because it suited her fancy. Not in what Pyotra thought of as the actual, ordinary, everyday world.

Although lately, she was no longer convinced she was still an inhabitant of that world.

It was the way Volk had offhandedly apologised for wounding—for *ruining*—her duck, as though she had given him a common cold. As though destroying a child's life was a minor inconvenience, an occupational hazard in the day-to-day existence of the obo—yes, she would use the term, if only in her head—the oboroten'.

She hadn't meant to *shoot* Volk. But she had been properly pissed off.

On top of it all, the bitch had the gall to laugh at her. The bark of her deranged guffawing rang out across the tundra, while Pyotra's mitten grew heavy with Volk's blood. She supposed she could just let her haemorrhage to death, out there on the snowy plain with nary a witness around. She could up and leave her, returning to Boris and Sergei and life as she knew it, where wolves were wily, menacing beasts, sure, but they were no more than that.

If Volk spoke the truth, however—and for all her infuriating aloofness, she didn't strike Pyotra as a liar—if Sergei was really *polluted*... If this was the case, inconvenient though it was, there was only one person Pyotra could trust to help him.

Whatever the outcome, Volk had already saved his life once.

When Pyotra returned with her first-aid kit and her hunting knife, Volk's boisterous mirth had ebbed to a quiet titter. Her spaced-out gaze was turned up towards the night sky. Before leaving her, Pyotra had stuffed her shawl underneath Volk's head, but half-melted snow still clung to her messy, tangled hair.

Pyotra tutted, kneeling to inspect the damage. She had left her soggy mitten draped across the wound, though it did little to staunch the flow. It didn't look as bad as she had thought at first. A flesh wound, as the nurse back home would have dubbed it; she did see her fair share of 'hunting accidents' among the village's male population, typically fuelled by a bottle of vodka or three.

Pyotra used the knife to cut through the fabric of Volk's haphazard clothing, asking herself if she had managed to do anything other than ruin her own clothes. One of her best shirts too. Pyotra harrumphed, exasperated, and Volk turned her black eyes on her. Her face looked so soft and relaxed Pyotra was taken aback.

"You smell *so* good," the wolf woman lisped, and Pyotra's face grew hot. "You smell like an incense-filled church, like fire and snow, warmth and gentleness." Volk nodded, closed her eyes, and drifted into unconsciousness.

*

"We are heading in the wrong direction!" Pyotra shoved her compass right under the oboroten's nose. Somehow, she had made the mistake of trusting to the wolf's inherent sense of direction.

To be honest, she had been too tired to argue. Sharing a sleeping bag with a storybook creature one has shot at could do that to a person.

Also, after the wolf woman's weird soliloquy on her olfactory assets, Pyotra had been acutely aware of the way Volk's nostrils flared, even in her sleep.

Whenever Pyotra had moved, a soft moan of pain issued from the freshly wounded. Not to mention that— inevitably—skin brushed against skin, thighs, hands, and hips squashed together. At one point, the sole of Volk's foot had slid down the arch of Pyotra's, and it had jolted Pyotra wide awake; it had—*bothered* her.

"We will be too slow on foot." Volk shrugged at the compass. It was almost impossible to tell which shoulder had been hurt.

All the same, Pyotra felt sick, remembering how she had dug the bullet out with the tip of her knife while Volk bit down on the leather sheath, beads of sweat forming on her forehead despite the glacial temperature of their surroundings.

Pyotra pocketed her compass. "We'll be too slow on foot, so you figured we'd take a detour for the hell of it?"

Volk's brows bunched together. It was the daylight hour—or half hour, to be precise—and in the vague, panting glow of the distant sun, Pyotra could scrutinise her companion thoroughly for the first time. She was downright ugly, Pyotra decided: short, stout, wild-haired and wild-eyed, with a broad face and weather-beaten skin. She had been graceful as a wolf, but now she trod on with an irregular, lopsided gait, as though she had not quite adjusted to having only the one pair of legs.

She was gruff too, and impolite. In short, she was nothing at all like beautiful, clever, well-mannered Tatyana Ivanovna. So why did Pyotra—

"We are stopping by my den to pick up skis," Volk answered patiently.

"Oh." Pyotra had no sarcastic comeback for this. "Well, why didn't you say so?"

Volk blew out her breath and turned to trudge on. "You didn't ask."

"I shouldn't have to ask. You should have told me anyway. It's common courtesy."

Rather than answer back, Volk rubbed at her wounded shoulder. It was a subtle gesture, but Pyotra saw, of course, like the damned woman counted on. And of course, she got the message, loud and clear.

Pyotra had shot her. To be fair, she had done her best to undo the damage, as it were, but... Asking your victim to be polite to you the day after you've fired a gun at them was maybe—really—too much to ask.

"You're a fucking wolf," Pyotra muttered under her breath, her eyes tearing from the bite of the wind.

And like a wolf—because no human being could have heard that, not from ten metres away—Volk turned, the corner of her mouth twisted up in a sideways grin. "I never claimed to be anything but."

Pyotra scowled.

Then, all at once, something broke within her. "I'm sorry! I'm so, so sorry—oh God! I could have killed you."

She didn't know how it happened, but rather than fall to her knees on the ground, she rushed forward and wrapped her arms around Volk's midsection, hugging her to her, bawling like Mashka Petrovna had bawled when her favourite, prize-winning Persian had gone missing the spring before last.

Volk repositioned herself in her arms. Pyotra felt the oboroten's nose press to her hairline, sniffing luxuriantly, and a hum of incandescent, intensely jarring arousal spread like a quick-moving infection from her neck to her groin.

It was—it wasn't—

She let go, taking a wobbling step back. Volk's eyelids fluttered; a flush darkened her temples. She cocked her head to the side and looked at Pyotra, the way the wolf had looked at her, as if gauging her, seeing right into her. After what seemed like an endless moment, Pyotra wrenched herself free of that gaze with what felt like physical effort, and turned away.

Volk said something, muffled by the snowfall and the wind and Pyotra's scarf, wound around her neck, wrapped across the lower part of her face whenever she wasn't speaking. She moved again, without looking back, trusting Pyotra to follow as usual. It seemed to be the firmament of their relationship.

But Pyotra stood petrified, perplexed. She started after her only as the falling snow threatened to erase Volk from sight, because even if the words had been only half meant for her, she had heard them, and they unsettled her, confused her. Exhilarated her.

You would have made a fine wolf.

*

They reached Volk's den, a cave in the side of a flat-topped cliff, after hours of hiking through darkness.

Pyotra had no idea where they were or how far—how mind-numbingly far—from all she knew; she had stopped checking her compass, stopped resisting—she knew not what. For the last half hour, she had moved in a torpor, letting herself be guided by Volk's lead, stepping in her fresh prints. She wondered if her old boots pinched the wolf woman's feet, if they kept the cold out. She had never meant to use them, adding them to her pack only as a superstitious precaution, a last resort. Volk wearing them had lightened her load considerably.

Kolya had used to scold her for overpacking, overthinking things. What were the odds she was going to damage the boots she wore on a hunt beyond repair?

Pyotra supposed they were about equal to the chances of needing to clothe a bare-naked turnskin out on the tundra.

Sometimes, not very often, but sometimes, being prepared for the wildly unlikely wasn't such a bad thing. Pyotra could almost hear her father laughing good-humouredly—as he had, in the days before Sima's brutal attack—and it made her throat constrict, her eyes well up.

Blinded by her whimsical tears, Pyotra walked right into Volk, who had halted abruptly. She fell on her rear, whooping and cursing with the surprise of it, the ignominy.

"You are tired, human." Volk handed her up without effort, as if Pyotra's lanky self and the rucksack weighed next to nothing. She brushed her off with an inscrutable expression, squinting from the glare of Pyotra's LEDs. "This is my summer residence. We will rest here tonight and start back on skis in the morning."

Volk was making an effort to share information, Pyotra intuited, although it precluded Pyotra having any differing opinion on the matter. She was too wiped out to argue, however. Well, almost.

"My name is Pyotra."

Volk smiled faintly. She pushed at something which Pyotra would have termed a Boulder Too Large to Move, except it slid away easily, revealing the opening into a cavern which was, if possible, even darker than the Siberian night.

"Welcome to my den, Pyotra." Volk spoke softly, so softly Pyotra bit back the snide remark on the tip of her tongue.

Instead, she craned her neck to shine her torch inside and gasped as she caught sight of the innocuous traces of human life: wooden shelves lining the rock walls; earthen crocks and pots; something that looked like a chimneyed fireplace, which she couldn't even begin to fathom how Volk had contrived to construct inside a natural cave.

Crude hunter-gatherer-style weapons and implements leant against the side of one of the shelves, and opposite it, most marvellous of all: a generous, low, wood-framed bed lined with fur upon fur.

It was like being thrown back through centuries—through millennia—and yet, it was so blessedly civilised, comfortable, safe, compared to the stark, indifferent world out on the plains.

Pyotra reached out and squeezed Volk's arm in delight. She didn't speak—she was too overwhelmed—but Volk could obviously read her emotion. Uncharacteristically bashful, the wolf woman turned her face away.

"There's some firewood left since...last time I was here. Will you get started on building up a fire while I check the perimeter and open up the chimney hole?"

Pyotra had begun nodding before she grasped what Volk was saying. "Wait, you're leaving me here?"

Volk scoffed. It was the scoff of the wolf, the haughty predator, and Pyotra felt her cheeks reddening, half in anger, half in shame.

She was about to lash out when Volk extended her hand and touched Pyotra's cheek, in a gesture akin to what one might use to comfort a child. Pyotra opened her mouth to protest, but the words hitched in her throat as Volk moved her rough-skinned thumb across Pyotra's bottom lip.

She couldn't speak. She couldn't think. All she could do was stare into the wolf's black eyes, as her pulse pounded at her neck, as her knees weakened, as her breath came in short bursts and gasps.

The wolf woman grinned slowly, and there was a knowingness to that grin, a recognition, which should have been infuriating. Instead, Pyotra smiled back, shyly, her hand coming up to press against Volk's.

"I'll be right back. I promise. No need to worry. You're in my den, human."

Pyotra had to admit, there was a certain kind of skewed logic to that.

"Don't you need the torch?" Pyotra made to take it off, but Volk shook her head, sweeping the tips of her fingers along Pyotra's jawline before she let go and slipped out into the pitch black, leaving Pyotra on the threshold, in every sense.

Chapter Thirteen

Volk had bitten the cub. She hadn't meant to—they were too fragile, these humans, too apt to bleed—but she had, and in doing so her fate had been sealed. All she could hope for now was that the female—Pyotra—had been mistaken somehow, or that Galina had been mistaken; in short, that everyone had made a mistake except she, Volk, the unhappiest mother-to-be this side of the Ural Mountains.

Because she would have to take him away. She would have to sever his ties with the humans, the village, the world as he knew it, or they would hunt him down and kill him, like the baby abomination he was.

Deep inside her were buried the memories of another such hunt, the stink of fear and adrenaline, the smoke of fires, Galina barking, goading her on.

Volk's teeth gritted as she began scaling the cliff, dislodging the snow from the roughly hewn steps in the rock wall as she went. Cold moonlight bathed her in an unearthly blue grey; yes, the colours, the nuances were returning.

She had bitten the cub. She should be sorry, and she was. For years now, too many to reckon, she had not met with a single, solitary creature she could have imagined having as a constant companion.

Until now.

The wolf inside her—the being that was more her than this frustratingly inept incarnation—bristled and shook with the urge to run back down to her den and do some serious biting, proper biting; biting as it should be done, with passion, with fervour, between two consenting adults.

As Volk had planned for it to happen, since she had first caught a whiff of Pyotra Nikolayevna's alluring scent.

She paused at the top of the cliff, watching the clouds of her warm breath forming and disappearing. It was painful. It felt like a betrayal, even now, but she had to admit it to herself: she had wanted Pyotra. Even in her lupine skin—*especially* in her lupine skin—she had craved her, lusted after her, right from the start.

Volk grimaced. The glow in her abdomen informed her that the past tense was just another vain attempt at coyness.

The unreasonably dogged woman had come after her, pursuing her through the taiga, tracking her across the tundra, crowning it all by actually, genuinely shooting at her. But she had also rescued her, several times over, from the tawny-legged loner; from starvation while her leg healed; from the elements when she had been reborn, a defenceless babe in the snow.

She had removed the bullet from Volk's shoulder. She had a temper on her, but she was fair-minded, Pyotra—Volk's fever dream come true.

Oh, she would have made a magnificent wolf.

You mustn't remain alone for too long after I am gone, lyubov. It is against your nature. Promise me you will look for someone.

Volk had bitten the cub.

She fell to her knees on the moonlit cliff and howled.

*

When Volk returned, Pyotra was seated in front of a burning fire. She had plaited her long yellow hair—startlingly yellow, like buttercups, like orange juice mixed from concentrate, like the overpowering crayon yellow of a child's depiction of the sun. In short, it was the yellow of high summer, the few weeks of the year when all of Nenets Autonomous Okrug, in unison, in wonder, turned their faces towards the open sky. The contours of her cheekbones jutted out as she bent over some task. Something in her hands consumed her attention.

Volk glided towards her, rapt by the sight of this woman, this human, this other being in her den, so nonchalantly comfortable and unperturbed. She peeked curiously over her shoulder.

Pyotra was holding her hunting knife in one hand and a whetting stone in the other, sharpening the glinting steel of the blade. Volk's mouth fell open. She snorted in derision.

Pyotra jumped, nicking herself on the knife.

"Ow!" The human put her finger in her mouth, and Volk's guts clenched. She blew out a gust of air through her nose. She wasn't used to this constant battle to control the predator within. When she wanted something, she was in the habit of taking it.

"You have to stop creeping up on me." Pyotra squinted at her. "I could have hurt myself."

Volk grunted. "I only told you to get the wood ready, not light a fire. You could have hurt yourself much worse from monoxide poisoning if you started it before I'd cleared the chimney."

Pyotra shook her head. By the low light of the fire, her eyes were like bruises, her pupils dilated, two angry red blotches forming across her cheeks. "I'm not an idiot, or a child. I've survived perfectly well without a personal oboroten' guardian for twenty-two years, thank you very much."

Volk had guessed she was young, but that—was very young indeed. She sighed. "Then why did you—"

"I heard you up there. I have to say, I thought wolves howling at the moon was a myth."

Volk frowned. The human certainly knew how to push her buttons. And the twitching of her lips betrayed that she was enjoying it too.

Volk seated herself, without a retort. It was a good fire, she had to concede, and it made sense, she supposed, to light it as soon as possible. She pulled off her borrowed gloves and held her paws out to warm them.

Hands. They were hands now.

Pyotra shifted beside her, and Volk shut her eyes and opened her mouth to taste the human's scent, all but tangible in the stuffy air of the cave. It wasn't right, but she didn't care; she was too tired to fight it. Surely she wasn't doing any harm?

Her taste buds swelled with pleasure as Pyotra drew nearer. Pyotra put a hand on her shoulder—her good shoulder—and Volk peeped at her through her lashes.

"I apologise, Volk. I know I can't... I would like to do something for you, if you will let me. I know I haven't been treating you the way you should be treated; you're a fellow creature, a fellow *person*, and I know whatever you did to Sergei—that wasn't your intention. I, on the other hand... I have a lot to make up for."

Her hand seemed to burn through Volk's layers of ill-fitting clothes, making her very bones tingle. She had to push her away, now, or she would be lost, she wouldn't be able to—

"I thought, if you would allow me, I could cut your hair."

Volk gawked at the pale apparition beside her, not sure she had heard her correctly.

"You—what?"

Pyotra dipped her head, her face pinkening, notes of embarrassment and something, something heady and disorienting, present in her smell. She held the knife up in the flickering light.

"I know it's silly, and I know it doesn't even begin to—but I'm quite good at it. That is to say, I cut Boris's and Sergei's hair. Usually with scissors, but..."

Volk began to shake her head in amazement, but changed it into a nod lest she should be misconstrued. "I guess I'm a little shaggy."

Pyotra's eyes sparkled.

Volk gave her a half grin to spur her on, and the human obliged, throwing her head back in helpless, tension-releasing laughter.

*

"Sit completely still."

Pyotra's hands pressed on the back of her head, soft but insistent, and Volk was already regretting saying yes, regretting that she had agreed to this meaningless, dangerous frivolity, when they had much better catch their rest while they could and be off again.

But how could she have resisted the earnestness in Pyotra's request? How could she refuse her—anything?

Volk had claimed her brother. She hadn't meant to do it, but there seemed to be only Pyotra and Sergei and—*Boris*—in that small izba by the pond, which Volk only dimly recalled. It was an effort, remembering details from her deep-wolf consciousness.

Who was Boris? Another brother, their father, a—lover? What species of Russian male would allow his woman to go scampering off on a wild wolf hunt, without accompanying her, or at least coming after her?

How—

Volk stiffened, her mind going blank, as Pyotra's cool fingers began threading and weaving through her hair, parting it this way and that. Her scalp came alive, aching with the minute sensual gratification of it, sending thrills down her spine, ripples that eddied and flowed through her system.

She couldn't think straight.

She couldn't think at all. She was entranced by the slow, calm way in which Pyotra untangled the knots and snarls so as not to hurt her—but it did hurt her. She couldn't not hurt with longing, with desiring what wasn't, what could never be hers.

"Are you okay?" Pyotra's face came suddenly before her, the damnable glare of her torch spearing into her eyes, and Volk opened her mouth and surprised them both with what came out: "What's wrong with Boris?"

Volk shut her mouth quickly, pressing her lips together, but the words had been spoken. They lay thick as poison in the air between them.

Pyotra bit her lip. Her eyebrows came together, and then she righted herself, returning her attention to Volk's messy mane.

They were silent for what seemed like an eternity, as Pyotra worked through the remainder of her hair—not quite as careful now. Volk welcomed the physical pain. It was a lesser pain, all things considered, than the ache of want from a moment ago.

She fixed her eyes on the cave wall opposite, where their shadows played by dint of the firelight. She watched the dark outline of the woman behind her raising a knife over her head, and she yipped in a sudden flash of atavistic terror as Pyotra brought the blade down to slice through the segment of hair she held stretched in her left.

"I didn't mean to startle you," Pyotra mumbled.

Volk smirked inwardly. "Yes, you did."

Pyotra let out a long breath that turned into a sweet little regretful laugh at the end. "You're right. I'm incorrigible. But so are you. How did you know about Boris? Did you stalk us? Did you—"

Volk's eyebrows rose, despite the fact that Pyotra was talking to her neck. She was more than talking to her neck, for that matter. She was caressing it, absentmindedly, as she spoke. The human just wouldn't give her a break.

"I knew nothing about Boris until you mentioned him before. You said you cut Sergei's and Boris's hair."

Pyotra tutted like an old *babka*, resuming her chore. The blade of the knife was—really—very sharp. *The better to cut your hair with, Wolf.*

Volk scratched her chin.

"And I am to believe that it was your supernatural werewolf senses that picked up on the fact that Boris is blind? How gullible do you think I am? You were watching—"

"Enough." Volk could hear the threatening snarl in her own voice. She took a deep breath. "I don't reason as"—*Myself* was on the tip of her tongue, but she abstained from using the term. They needed to make some headway towards levelling with one another—"as a wolf. I am not a human in wolf's clothing, so to speak. I had no idea your Boris was blind, nor even that he existed. I only surmised, now, in this...form, that any man who would let his woman—"

Pyotra's fingers curled around her shoulder bone. *Not* her good shoulder. Volk hissed.

"Boris is my dedushka," Pyotra said unexpectedly. Then, just as unexpectedly, she sniggered. "I guess I can scrap the theory of your supernatural wolf senses."

The relief that flooded her on finding out Boris's identity in relation to Pyotra was almost more frightening, more harrowing, than if she had been right. She had no rival. There was no one, nothing, that stood in her way.

Except that, in another three weeks, Sergei Nikolayevich would go through his first change.

Except that Boris, Pyotra's grandfather, was blind, living in a cabin outside a nondescript northern Siberian settlement, in the taiga, with no one but his two grandchildren to depend on, of which Volk had already claimed one.

She had bitten the wrong grandchild.

"If you don't reason as a wolf, why did you take it into your head to save Sergei?"

Pyotra had let go of her shoulder. She was chopping away at Volk's hair with swift, precise movements, thick, black coils falling to the floor of Volk's den.

Volk caught a wisp of hair in her hand, unsettled. This part of her that had so recently been a living thing, now ruthlessly, dispassionately shorn away. It was not unlike how her life had changed, sharply, from one breath to the next.

"He was just a cub. The instinct to protect younglings is not species-specific." From force of habit, Volk held up the hair to her nose. "Besides, he smelled of you."

Chapter Fourteen

Pyotra didn't know what to say. Navigating a conversation with a turnskin—with Volk—was akin to walking across a minefield, even at the best of times. And here she was, in the very lair of the beast, cutting the wolf woman's hair with her hunting knife, while said wolf—again—pointedly commented on her smell.

She really cold use a bath, at that.

"You have books," she blurted at last, grasping at straws, her LEDs flitting towards a shelf in the corner.

"I have books," Volk agreed, a hint of amusement apparent in her otherwise flat, rather gravelly voice.

"Where did they come from?" Pyotra struggled to keep her tone level, sawing away at a thick strand of hair. She couldn't think why Volk had to have this effect on her. She had never considered herself a particularly irritable person. Well, apart from where her family were concerned; wolves and her family was a sore spot with her.

"Where do books come from?" Volk raised her shoulders but managed, Pyotra noted, to keep her head perfectly immobile. "Most of them were Galina's. Some I have picked up myself, bartering. I get bored, you know, in this skin."

The knife had stilled in her hand. Mortified, Pyotra realised she was gripping Volk's hair, aimlessly running her fingers through it, as though it were Sergei sitting in front of her and not a stranger—a woman—a wolf— "Who is Galina?"

Volk was silent. She was silent for so long Pyotra was unsure whether she had asked the question out loud or not. Then a shudder went through her—through Volk and into Pyotra—and she knew she had asked a question too many. She was trespassing. She was—

"Galina was my maker. My lover. My...mate."

Volk didn't turn around as she spoke. She didn't change her position nor her tone of voice, for which Pyotra was infinitely grateful. It was enough that Pyotra's knife had clattered to the ground, that she had to stoop to pick it up, her mind racing, her *heart* racing.

Clumsily, she took up her self-assigned task anew, because she couldn't think what else to do. Also, a haircut wasn't something you left off half or two-thirds of the way through.

"What—" Pyotra cleared her throat. "Why—where did she go?"

"She was shot. Gutted. Probably what remains of her hangs on the wall of some hunting lodge."

The wolf woman's reply seemed to come everywhere and nowhere at once, its import hitting Pyotra like a fist to her solar plexus.

"Oh, Volk!" Somehow she slipped with the knife; a faint red line became visible on Volk's newly exposed neck. Pyotra gasped, horrified. "I'm sorry! I'm sorry for your loss. I'm sorry—I—"

She threw the offending knife down and bent over Volk's neck, wanting to stem the blood. And it was Sergei's wound, Sergei's neck, all over; *an accident, just an accident*, her mind screamed as she pressed her thumbs around the thin, yet vicious-looking gash, as she put her lips—

"No!" In one quick, peremptory motion, Volk turned and shoved her aside, the whites of her eyes showing all around her irises, her mien fierce, desperate. Savage.

Pyotra stumbled and fell, and Volk stood over her, her hand holding the back of her neck, her jaws working.

"You don't want my blood in your system, human."

Pyotra mewled with fright, and Volk's lowering eyes softened. Her face fell.

"Pyotra..." Volk knelt by her side, and Pyotra stared at her in wonder. Never before had someone made the harsh consonants of her name sound like a caress. Something inside her quailed, as though the werewolf had indeed touched her, had reached inside her and stroked her soul.

"I didn't mean to cut you. I never meant—" The words died on Pyotra's lips.

Volk nodded, simply, and drew her into her arms, tucked her against her chest. For the first time, Pyotra noticed that her cheeks were slick with tears, her eyes sore and stinging.

She was so very, very tired.

Sighing, she let the side of her face press against Volk's torso; she let those strong, knobbly hands pat her back. She could hear Volk's heartbeat, forceful and steady, if a little quick, as if she had been out running across the tundra, her two—or four—feet drumming over the ice crust.

"I should be the one comforting you," Pyotra muttered sleepily, speaking as much to that heartbeat as to Volk herself.

She craned her neck and looked up, meeting the inky depths of the oboroten's gaze, feeling herself surrendering to it, at last—or maybe as she had done, from the start.

Volk pressed her lips to Pyotra's forehead, mouthing the words, "But you are."

*

Pyotra didn't remember getting into bed. Her mind was a mess of disjointed recollections; but removing her outer clothing, slipping between the furs of an unknown bed— surely, she would have remembered that?

She scrubbed the last sleep out of her eyes, stretching her legs, her toes curling in upon themselves in her woollen socks. The last thing she remembered with any degree of certainty was a feeling of utter safety, of peace, such as she hadn't felt since—since forever, as her head drooped onto a sturdy shoulder, as her body relaxed and let go.

Volk.

Pyotra sat up, blood rushing into her head, her face. She had been in the arms of the werewolf; she had... Well, she was still in her underthings, at least, even if her nipples pointing through the fabric of her vest made it look like she'd had a very good night indeed. But she was in a cave, a cold-as-hell cave—if hell had frozen over, that was.

"Good morning."

Her head snapped up and there was Volk, removing a pot from the fire, dressed in animal hides from head to toe.

She looked like—

"You're Nenets," Pyotra exclaimed, amazed that she hadn't put two and two together before now.

Volk looked as closed off as ever, as if nothing whatsoever had happened between them.

Pyotra didn't know whether she should feel relieved or piqued. What she felt, if she were to be honest with herself, was something uncomfortably close to regret.

"I'm Volk," Volk rejoined, her lips compressed into a line, as she ladled something from the pot into two battered tin plates. "Come. Eat. We haven't got all day."

"Fine," Pyotra replied in as neutral a tone as she could muster. She was done with being baited, done with her days being a constant tug of war. The future looked murky and uncertain, but she didn't want to fight with Volk—not really. What she wanted was something too complicated to be expressed, clearly, even to herself.

Pulling on her trousers and fleece jumper, which she found neatly folded by the side of the bed, she glanced surreptitiously over at her strange companion. The wolf woman's eyes were hooded; vertical lines ran down the sides of them. She didn't look like she had slept well. Or at all.

Her hair...looked fine, actually. Evenly trimmed to the line of her jaw, despite everything.

Pyotra laced up her boots. This was madness. If she was doomed to share her duck—the thought still made her mentally shy away, as if from fire, but—if she had to share her brother with this creature from now on, it wouldn't hurt to try to make friends. A fresh start, let bygones be bygones. No hard feelings. Please forget about the small matter of my trying to kill you, several times over, Mistress Wolf.

She rose and drew back her shoulders. It was worth a shot.

Pyotra strode over to where Volk was seated, and the wolf woman scooted, making space for her on what appeared to be a sheepskin rug. Briefly, she considered asking whether Volk had slain the hapless critter as a human or as a wolf. She decided it was better not to know.

As she sat, Volk pushed one of the plates towards her. It was some kind of porridge with an amber-coloured jam.

"Cloudberries," Pyotra enthused, "my favourite."

Volk looked at her out of the corner of her eye and offered the ghost of a smile. "It's the last of Galina's preserves," she mumbled.

Pyotra felt a tug at her heart, a compassionate, companionable grief. She comprehended next to nothing of her present situation—but she did understand loss. She was fairly steeped in it, moulded by it.

"My mother was killed when I was ten years old." Pyotra stared down at her plate of porridge, taken off-guard by her own admission. It was the first time, she realised, baffled, that she had spoken those words out loud. It had never been necessary; everyone knew.

Volk inclined her head. Her spoon clanged against her plate. "How?"

Pyotra shivered in spite of the warmth of the fire, the porridge, the fell underneath her that retained Volk's body heat. Ten years had passed and still the hurt was overwhelming: a pus-filled, irregular wound.

"She was attacked by a pack of wolves. There wasn't much left of her when the trackers found her. Papa drank himself into an early grave, afterwards. It took him a little less than two years; a congenital defect of the liver."

They finished off their porridge in silence. But something had softened between them, Pyotra sensed, as the wind continued to howl outside and the fire crackled inside.

Finally, Volk took the empty plate from her hands, and their eyes met in quiet recognition.

"I see," the werewolf said, and it was the right thing, the only thing, she could say.

*

Volk appeared to have been born on a pair of skis. She shot across the snowy expanse in the grey twilight, stopping every five minutes or so to give Pyotra the chance to catch up.

It was the wolf and the girl in the forest all over again; the bitch stringing her along, all the while being perfectly able to outrun her, but choosing not to.

Why *had* she chosen not to?

The question had been weighing on Pyotra's mind. Why would the beast risk its life to lead her on a merry chase, to lead her, in effect, towards her home, her—

Pyotra almost stopped in her tracks as the kopek dropped, except Volk was a hundred feet ahead of her; if she allowed the distance between them to grow, she would have to put up with the humiliation of the wolf woman turning back to look for her.

No, she didn't stop, she didn't slacken her pace, but her insides quaked. Her stomach seemed to have dropped to the ground, frozen stiff in the space of seconds.

The wolf had never been after Sergei—she had known this; in her heart she had known this. Maiming Sergei had been an accident; turning Sergei into...whatever it was he was doomed to become—none of it had been intentional, all of it prey to circumstance, worse, a Russian roulette.

But the pursuit of Pyotra, or rather, the herding of Pyotra... The frigid air stung her throat as she gasped, putting one pole in front of the other, sliding her skis— *Galina's* skis—over the furrows and ridges left in the snow by Volk. Volk, the wolf; Volk, the oboroten'; Volk, the...person. She had wanted *her*.

Pyotra felt like a halfwit. A sheep. The luckiest girl in the world.

Chapter Fifteen

The human would not quit ogling her. Ever since Volk had come to a halt at the edge of the taiga, suggesting they set up camp for the night, she had felt her eyes on her, an unerring prickling of her skin as they pitched the tent, took care of their necessities, brewed their evening chay.

Volk had remembered Pyotra's enraptured reaction to the aurora borealis, even if the memories she retained from being in her lupine form were more like dreamy impressions, unprocessed imagery: a sleepwalker's awareness of the world around her. But the raw emotion on the human's face had tugged at her enough that Volk had stored the sensation, eager to revisit it irrespective of which corporeal manifestation she was presenting to the world.

Tonight, however, the enigmatic woman had barely given the Northern Lights a second glance as they rolled across the night sky, reflecting against the snow-covered tundra. Tonight, all her attention was lavished on Volk, following her every move, and it was unnerving, confusing—perversely gratifying.

Volk didn't think she had done anything to warrant it.

As they sat over their tea, Pyotra kept opening her mouth as if to speak and snapping it shut again. She licked her lips and took another sip of the hot beverage.

"Spit it out," Volk growled, surprising both herself and Pyotra. She hated suspense.

Pyotra's lips moved, and Volk wanted to taste—to suck—to nibble— She had to restrain herself.

"You said Galina was your maker."

The statement, spoken in a strained hush, seemed to spell itself out in the air, glittering faintly in the moonlight.

Volk huffed, but nodded, unsure where this was going.

"So she—" Pyotra faltered, swallowed. Resumed. "—bit you? That's what you're saying? She bit you to turn you into—her mate?"

Volk's eyebrows rose. She wasn't looking at the human, but she didn't need to. She could feel the avidness of those big ice-floe pools on her, teasing her. Warming her.

"I was born to be a wolf." Volk shrugged. "It wasn't a hard choice."

Pyotra fluttered beside her. Stubbornly, Volk kept her gaze averted.

"She gave you a choice?"

Ire rose like acid in her throat. "Galina wasn't a monster. I was young, but I knew what I wanted."

A weight came to rest on her thigh; Pyotra's mittened hand stroked her soothingly. A flash of movement at the tree line beyond their—*Pyotra's*—tent startled them both; but it was nothing, or nothing more threatening than a black-nosed, snowy-white tundra hare.

"Don't be angry with me." Pyotra's voice was low but steadier now. "I thought it could have been an accident, like with Sergei. Volk, will he be your ma—"

"He's a child!" Aghast, Volk turned, provoked at last into eyeing the human. A faint smile flickered over Pyotra's lips; her eyes gleamed; something in her scent told Volk—

Pyotra slipped off her mitten and glove, and placed the dry flat of her hand to Volk's cheek. A thrill shot through Volk, a shiver that had nothing to do with the Arctic cold around them, and everything to do with this: the possibility that—but—how could it be?

"You chose well." Little by little, Pyotra closed the space between them. Her scent was impossible to ignore. Volk didn't want to ignore it; she wanted to revel in it. She wanted to be encompassed by it. "I would have chosen the same."

Volk's fingers curled. Her toes curled. Her entire body curled as the yellow-haired female pressed her mouth to Volk's with an inimitable mixture of defiance, shyness, and resolve.

Her ears buzzed. There were a million and one reasons why this should not be happening, but Volk was hard-pressed to remember a single one as Pyotra's hand moved from her face to her neck, as Pyotra's lips parted and let slip a noise, a small, appreciative sound that pierced Volk, that aroused her in a way she had never experienced, not like this—like the aurora had descended and become stuck in her groin.

She couldn't think. She stood and held out her hand, pulling Pyotra to her feet. Mutely, they made their way to the tent, Volk's hands shaking as she unzipped the front, as she removed her boots and waited for Pyotra to follow suit.

Pyotra giggled, her hair snagging on the zip on her way in. Patiently, Volk released her and closed up the insulated weave against the worst of the cold.

"Volk, I..."

Volk shook her head, drawing Pyotra back into her arms, onto her lap. Pyotra sighed, then sucked in her breath as Volk pushed her hands under layers of shirts and tops, finding her warm, soft skin, at last.

At last.

"Pyotra..." She spoke the human's name in a thick rasp, and even she could hear the wolf in her voice. She drew a ragged breath, stilling.

"I want this," Pyotra whispered in her ear, her voice equal parts strangled and urgent. "I want this more than anything. Please, Volk. *Ya tebya khochu*. I want *you*."

The wolf sprang free.

With a low rumble, Volk caressed the human's belly, nipped at her lips, and Pyotra responded quick as anything, pressing closer, knitting her fingers into the newly shortened hair at the back of Volk's head.

Volk groaned deep in her throat, pushing Pyotra back onto the floor of the tent, where Pyotra had placed out her sleeping mat and Volk had arranged her fells. In an instant, she was on her, her fingers digging into Pyotra's hips, her lips claiming Pyotra's as her own.

Pyotra rolled beneath her, humming, raising herself up to allow for Volk's roving touch, the removal of her upper clothing, until she was bare from the waist up.

Her skin was flushed. Her small breasts beautifully, wondrously puckered. Volk ran her hand from the waistband of Pyotra's trousers up her torso, her rough palm creating friction against Pyotra's smooth curves. Pyotra's gaze grew hooded. Her mouth opened in a breathless "Da."

As Volk fumbled with her button fly, Pyotra angled her hips up. Volk's head, her heart, her very centre was in thrall to the full-bodied scent of the human's—of Pyotra's—readiness.

She couldn't wait.

She couldn't wait even to remove her own clothes, to prepare and to tease, the way Galina had taught her. No, overpowered by greed, by the throbbing heat of the moment, Volk gripped the crest of Pyotra's hip and thrust inside her in a single stroke, her digits instantly coated, instantly squeezed and welcomed, as Pyotra threw her head back and all but lifted off the ground.

Volk thrust again. And again. She was being too forceful, too feral, some deep-buried human part of her protested, but this one-of-a-kind woman was more than game, meeting each thrust with one of her own, hugging Volk's fingers so tight she was groaning with the ecstasy of it. The rapture of it.

Volk slid her thumb up Pyotra's slick sex, circling her swollen nub, and Pyotra clutched at her own head and cursed. Her thighs trembled.

Her thighs trembled, and Volk's mind unspooled; she cupped Pyotra's luscious bottom with her left paw and felt her inner walls go spongy as she rubbed at them with her right, twisting her fingers to reach as deep as she could.

"Volk!" Pyotra cried out, loud enough that the sound must have ricocheted between the trees at the entrance to the boreal forest. Volk would have given anything—everything—to have claimed her then, in that moment, to have sunk her teeth into the soft, infinitely tempting flesh of Pyotra's belly as it rose towards her, as Pyotra juddered and stuttered through her climax.

As it waned, little by little, Volk held her, drawing lazy circles around her tail bone, close to weeping with the beauty of *her* human: her abandon. Her trust.

She wanted to do it again. Volk wanted—she wanted to consume her, to make her part of her: to hold her and keep her and—and she would. In her vulpine skin she would, because the wolf had no compunction whatsoever—

"Stay."

Pyotra was sitting up, squinting at her; the human couldn't see in the dark. Volk was hyperventilating. She hadn't realised. She was—

"Stay with me." Pyotra spoke again, though her voice seemed to come from far, far away.

Volk barked an alert. Pyotra, *Pyotra*... Pyotra had to open the door flap, push Volk outside, grab her rifle, because the wolf wouldn't be able to hold back; she would want to take—to possess—

"Don't." The human's arms folded around her. Her mouth pressed to her ear. "I want you to stay like this, Volk. Can you do that for me? I don't care what happens; I am not letting you out of here. But it would be more practical, I think, if you stay with me. I can't make love to a wolf."

Volk snorted. Pyotra rubbed her cheek against her neck and somehow, miraculously, the tension subsided. The pressure on her skin lessened; she felt hands—not paws—at the ends of her arms.

In wonder, she ran them up Pyotra's nude, shivering back, and Pyotra made that little appreciative noise again, like the coo of a pigeon.

Volk's heart contorted. She felt, of a sudden, utterly drained and at peace.

Pyotra gave her a lingering kiss, as shy and as brazen as the first: the one that had unleashed the spring-flood of Volk's desire, that had robbed her of her senses, overwhelmed her with pure animal lust.

"Come to bed with me, wolf woman. I don't know if you've noticed, but it's freakishly cold. If it hadn't been for your special brand of body heat, I'd have been a stiff by now."

Volk laughed quietly. She was too light-headed, too relieved for words.

Chapter Sixteen

She had been shagged by a werewolf. That had happened. She, Pyotra Nikolayevna Kulakova, daughter of Serafima, the wolf-slain. She had kissed Volk as an experiment, to see if— Oh, but she had known, as soon as she had figured out what, admittedly, should have been obvious from the outset. The wolf had wanted *her*.

Pyotra turned in her sleeping bag and was met by Volk's searing gaze. Heat crept into her face. She felt herself squirm, felt her nipples contract; her cheeks, no doubt, brightened further.

Volk's square hand emerged from under her fells and stroked Pyotra's face, brushing back her sleep-mussed hair. "You're gorgeous when you blush. More gorgeous. You are—"

"You too," Pyotra broke in, her whole body aflame. She zipped open her bag and crawled under the fells Volk was holding open for her. The fur tickled her naked skin in a way that shortened her breathing. Volk quirked an eyebrow, pulling Pyotra flush against herself.

For a second, Pyotra could think of nothing but this: their bodies aligning, their thighs entwining. She placed a kiss on Volk's rounded jaw, and then another. "I think I have been attracted to you since the moment you—changed—but I— It was your eyes. I couldn't bear not to be— The way the wolf looked at me, it wasn't...normal."

She hid her face against Volk's neck, and the turnskin tightened her hold on her. What she had said made little to no sense, but perhaps, if she was lucky, the wolf—the woman—both understood.

Volk slipped her hands around Pyotra's rear, pressing her to her. Pyotra gasped as her thigh brushed the wolf woman's wetness. Instinctively, she pushed into that melting heat, and Volk's throat clicked and rumbled.

It was the loveliest sound she had ever heard.

"Lie on your back for me."

Volk's eyes bulged. Pyotra had to snigger.

"What are you—"

She put a finger to the oboroten's lips, hushing her. "You know very well," she murmured, as Volk twisted onto her back and pulled Pyotra on top of her. "You don't mind, do you?"

Volk's smouldering eyes—darker than ever—told her *no*, emphatically. Pyotra grinned from ear to ear.

Taking her time, she began working her way down Volk's body, touching, nibbling, running her tongue over warm, salty, slightly musky skin, dipping into every little crease and fold she had felt rubbing against her, torturing her, on their first memorable night together inside this tent.

Well, their second night. Their first, she had held the wolf in her arms like it was an oversized teddy bear.

Volk said nothing, but her hands twitched, her torso twisted, her entire form responded to Pyotra's touch.

Pyotra's heart thrilled. Arousal coated the insides of her thighs, burned in the pit of her stomach as she reached her destination. She nestled her nose in the wolf woman's bush and inhaled deeply.

"Pyotra." Her name seemed to have slipped between Volk's lips of its own accord, husky and redolent with need.

Pyotra smiled. She smiled and pushed herself between Volk's well-knit thighs until she found her, moist and ready, her labia puffed out, her clitoral hood drawn back so far it seemed to verge on the painful.

"*Prekrasnyy*," she whispered reverently. "I knew it."

Volk growled. Pyotra smirked and took pity on her, describing the marvel of her not in so many words, but with her lips and tongue, her fingers, and even the edges of her teeth, until she was well and truly soaked in her juices. Volk panted; rocked; gripped the back of her head.

"Yes, lyubov, do," Pyotra lilted, half smothered, and drove her tongue home, into the tart, sharp, ridged centre of all that was Volk: her trekking companion, her shape-shifting lover. Her wolf.

Volk came without a sound, yet unmistakably; her legs shook, her hips lifted, her fingers curled into Pyotra's scalp, and it hurt, but it wasn't the pain that made Pyotra cry out—made her howl, quite frankly—but the sheer bliss of the experience. The pride. The honour.

Yes, honoured was how she felt, as Volk dragged her up and into her arms, as she kissed her deeply, a low whine reverberating in her chest, and Pyotra giggled and wept and gave herself over to it. Again, again.

*

Three days had passed since they had entered the taiga. Volk hadn't decreased her pace, but she glanced back at her, every so often, in a way that kept Pyotra warm and fighting. They didn't speak.

Or they spoke, but only as new lovers speak: in stops and starts, in sighs and sweet nothings, in gasps and grunts and groans.

They made love each night as if making up for lost time, which they were, in effect, and as if there would be no tomorrow, or a tomorrow that would come between them: a tomorrow where their tracks in the snow would diverge.

It made Pyotra start awake at unseasonable hours, unable to shake off the sense of impending doom, but Volk was there, pulling her close, saying nothing as Pyotra cried herself back to sleep.

So much was left unsaid, Pyotra could not even begin to shape the things she wished to say with her mouth, her vocal cords. Like:

I'm worried about Sergei.

I wish I had met you before.

I wish it was me you had bitten.

I think I want—

No, no, not even to herself, in her head, which was a jumble of Sergei and Boris, Kolya and Serafima, the unknown Galina and Tatya, or the idea of Tatya, fading and becoming little more than an abstract concept, a red dot on the map like St Petersburg, St Petersburg on the shores of the Baltic Sea.

Too fast and too slow. Nothing had ever happened to her; everything had. The oboroten' nipped at her earlobe. She felt at peace and at war and at odds, all at once.

"Fuck me," she said, in lieu of what she couldn't, and the werewolf complied with fervour.

They didn't speak.

*

"How far have we left to go?" Pyotra asked, on the fourth day, crossing her poles and looking up towards the stars. The quarter moon's pockmarked visage seemed so close she felt as if she could reach up and touch it, will it to remain like that.

Volk was on edge, restless in her bones. She had said she wasn't affected by the moon's phases; only young wolves were. Looking at her now, Pyotra wasn't so sure about that. The woman reeked of wolf.

"We're close," Volk replied, her voice thick and distant. She was sniffing the air. "Something's—" Volk shook her head and fell silent.

"What?" Pyotra inquired querulously. "What are you not telling me?"

Volk shifted on her skis. "We should keep moving. Or are you too tired?"

"I'm exhausted." Pyotra uncrossed her poles. "Let's go."

Volk nodded, but she didn't move; her midnight eyes bored into Pyotra, soft, caressing, wistful. Clawing at her soul.

I'm worried about Sergei.

I wish I had met you before.

I wish it was me you had bitten.

I want—

Pyotra closed her eyes. The snow crunched and groaned as she pushed against it, pushed off.

*

That night, she found Galina's mark. She had made Volk turn from her so that she could kiss her way down her spine, admire the muscular build of her shoulder blades, trace the constellations of birthmarks and liver spots, those little blemishes that somehow she found so much more endearing than if her lover's back had been a perfect blank. There were faded scars from teeth and claws— accrued, no doubt, in her wolven shape. Pyotra didn't quite understand how it worked; she couldn't. For all she knew, Volk didn't either, despite it being her body, her story. Where did the wolf's fur hide?

Pyotra outlined each vertebra of Volk's spine, near falling asleep with the ease of the moment, yawning. Her fingers reached an odd indentation across Volk's tail bone. She rubbed at it and Volk stopped breathing.

"What's this?" Pyotra snatched up her LEDs to take a closer look. It was an oval-shaped aperture, missing flesh, white scar tissue. Even as she peered at it, transfixed, the image of the wolf's white-circled tail flashed before her. Volk's tail.

She touched the mark again, and a small but distinct shudder went through Volk. Pyotra couldn't keep silent. Something in her had to know; she would ask herself, later, why she had pressed the matter, literally, metaphorically, like a child who suspects that the fire will burn them, but the flame, the flame... "Volk, what is it?"

The werewolf took a deep breath. Otherwise, she lay immobile. "It's where Galina bit me."

Pyotra should have guessed. Perhaps she had, but she had needed to hear it spoken out loud. There was something so deliberate about this scar, something close to artistic, as though Galina had known how her mark would be expressed when Volk was—well, Volk.

She had put her ring on Volk as she had completed their union. Pyotra couldn't pretend like she didn't know it must have been in the course of an intimate act—their wedding night, in essence—and it was beautiful and heartbreaking and it hurt her, like a physical blow to the guts, a vicious, stabbing pain in her chest.

She wasn't sure if she had ever known the precise taste of unmitigated jealousy until then. The edges of her vision blackened; a self-pitying lump lodged in her throat; a feeling of utter and absolute inadequacy pooled in her stomach because she could never, ever...

"I want you to bite me."

It came out of nowhere. Volk turned around.

She turned, and something was off about her face: She had an unhinged look to her. Her lips were thinner, her canines sharp, elongated points. Fine, fuzzy hairs sprinkled her cheeks, stealing up towards her temples. Pyotra's mouth fell open. A heady mixture of fear and want made her stiff and inert.

"Yes," she gasped, but Volk shook her head wildly; she was fighting it, desperately, on the pivotal point between human and wolf.

The wolf would not think twice about turning Pyotra. She could see it in its eyes: the lust for her, the longing for her. But Volk—

This wasn't how she wanted it. She wanted consent, mutual consent. Mutual trust.

Pyotra gripped Volk's face in her hands, Volk's baby-soft fur tickling her palms, stirring her. Volk snarled, her teeth clicking together. She might be too far gone this time, but Pyotra didn't care. Human or wolf or both or neither, with every and any facet of her being, the infinite variety of expression that is life, life, Pyotra wanted—

She put her forehead to the wolf's. The wolf whimpered.

And then Pyotra felt Volk's hands on her, scalding, feverish hands, burning her skin wherever they touched, sending excruciating flickers through her as they grabbed her roughly. And yet, she welcomed the touch. She wanted to be burnt, branded, to her core.

Volk flipped her around. Disoriented, Pyotra found herself on her hands and knees, gasping, as some primordial part of her made her push back, back, until she was met by that overpowering warmth again, until she felt hard, hot fingers pushing into her, filling her, as the oboroten' bent to kiss the nadir of her spine.

It was a promise. Volk licked her suggestively, grazing her tender skin with the tips of her fangs, and Pyotra shuddered and paroxysmed, her cunt contracting helplessly from the onslaught. She hollered out her climax in the dead of night.

Chapter Seventeen

She was a wolf. Volk could feel it; her sense of time was out of joint; her language had exploded into a thousand unintelligible constellations. Except, she wasn't. Her chin rested on soft human skin. Her fingers were lodged in velvety moisture, in...

"Pyotra." The name erupted from her in a half growl, pulling the scattered remnants of her back into herself, into this: Volk.

Warily, she raised herself up. The human—the woman—Pyotra was alive, thank the moon. She turned to face Volk, her eyes blinking, her expression calm and relaxed.

Volk tasted the wolf's yearning in her mouth. She had to mentally shove it aside. Her hands trembled where they held Pyotra, inside and out.

"Sweet saints in heaven." Her lips did not care to move. She rumbled in frustration, and Pyotra sat up, wrapping her long arms around her, filling Volk's nostrils with her soul-pinching scent. Volk tried again. "Did I... Did I hurt you?"

She didn't want to know. But she had to.

Pyotra trailed her fingers through her hair, along her jaw, which—Volk's world tilted a little further—was fuzzy with the traces of fur.

"You were so hot." Pyotra pecked her neck. "I thought you would burn me to cinders."

Volk swayed.

"I wanted you to." Pyotra smoothed Volk's hair back, encircling her face with her hands. "You did nothing wrong. I pushed you. It's a bad habit of mine."

Volk shook her head: the human—still human, though not thanks to her—didn't understand. "I wanted to—" Volk couldn't say it. Her stomach lurched.

"I asked you to." Pyotra caught her gaze and held it. "I wanted it. I want it. I will want it. When it's time."

"To be a wolf?" She flinched at the note of something akin to resentment in her query. It was what she herself had wanted, passionately, all those many, many moons ago. It was what Galina had offered her: freedom, in animal form. With the caveat that she would be her bitch, and Volk...could live with that.

Pyotra nudged her head between Volk's jaw and shoulder. "To be with you," she said simply, and Volk felt as dazed and bedevilled as Pyotra herself had appeared, kneeling before the Northern Lights.

*

Something had changed between them. Something had clicked into place; in awe, Volk studied her companion as they continued on their journey.

The wolf had wanted this; had planned this; had homed in on this particular human from the first. Yet the reality of Pyotra surprised her, amazed her, left her dumb. Not that she—no, not even in her lupine skin—had considered taking her without her being a willing participant, but... She had assumed she would have to work on her the way Galina had done with her, presenting it to her as an escape from narrow conventions and gender roles, a means of survival, longevity, superhuman strength. A business deal of sorts, with certain terms to fulfil, which Volk had done readily, wantonly, in heat and lust. She had come to care for Galya, yes—but the wolf had come first: to become herself. To be herself. To be...

To be with you, Pyotra had said, and Volk had felt it, smelled it: the sincerity of this avowal, the easy truth of it in all the ways that Pyotra gripped her, touched her, respected her. Could it be? She would not have deemed it possible for a creature like her to find—this.

But truth was, Volk had been smitten. Smitten from the first sniff.

*

It was dusk by the time the little pond came into view. Pyotra gasped and plunged ahead; if she'd had a tail, it would have been quivering.

Volk brushed the thought aside. More and more these images—these fantasies—came to her: the sleek, white bitch her love would make. Yes, her fur would approximate their snowy surroundings, Volk would bet her canines on it. She would be playful, impulsive, swift, and skittish. Perfect. Carrying Volk's mark on the soft flesh of her underbelly, hidden from plain sight, but always there, indelibly.

Volk sighed. First, she would have to deal with the matter of the accidentally moonstruck juvenile.

"There's smoke coming from the chimney," Pyotra called over her shoulder, her skis slicing through the drifts with barely contained impatience. "Come on, don't fret about Boris. I guarantee you, his bark is worse than his bite."

"You are a comic genius, Pyotra Kulakova," Volk returned, the corners of her mouth turning upwards, for all that. She loved the smell of Pyotra's unbridled, palpable excitement. She loved—

"You'll love Sergei, I know you will," Pyotra averred as she kicked off her skis and reached for the door, reminding Volk yet again of what the purpose of their visit was. This was not a meet-the-family. This was damage control.

"Ded!" Pyotra called as she rushed inside. Then, hesitantly, "Ded?"

Volk came up to the doorstep. The fine hairs at the back of her neck had risen. She peeked inside.

*

Her first impression of Pyotra's grandfather's house was of an unlikely green-and-yellow bird—a budgerigar, Pyotra would explain to her later—perched atop a bust of Lenin on a shelf. The second thing she noticed was a yowling furball of a cat, flying before her and under the empty cot in the farthest corner of the room. The third—

"Wolf!" the old man cried, the nostrils of his big red nose flaring, the chair he had been sitting on tipping backwards onto the floor.

At the centre of it all stood Pyotra, her chest heaving. Her hands were balled into fists.

Volk growled. The bird lifted from Lenin's ear and flapped about in the sincere panic of the likeliest prey.

"Ded," Pyotra said for the third time, even as she glanced over at Volk and shook her head, close to imperceptibly. Volk's face warmed. She hadn't meant to growl. It was pure instinct. Something was seriously wrong. "It's me, Pyotra, your granddaughter. And—my friend." Pyotra gestured for Volk to enter, beckoning her to her side. "No wolf."

Volk's eyebrows shot up. *Not the time*, Pyotra mimed.

"Pyotrushka…" The old man's face fell. The weight of the world seemed to have collapsed onto his shoulders, from one breath to the next. "Pyotrushka, I thought—I thought I had lost you. I thought I had lost you too."

Pyotra recoiled. Volk put a hand on her arm to steady her. The old man—Boris—turned in Volk's direction and scowled. His eyes were not quite open, not quite latching onto her, but the effect was there just the same.

"What sort of creature lurks about the taiga preying on young, defenceless women?"

Defenceless women her arse. It was painfully obvious that he was deflecting, goading her, pushing her to show herself for what she was. She had read about this kind of strategy in old folk tales. The man believed in werewolves, all right. Volk bristled. Only the feel of Pyotra by her side grounded her.

"I am a hunter. A nomad. My name...is Evane."

Pyotra sucked in her breath. Volk couldn't blame her. They should have discussed—so many things.

"That means 'orphan,' if I'm not mistaken." Boris took a step closer. He was wringing his hands.

Volk cleared her throat. "You speak Nenets, *gospodin*?"

Boris opened his mouth to answer, but Pyotra interrupted in a calm, clear tone of voice that belied the fierceness in her eyes. "Ded, where is Sergei?"

Chapter Eighteen

She had felt his absence the moment she had crossed the threshold. It was like a visceral lack; her skin crawled as she entered the home she had left almost two weeks ago. The buoyancy that had carried her to the door of the cabin abruptly ebbed, leaving nothing but a faint, indefinite nausea in its wake.

Sergei was missing. She had known it, and she hadn't; she had feared it, and she hadn't.

Volk must have known. There were scent traces, surely; what else did you have those wolf senses for?

She was being unfair. Volk—*Evane*—wasn't responsible for this. That prize went to Boris, her dedushka—*his* dedushka. The Judas who had sold what he thought was his last remaining grandchild for a few silver roubles.

She couldn't stomach it. She couldn't bend her mind around it. It was too rude an awakening.

"They came for him," Boris admitted, when even that ridiculous budgie—Mashka's cheer-up gift—had fallen silent. Perhaps the cat had eaten it. Pyotra did not turn to investigate.

"They?" she pressed, and she had prayed fervently, madly, that *they* were medical professionals, an ambulance helicopter, anything, anyone but the village undertaker.

And yet, that might have been a mercy. At least Pyotra would still have had her grandfather then.

"He smelled—he was starting to smell," Boris whispered, and Volk's arm around Pyotra's hip was half restraining her, half propping her up. "He wasn't right, Pyotrushka. He wasn't...Sergei any more."

She began to shake. Scrambling for some semblance of control over the situation, or perhaps simply to prevent herself from passing out, she trained her gaze on the lighted candle that stood on the table by the samovar, its flame reflected in copper. Why Boris continued the ritual of lighting candles when there was no one in the izba to see by them was beyond her.

"Who—are—*they*?"

"You can't fight them. You can't refuse them. They are a law unto themselves. You know that, Pyotra, lyubov, my heart; you are all I have left in this world!"

Boris had sunk to the floor, his hands outstretched towards her. Like a frail old man, impotent in the face of adversity. Like the frail old man he was.

They came for the cub, she heard herself think, Volk's odd turn of phrase ringing in her ears; her duck had been gobbled up, swallowed down. Turned inside out.

"They were generous." Boris scrabbled for the wooden box he kept in a drawer of the side table. Crumpled pieces of paper, hundred-rouble bills, flew about. "They will take care of him. They will cure him, Pyotrushka. We don't have to worry about anything. Everything's provided for."

There was no point in arguing. He didn't believe himself.

"Boris Ilyich." Volk had not raised her voice; the razor edge of it was enough to stop Boris in his tracks. Pyotra's grandfather's name had never sounded so ominous as it did coming from the lips of an irate oboroten'. "Who took your grandson?"

He was weeping, Pyotra noted dispassionately. This man who had been everything to her and Sergei. This man who would have chosen the gulag rather than betray them, or so she had thought. Who should have protected them with his dying breath.

"It was Oleg Gudkov. Oleg Gudkov's people."

Pyotra slumped against the werewolf. Boris buried his face in his hands.

*

How would she even begin to explain the phenomenon of Oleg Gudkov to a tundra wolf? Pyotra didn't know how to explain it to herself; what did Gudkov want with Sergei? Who was his informant in this nowhere settlement in the Nenets Autonomous Okrug? What exactly had they told him?

There is this boy who was bitten by a wolf...

Pyotra had heard stories about the recluse oligarch. He was the stuff that stories are made of. Rich beyond her wildest imagination, with businesses embedded in every golden pot Siberia had to offer: oil, metallurgy, chemo-technical exports, the banking system. He had a legal team to fill up the residences of a minor town on his payroll, including corrupt judges and a lesser legion of friends-in-high-places. Oleg Gudkov was not just a law unto himself. He *was* the Law.

If Gudkov wanted you to disappear, you were already gone. If he wanted you dead, your eulogy was written.

But why, for the love of reason—

"He wants the wolf in him," Volk stated phlegmatically, as they were preparing for bed.

It was strange, going to sleep in Boris's cabin as though the last two weeks had been nothing but a demented dream. Except Sergei wasn't there. Volk was.

"How could he even know... No one knows! You're a...a...a fictional character, for crying out loud. Who in their right mind would think—"

Volk sat on Sergei's cot, and Pyotra's heart ached so badly, for such a troublesome multiplicity of reasons, she feared it might stop beating altogether. Her otherworldly lover glanced over at the sleeping form of Boris, and Pyotra tasted bile in her mouth.

"There's always been those who believe," Volk said quietly. "Your ded is one of them. If he cried 'wolf' loud enough for others to sit up and take notice..." The wolf woman's face showed deep lines of worry, across her forehead, accenting her temples, parenthesising her closely shut mouth.

You are the cause of all of this, rang through Pyotra's head. But she couldn't regret—no, she was no better than Boris. If there had been a choice...

"I can't be sorry for not leaving your brother to die," Volk spoke defiantly, as though she had read Pyotra's mind. But there was a world of pain in her eyes, an ashen tint to her features.

"I can't be sorry either, Vo—Evane. What will we do? What *can* we do?"

Volk reached for her but stopped herself. Pyotra swallowed hard.

"We find him. I'll get him back for you, I swear, even if I have to offer myself in exchange. It would only be right."

Pyotra bit her lip. She had no argument against this, but dear God... She hated what was right.

"Outside Arkhangelsk, on the beaches of the White Sea. That's where Gudkov's mansion is, or so I've heard. I...I suppose we could take a plane from Naryan-Mar?" Pyotra rubbed at her tired face.

Volk pursed her lips. "I've never flown," she confessed. "And I've never been to a...a city. In different circumstances, I would tell you to stay with Boris, but..."

"When hell freezes over."

Volk shook her head, but for the first time since their arrival at the cabin there was a glint in her eye—a sparkle of vulpine vivacity that Pyotra had come to appreciate. So much.

"You are no Penelope, are you?"

It took her a moment to place the reference. Then she laughed, with the pure outlandishness of it. "You have never been to a city, or on a plane, or anything, but you have read *The Odyssey*?"

Volk scratched herself behind the ear. "It was on the shelf."

*

Boris looked about ninety years past his prime. His cheeks were hollow, his skin drooping off his bones; he hadn't been eating properly since Pyotra had gone away. Pyotra felt a pang of guilt, despite the bitterness of her fury with him. There was a fine tremor to his large paws as he stroked the tortoiseshell Persian that clung to his lap for dear life. Volk had gone out, but Pyotra had no doubt that her peculiar scent lingered, confusing and disturbing Boris's recently acquired pets.

"I take it Mashka has been to visit?"

Boris's hands stilled. The cat glowered at her.

"I thought you had perished, Pyotrushka. I didn't know how I was to make it on my own."

Her cheeks prickled. Her grandfather's statement held nothing accusatory per se, but she had rarely heard him speak quite so frankly before. Even when Kolya had passed, he had said nothing, nothing. The budgerigar alighted on the table and pecked at the leftover crumbs from their morning repast.

Boris wetted his lips. His iron-grey hair was in disorder. It had always been Pyotra who combed it into submission at the start of the day. It had been more or less an unconscious act—one of those behaviours one doesn't notice one engages in, until one doesn't.

"I thought there would be no one here to take care of Sergei. When I was gone."

"So you auctioned him off to the highest bidder? Children are not for sale, Boris Ilyich!" Pyotra wanted to spit on the floor. She abstained, however. She could envision her blind dedushka slipping on the puddle, and her conscience was bad enough as it was. "You are not dying." It came out as a command.

"Your friend... Was she the one that bit him?"

"Evane? Have you gone—?"

"But that's not its true name, is it?" Boris's voice had taken on something of its old bearlike bassoon quality. "Its name is Volk."

Goosebumps erupted all over Pyotra. Her spine tingled.

"I did not raise you to consort with the devil incarnate," Ded pressed on.

Pyotra's fist crashed onto the tabletop hard and loud enough to make them both jump. The budgie sought refuge with Lenin. The Persian hissed and latched onto Boris's shirt with her claws.

"I won't hear you call her that again. You are an old fool, Boris Ilyich. I have had it with your superstitions. Vol—Evane has come to mean a lot to me. She is the only one who can help Sergei. If you had just waited—"

"It has you under its spell. But you don't smell—" His great nostrils widened. "—you are not one yet."

He had punched her in the viscera, found her sore spot and thrust his fist into it. A bleeding wound, that was what she felt like. The entirety of her, physically and mentally. She wanted to slap him, to snap him out of it. Her beloved ded—how had they come to this?

She stood and went over to the not-so-secret wooden box.

"I am taking some of your blood money for our journey. You will have more than enough to last you until our return." She counted out the bills, her mind reeling at the sum total. From what she could tell, Gudkov wouldn't have needed to pay a pittance of it to relieve Boris of his 'unholy' burden.

Her baby brother.

She folded up what she reckoned they needed—there would be bribes to pay on top of the regular costs—and crossed back to Boris, standing behind him and smoothing down his unruly shock of hair. She bent to whisper in his ear, a harsh threat threaded through her hushed voice: "You better not die while we are away. I am not finished with you, Dedushka."

Her fingers dug into his shoulders.

Chapter Nineteen

Outside Arkhangelsk, on the beaches of the White Sea...

The words meant nothing to Volk; they could have been something out of a fairy story. She retained only the dimmest recollections of her childhood—of Evane. She knew what a map was, but she couldn't remember being taught to read one. She and Galina had never used a piece of paper to negotiate their territory.

Where she stood outside Boris Ilyich's izba, Volk hugged herself against the cold, reluctant to go back where her olfactory senses would be assaulted by the plurality of odours trapped behind the caulked window. Boris's cabin had no *fortochka*. The only air that seeped into it came from the chimney and from the opening and closing of the door.

She scratched her nose with one of her deerskin mittens, at odds with herself. As Volk, she had always known exactly who and what she was. As Evane... Resurrecting that name had been a mistake. Evane had been dead and buried these last twenty winters or more. To have her spoken about now made Volk feel disoriented; it made her feel like she was haunted by her own ghost.

She wasn't human. She had never been meant for a human life. If it hadn't been for Pyotra's grandfather—but little good it had done her, laying herself bare. Boris saw only the wolf, casting aside her Nenets origins as inconsequential. He acknowledged only her lupine self and he hated it. It was as simple as that.

She could almost have adored him for it. She loved how he took the oboroten' at face value, not allowing himself to be fooled by a human shape his eyes couldn't see. He made her feel pure, unadulterated. A born Volk.

Pity her wolf skin had him consumed with fear and loathing. How Galina would have laughed at this predicament. Right before she killed him.

Turn them or kill them had been Galya's motto, her golden rule for how to survive as a were. *Do not get attached to anyone you are not willing to bite, and do not let anyone live knowing what you are.*

Evane would have been dead regardless of the choice she made. How many years had it taken Volk to reach this inescapable conclusion?

Volk huffed, watching her breath swirl through the frigid air.

She had loved Galya. She had been—in awe of her. But she had never had the intention of making Galina's ways her own. Hence, she had avoided humans at all costs. Right up until a little over two weeks ago...

Volk had more pressing concerns than Boris Ilyich, however. This Oleg Gudkov—he was not on a mission to eradicate the Russian oboroten', of that she was certain. He could have had the cabin burnt to the ground with Sergei and Boris in it; an accident, people would say, such a shame. It would have been easy, efficient. Remove the cub from the equation, then come after her.

No, he wanted something else, she could feel it; the suspicion weighed on her, chilling and warming her with anger, with apprehension, in turn.

He wanted what a fledgling turnskin would not be able to offer him for twelve moons, at the very least. But that—Volk was willing to stake her life on it, such as it was—was something Oleg Gudkov was not aware of.

What would happen to Sergei when he found out? What would happen to all of them?

Outside Arkhangelsk, on the beaches of the White Sea... Neither Volk nor Evane had ever seen the sea. But she had to go. Even had it not been for Pyotra, for— everything, she would have had to go.

Because of the pull.

It had started so faintly, almost like an abstraction, she had failed to recognise it at first. With Galina—oh, but she had been a hopeless romantic back then, passing it off as the pull of love, the indelible bond between two mated individuals, irrespective of species.

But that hadn't been it; she saw that now. If Galya had known better, she had taken the secret with her to her grave.

Volk shut her eyes. Inside her, clamorous, insistent, growing stronger by the hour, was the wordless call of the cub. Trapped, confused, wolf hormones kicking into overdrive; he was so close, so close.

And he was mad. He was furious. He was baying for blood.

How did the idiot Gudkov expect to contain a first frenzy? Even Volk was not sure how to contain it; she would have had to bring him out to the tundra. Her wolf self would have been there to pick up the pieces, to quell him by tooth and claw—the only language with which one could hope to reach a newly shifted.

From instinct, the cub pulled at her, voraciously—*wolfishly*. To Volk, it felt like she was being devoured. She pushed him away, but he returned all the more forcefully. Was this the essence of motherhood? To be eaten alive, for the sake of a split-second decision, one single mistake?

Oh yes, Galina would have laughed.

"The blood will run its course, Evane."

"Don't call me that."

"Oh? What shall I call you then?" That knowing smirk.

"Just... Just call me Volk."

*

"What's wrong with you?"

Volk looked up. Pyotra's eyes were lowering. Of course they were: she was Pyotra Nikolayevna Kulakova, poster child for the worldwide association of Loose Cannons.

Volk essayed a smile. "I'm not used to this." She waved her hand vaguely at the four walls enclosing them. As usual at this hour, Boris slept. That man would sleep through anything. It would have been a very small matter indeed for Gudkov to have had the cabin torched.

Pyotra looked unconvinced, but nodded. "I can't abide it either, this inaction, this waiting. I want to set out at once, but we won't be any quicker on foot. Well, you would, I guess... I wish there were any other means for us to go to Naryan-Mar rather than having to wait around for the postal service."

Volk sighed and pulled her would-be mate to her. She wanted more, needed more. She wanted to be subsumed in Pyotra, engrossed by her; she wanted skin-to-skin, scents mindlessly entangled. She wanted some semblance of peace in the midst of chaos. "I wish I were a shape-shifter."

Pyotra's peal of hysterical laughter nearly roused Boris. Volk covered her mouth with her own, nibbling at her lips until she felt Pyotra's mirth recede in the wake of a spring of desire.

It took every last resource of self-control she could muster for Volk to pull away, quirking an eyebrow at the slyly grinning human female.

"You *are* a shape-shifter. I'm pretty sure you are the textbook definition of a shape-shifter. You are the impossible come true."

Volk's face heated. It was not how she saw herself, not in the least, but she couldn't expect Pyotra not to have her own interpretation of their new, shared reality. She was allowed to have her own version of Volk; she was the first human being to have been invited to have one. It was weird, but not altogether unwelcome, this being *seen*. It made Volk's chest expand.

"I didn't mean... I meant, you know how in fairy tales witches and wizards can transform themselves at will? I can't do that. I change with the seasons, with certain levels of...stress, but I can't—I've never been able to control it. I can be triggered; if—*when* Sergei shifts, I will too. This time of year, I would still be a wolf most of the time. I would be pushed over the edge if I was...alone. But I can't mentally will it to happen. That's what I mean."

Pyotra gaped. Her warm breath stole across Volk's cheek. Not until she had tried to summarise her nature had it occurred to Volk what should have been glaringly obvious: Pyotra was the one anchoring her to this skin. Pyotra was the one who had called it forth earlier than was to be expected; the one who had roped her in and secured her, literally and figuratively.

The wolf wanted Pyotra, without a shred of doubt, but so did...Evane. All that was her—Volk—seemed to be falling apart.

Pyotra furrowed her brow. "Sure you can."

"Excuse me?" Volk's head was spinning.

"Twice, at least, you've stopped yourself from shifting into a wolf. I don't see why that couldn't go both ways."

It took her a moment to come to grips with what the human was referring to. Then, she slowly let out her breath.

"I didn't do that, Pyotra. You did."

Pyotra shook her head, her eyes gleaming for the first time in days; for the first time since they had entered the forlorn little izba, Pyotra's and Sergei's and Boris's home.

Volk felt the response to that gleam flickering within her: a tender, steadfast flame. Her mate. Here she was. With an inward start, it dawned on her: she didn't have to turn Pyotra to be bound to her. Somehow, against reason, against all she thought she knew about herself and the world, she already was.

"Maybe I will shift if you tell me to?" Volk teased, as she burrowed her nose in the intoxicating scent of her lover's—her mate's—scruff.

Pyotra vacated their shared cot so swiftly Volk gave a yelp of surprise.

"Only one way to find out, *volchonok*. Come on, get your kit off. We're going out."

Volk's eyes widened as Pyotra began pulling at her shirt. "What are you talking about? I'll get frostbite."

"Oh no, you won't." Pyotra treated her to an inconceivably sexy grin. "I'll have you swathed in the most luxurious fur coat in the world before long."

*

Volk's teeth would not stop chattering. Her skin had been numbed, then started to hurt in a way that seemed to wrench her heart out of her body, then numbed again, as she stepped outside in minus thirty degrees Celsius, in her—in Evane's skin, wearing absolutely nothing. At all.

She supposed she could see Pyotra's point. The cold alone might bring forth the wolf, if only for the sake of survival. *Change or die*, she tried to convince herself. But she knew Pyotra would not let that happen. Not before and not now. It wasn't going to work.

"Could we please—"

Pyotra spun on her heels. She had walked off a ways into the dark, towards the pond, which made Volk's stomach flip uneasily. Her mate's face was unmoving and white beneath the gibbous moon.

"I remember where the drill hole was, wolf. Do you? I bet the ice is still thin enough to let me through if I stomp on it. You should come out here and stop me. Naked, freezing Evane will be too slow."

"What? No! Pyotra—"

But she had already taken off at a run, the madwoman that was Pyotra Nikolayevna, and Volk heard her own shout of dismay turning into an angered growl. She started sprinting on her bare feet, but Pyotra was right, the bloody hare-brained, suicidal bitch of—

Volk didn't pause for a second as her bones began to contort, her insides churn, her entire body—her two-bodied, impossible self—shaking, stretching like a strain of music that was suddenly played by a different instrument. Her front paws hit the ground running.

Part Two

Chapter Twenty

Sweat poured down the back and front of the solitary man sitting on a square piece of cloth on a bench in his private sauna. His eyes were closed against the sting, the drip, the rawness of the swelter that scalded his airways with each laboured breath. It annoyed him that breathing was necessary; that in spite of all his financial power and personal authority, there were things that were out of his control. He had to breathe. He had to eat. He had to shit.

Oleg Vladimirovich smirked. He squinted at the thermometer attached to the wall by the door. The sauna was subtly lit by spotlights that glowed from underneath the seats. Ninety-five degrees Celsius. Five degrees below boiling point. He dipped his *venik* in the bucket of water at his side and slapped it over his shoulder, lashing his own back with the springy twigs harvested from the birch saplings in his conservatory. The non-feeling when he hit his old scars tickled him. He had endured. He would endure. He was—untouchable.

The *banya* hat lay abandoned in a corner. Oleg refused to wear it once he was inside, but he kept up appearances; he brought it with him, always. Sometimes, he felt like his life was one long ritual, from morning to night, unbroken by crude reality.

Only sparks and flashes of recollections could get to him, unvoiced, unheard, tearing him from his sleep or making him ignominiously wet his bed.

The boy would fix it. The boy was the key. The boy would break the spell.

Oleg threw the whisk aside and rose, stretching his limbs before he wrapped his hand around the door handle. Every time he did so, for a split second, he was thrown back in time, in space; he hurt all over with the momentary dread of finding the door locked and bolted.

Silly Olezhka. Babushka needs to work.

As the door creaked open, he wiped the dew from his face, blinking against the brilliance of the overhead lights. This time of year, he could have taken his ice bath in the sea; it would have made sense, been more economical. But Oleg Vladimirovich did not spare any expense where his own convenience was concerned. It was a matter of principle with him.

The artificial ice pool beckoned to him with its promise of a full-body shock to his system, a freezer jolt to his lingering heat. Yes, he could have stepped outside, into the White Sea, but this—this was altogether better. Besides, Olezhka was shy of going out.

*

"You are carrying a lot of tension in your shoulders, gospodin Gudkov."

Oleg steeled himself for the assault that invariably followed upon this observation. Ludmila Andreyevna rarely let him down. She was ruthless, hard-fisted, unyielding as an iceberg—a masseuse of the myofascial-release persuasion.

The first and only woman he had allowed to touch him since his grandmother.

His breath came out in a whoosh as she bore down on his upper back, knuckles first, all one hundred and twenty kilos of her. Oh, she was formidable; built like a discus thrower, her one concession to femininity was the tightly pulled rope of a plait that hung from the top of her head down to her buxom, taut-muscled behind.

He could almost have been attracted to her, he had caught himself thinking groggily on more than one occasion after she had helped his rubbery loose, momentarily incapacitated self up off the table. She had worked with the Russian Winter Olympics team and was firm on keeping their sessions short and brutal.

Almost.

"I suppose it is the fate of the hard-working businessman, Ludmila Andreyevna."

She grunted, and with his face plastered to the baranka-shaped contraption at the top of the table he couldn't see her; but he would bet half of Siberia her cheeks blazed.

Her fingers skimmed his terry-cloth-covered buttocks. Oh yes, someone would be getting very lucky with Ludmila Andreyevna tonight.

But it wouldn't be him. His stomach roiled in protest at the mere notion of sinking himself into that ravenous, insatiable hole.

As if she sensed the slight, sensed the stubborn slackness of his cock against the vinyl padding of the table, Ludmila put her elbows to work. She paid no heed to his scars; the first time he had removed his shirt in front of her, she had given them a once-over and announced that they would not affect her work.

He had taken her into his private service on the spot.

Oh, but she was formidable, formidable. If he should ever concede to die, he wanted death to be administered by the capable hands of Ludmila Andreyevna.

But Oleg Vladimirovich Gudkov had no intention of falling prey to an early demise.

*

After his judo practice, his sauna and ice bath, his session with his masseuse, Oleg Vladimirovich felt nearly human. It was not his most coveted state of being, but it would do; it would have to do, for the present.

His contact at the Kremlin had warned him only this morning that another exorbitant bribe—an administration fee—would be required for the authorities to look the other way as he pursued his latest venture in the Caucasus region; and he would pay, however much it rankled. There were thousands, millions of these pesky gnats bleeding him, one rouble at a time. It was the price he paid for staying off the radar.

But the hour of the wolf would come.

Oleg Vladimirovich frowned at himself, gripping the gilt frame of the mirror in his walk-in closet. His silk Armani suit fit him like a second skin, cleverly tailored to make the most of his shoulders while concealing the slight sunkenness of his chest. He had been ranked number one among Russia's most eligible bachelors for ten years running, but always with the caveat that he was a recluse, perhaps a deviant.

To improve his image, and to throw the journalists off his scent, he'd had Yegor bring him a gaggle of impressionable young women on a bimonthly basis, who were summarily shown into one of his guest apartments and drugged out of their senses.

His Sleeping Beauties, he called them. They all awoke with drying trails of semen down their sequined dresses. Not his, but no one would be the wiser. He always made sure he was the last person they had seen—the first person they would blab about.

Now, he was just a regular oligarch, given over to the humdrum perversions of his set. It'd had the added benefit of testing Yegor's loyalty, too; and he had passed with flying colours.

Oleg called him his right-hand prick in private, and they laughed like two schoolboys sharing an inside joke.

No, Oleg Vladimirovich couldn't care less about the women. All he wanted was the boy or, rather, what the boy was to become.

Touching the hidden spring mechanism on the side of the frame, Oleg watched the mirror surface slide back, revealing a dark corridor, all raw concrete and buzzing strip lights.

In the distance, muffled sobs could be heard, and the hair at the back of Oleg Vladimirovich's neck tingled. He stepped into the corridor, unfazed by the wall closing up behind him. This was his domain. His tsardom. The part of his mansion not even Yegor knew about.

Oleg stopped at a brushed-steel hatch in the side wall and brought out a steaming tray of food sent up from his kitchens. The boy had a passion for blinis and was slowly coming around to the sturgeon caviar Oleg insisted on incorporating into his diet. That was not what was on the menu for tonight, however. He lifted one of the metal lids and sniffed expectantly. Chicken legs cooked in bouillon, like Babushka used to make them. Oh yes, they would dine well tonight.

"Olezhka?"

His heart lurched uncomfortably.

"Olezhka, is that you?"

Oleg Vladimirovich cleared his throat. He had very nearly wet himself. "Yes, it's me, Seryozha."

His voice was brittle and high-pitched, nothing like the register he used in the outside world. He tripped down the corridor, searching his pocket for the key.

The moment he opened the door on the far side, the boy fell upon him, his slender arms wrapping tight around him, his tears staining the front of Oleg's shirt.

Olezhka held the tray with one hand and ruffled the boy's dirt-blond curls with the other.

"Olezhka, I've been so lonesome. I've had such bad dreams! Oh, why do you always have to lock the door behind you? Why can't I stay in your cell with you?"

Oleg placed the tray on the table and gently released himself from the boy's arduous hold.

"I wish you could, Seryozha, believe me. But they would have me killed if I didn't obey their rules, and then you would be all alone in this world. We wouldn't want that, would we?"

The boy blew his nose on his sleeve. Olezhka cringed.

"My sister will come for me. She'll come for us both, once she knows you're my friend."

Oleg Vladimirovich sighed. He sat on one of the rough-hewn chairs and motioned for Sergei Nikolayevich to take the other. "I hope she does, but from what you've told me, it doesn't seem very likely she is alive, does it?"

Seryozha shook his head and nodded it, ambiguously. He gripped his fork and knife.

"She is alive. You don't know her. She wouldn't do that to me; she wouldn't die like— Besides, I can feel her—" The boy stabbed at his chest with the butt of his knife. "—in here."

"Is that so?" Olezhka raised his eyebrows, tucking into his portion of the chicken. "I hope you are right."

Chapter Twenty-One

"I love you." Pyotra had not meant to say that. She hadn't meant to say anything of the sort; it was the sight of her lover—her wolf—stretched out and panting on the fells after a hard day's run that tore the words out of her.

She flushed.

Volk turned, studying her with Evane's expressive, inky eyes out of her wolf face. *I know you do*, her gaze seemed to imply, and Pyotra huffed and plonked onto her sleeping bag.

She wasn't used to this—whatever this was. She had never uttered those words to anyone, not even her duck. Certainly not to Tatya.

Volk placed her chin on Pyotra's lap, rubbing it over her folded hands. They were cold as ice from having held onto the reins all day.

She hated that part—hated how demeaning it was to Volk—but they had to keep up the pretence of her being in charge. Having her old dog sled pulled by just the one wolf rather than pairs of huskies was odd enough; they didn't need some macho hero trying to rescue her from being carried along at a breakneck pace with no apparent means of controlling where she was going.

So, she held the reins, like she had held on to that rope the first time Volk had changed before her, out on the tundra. Weeks ago. A lifetime ago.

"I miss you." She dug her fingers into the thick fur at the scruff of Volk's neck, drawing a small, poignant whine from her.

The wolf wasn't subtle. Her snout was burrowing into Pyotra's crotch.

"Hey!" Pyotra pulled at the beast's ears. "Don't do that; it makes me—"

The telltale heat radiating from the wolf made Pyotra recoil. Volk wasn't supposed to shift. They had talked about this before they set out, and Volk had agreed, unwillingly, that changing forms every night would probably take too much out of her.

The oboroten' was strong—inhumanly strong—but pulling Pyotra, the sled, and all their gear across the snowy plains to Naryan-Mar was no walk in the park. Even Volk had her limits. And something else was draining her too; Pyotra could feel it, although Volk had not spoken of it. Well, she couldn't, in the shape she was in.

"Don't," Pyotra whispered, but she wasn't very convincing. Her whole lovesick frame seemed to scream *yes*. She pushed at the wolf's shoulders, but they weren't the wolf's; Volk's rough yet supple skin met her palms, and Pyotra sobbed with the dizzying relief of it.

"Lyubov," she sighed, and Volk rumbled, a low, loving sound that burred through Pyotra, lighting glowing fires where it went.

Although it was Evane's hands reaching for her, Evane's chest that met hers as Volk pulled her to her, Pyotra sensed that her lover was still mostly wolf. She gasped. From one moment to the next, Volk had her pinned on top of her fells, grinding into her as she continued to change.

"Oh, please," Pyotra heard herself plead, grateful for and exasperated by her extraneous layers of apparel. She wanted Volk's skin to hers, her hips to hers, her mouth devouring her—but she could feel the merciless sting of Volk's shifting heat even through her anorak and trousers.

She didn't care. She trapped Volk's incongruent face between her hands and kissed her, tasting the predator on her, but not minding, not minding in the least.

She was probably a pervert. So be it.

Volk's hands were at the lining of her trousers, all but ripping them, and Pyotra wormed her way out of them, obliging, knowing her eager dampness was filling the werewolf's nostrils, threatening what little self-restraint Volk possessed in this fraught state of in-between.

She angled herself up in brazen invitation, meeting a warm, fuzzy abdomen that had every nerve ending of her sex firing up at once.

Enraptured, she cried out, and Volk answered with a groan before pushing her down, splaying her legs as wide as they would go inside the domed tent.

"Need," Volk ground out through gritted teeth, and Pyotra nodded *yes, yes, without question, whatever you need*.

With the flats of her hands pressed to Pyotra's inner thighs, holding her open, Volk slid down her so fast Pyotra didn't quite follow what was happening before a thick, wet tongue lapped at her. Volk laved her with abandon, with such manifest pleasure in the act it multiplied through Pyotra, blurring their boundaries, making her uncertain of what was Volk's mouth and her cunt and sweet saints, it didn't matter in the least.

Volk drove her tongue into her, pulled out, and licked from the edge of her perineum to the tip of her clit. The wolf woman made a sound that was a ravaging mixture of howl and moan, repeating her move, over and over, as phosphenes littered Pyotra's vision, as her hands fisted in Volk's cropped mane and she was spilling into her, flooding her lover's mouth, barely holding on to consciousness as she surfed the crest of each consecutive orgasm.

She didn't want it to end. She never wanted it to end, but at last, she was all used up, raw and aching and indecently fulfilled. Volk lifted her gaze to hers, holding her tenderly, reverently, and said, "I love you too, mate."

Pyotra started to cry. Volk crooned and stroked her, wrapping herself around her, wrapping them both in the dishevelled sleeping bag on top of the fells. She was humming a wordless song, some old tune which Pyotra only vaguely recognised as Nenets, before she drifted off.

*

In the morning, there was half a hare outside the tent. Pyotra couldn't keep a grin back, even as regret tugged at her; Volk had shifted back, and it made sense, as much as any of it made sense. Her brother turning into a wolf; her setting out to retrieve him with a wolf; her sharing her sleeping quarters with a wolf; her loving—a wolf.

She wished her mother had been killed by wild boars.

"Volk!"

The wolf cannon-balled out of the firs like a great big pup, eager to please. Pyotra stooped to pick up the hare hindquarters.

"You spoil me," she chided the wolf, and caught herself scratching Volk behind the ear, the wolf's eyes closing in appreciation.

She stopped abruptly.

"I need to cook this. I don't eat raw meat." It came out harsher than she intended.

Volk put her muzzle in Pyotra's hand and Pyotra relented; she hunkered down, bringing herself eye to eye with the beast.

With Evane.

"I'm sorry, Volk." She put the hare down and held her lover's lupine face instead, touching her fur-covered cheeks and temples. The wolf's face was beautiful in its own right—majestic, really. It had an entrancing, enigmatic quality of which Pyotra was only too aware of the cause.

"I don't know how to treat you," she sighed. "I don't want to, but I keep catching myself treating you like a dog, like—like you are my pet wolf. I don't mean to do it, but it just...how am I supposed to—oomph!"

Her speech was rudely interrupted by the wolf licking across her chin, mouth, nose, and forehead. Volk sat back on her haunches and grinned.

Pyotra wiped at her face, trying to scowl but knowing she was woefully unsuccessful. The tension eased inside her. Without words, and summarily, she saw that Volk had given her permission to be—herself.

"Oh, is that how it is? Cheeky volchonok. You think I can't take you, puny human that I am?"

Volk's ears shot forward, and a happy yip escaped her as Pyotra threw herself over her, surprising even herself with her ability to wrestle the muscular beastie to the ground.

"Gotcha! Ey—what—that tickles!"

Volk's snout was in her face, her whiskers playing over Pyotra's sensitive skin as she nibbled along her jawline, her lips carefully covering her fangs.

And yet, Pyotra felt the outline of them, and it made her shiver, deliciously, as Volk in the wink of an eye reverted their positions, and Pyotra found herself flat on her back in the snow, two paws on her chest and a leering maw inches from her neck.

She knew this move. She had seen it enacted time and time again by the pups of the village mutts.

Pyotra bared her throat in surrender, and Volk sat back, jaws snapping shut. Her black eyes bored into her, and Pyotra heard the wolf woman's night-time profession reverberate through her: *I love you too, mate.*

She covered the wolf's paw with her mittened hand. Pyotra Nikolayevna Kulakova was in love—with Evane, with Volk. With the wolf.

*

"You taste of blood. I have hurt you—" There was panic in Volk's voice. She was shaking as she drew Pyotra to her in a hard embrace, her hand pressed over her genitals, as though to staunch the flow of—

"Oh, crap. Sorry, Volk, I forgot!" Pyotra bit her lip in embarrassment, hugging Volk back as she mentally rifled through their packing. Surely, she had thought to bring... "I knew it was supposed to start around now, I've just—I've been preoccupied."

"Start?" Volk looked at her blankly. "You're bleeding, Pyotra. I—I was too rough—"

Pyotra giggled. Volk had been anything but. "No, silly. It's my period."

"Your period? Of what?"

Pyotra clicked on her LEDs, revealing the incomprehension on the oboroten's features.

"My menstruation?" she essayed. "My monthly trouble?"

"You bleed regularly?" Volk's mien morphed into a look of concern. "Is it... Is it some kind of disease?"

Pyotra shook her head in bemusement. She sat up and opened the left-hand pocket of her rucksack, bringing out a pad. Volk's lips formed the most adorable lower-case *o*.

"Are you trying to tell me turnskins don't have menses? Don't be ridiculous. Even dogs in heat bleed." She grimaced. "Sorry, I didn't mean to say—"

"You're in heat?" Volk closed in on her, nostrils flaring. "You're... You do smell different. I didn't—how close are we to any settlements? Human males have an underdeveloped sense of smell, but—"

Pyotra's blush was verging on the painful. "Please, stop smelling me. I don't exactly feel like a budding rose in winter. I'm not in heat, not like that; no one is going to come scampering out of the woods to have their way with me."

She pulled on her padded underwear, checking to see she hadn't left any marks on Volk's fells.

"I would slay them." Her lover's words held a sober finality that chilled her.

"Well, you won't have to," she said guardedly. "But, Volk, you're an adult female, you're—have you really never bled?"

Volk shrugged, gathering Pyotra to her. She was being subtle about her sniffing now, at least. "I have been in heat as a wolf. It's—inconvenient."

Pyotra gave her a wry smile, snuggling closer. She toyed with the patches of pelt left on Volk's neck and shoulders. How quickly she had got used to them. How effortlessly they had become part and parcel of this strange creature to whom she belonged. "I can't argue with that."

"Great sex though."

Pyotra gnawed the inside of her cheek and hid her face against Volk as the images came slamming into her: of two werewolves, two werewolves who—

"I can imagine," she said thickly, and Volk grabbed her chin, forcing her to meet her gaze.

"You misinterpreted me. Lyubov, with you... It's like I've been in heat since I first scented you."

"Yeah?" Pyotra blinked her stupid, jealous tears away and tipped them both back onto the fells. "I think I had better take pity on you and help you with that, then. It's the least I can do."

She pressed her lips to Volk's, and Volk's immediate response, the hum that settled in her chest, chased everything else away on its tail.

Chapter Twenty-Two

Everything was white, white, and more white. Volk's muscles ached with exertion, but it thrilled her, too; she could feel her tenacity, her resilience growing by the hour. It helped her sleep at night—well, that, and shifting and all that it entailed.

She couldn't be in the tent with Pyotra and not change. It felt physically impossible, as physically impossible as not being aroused by her touch. Pyotra was uninhibitedly physical with Volk in her wolven form.

It made Volk happy in a way she could not explain, but perhaps it was that her mate seemed to love the wolf, as well; not love Evane despite the wolf.

Volk could never have imagined— No, it seemed much more fantastical to her, this love, much more like a fairy tale than that there were oboroten' prowling the Siberian tundra.

Or one oboroten'. For all she knew, she might be the last one, the endling. She might have been. Because now, there was Sergei.

Volk leant into her harness, increasing their speed fraction by fraction. She would be tired tonight, but so would Pyotra. This bleeding business took its toll on her. It was a peculiar condition; Volk wasn't sure how she felt about it, nor about the fact she herself had never bled as Evane. At least, not since she'd been turned. What did it mean? Were werewolves sterile? Or could she only conceive and give birth to...cubs? Cubs that would be wolves forever, one-bodied beings with no particular affinity to the moon?

There was so much she should have asked Galina; so much Galina should have told her of her own volition. If she had even known, that was. Perhaps the sum total of the insights Galya would have brought to the table would not have stretched much further than her own.

Volk almost wished that was the case. It made her feel less cheated. Although this preoccupation with heritage, with history, with the bigger picture was thoroughly, painfully human. In deep wolf, what did Volk care? How swiftly Evane had gained dominance, in spite of the years and years she had spent suppressed by Volk.

Pyotra loved the wolf too.

Volk felt suddenly giddy. The sun was out, making the world eye-clawingly bright and glittering around her. She was thinking too much. *Outside Arkhangelsk, on the beaches of the White Sea...* Volk picked up her pace once more.

*

Seryozha was all alone. He was in a room with a bed, a small and rickety one, like the beds he had seen in black-and-white photographs from the Great Patriotic War. There was also a table and two chairs, and a bright naked lightbulb to which he didn't have a switch. It came on of itself and it turned off of itself; he suspected they had rigged it up to emulate the passing of night and day.

He was afraid of the dark, but he hadn't worked up the courage to tell Olezhka about it. Only his sister knew; his sister who had ordered a night light for him from Mashka, and who hadn't breathed a word about it to Boris—not even when Sergei drove her half up the wall with his cockiness.

He had been doing that a lot lately. Because—well, because she was babying him; because she kept calling him stupid things like Duckling or Duck when he was almost a man. Dima had told him so.

Dima had let him drive his snowmobile and taught him to drill his own fishing hole in the ice. He understood that an almost twelve-year-old boy wasn't a baby.

Seryozha felt like a baby now though. He had even let Olezhka call him Seryozha. It comforted him, somehow. It made his present situation seem less real; Sergei was still in the cot at Ded's. Sergei's dedushka would never let the bad man—Yegor, he had called himself—take him away. What had he done, anyway, to warrant being carted off to prison?

None of it fit together.

Whatever Olezhka said, this couldn't be a prison. Not a state prison at any rate, or Pyotra would have been here already. He knew she would, in the marrow of his bones.

But she wasn't, and he was alone in the dark, and the fear was morphing into anger, a seething rage that made him tear up his bedsheets, claw at the walls.

When the light came on, he was consternated by the scratch marks. They didn't look like anything he could have accomplished with his fingers and nails. And the tooth marks in the fabric—they couldn't be his, despite his recollections of having been responsible for them. They looked like his worst nightmares come true. They looked like the monster under his bed had moved right in here with him.

The monster under his bed seemed just as pissed off as Seryozha was about being locked up.

Seryozha was all alone. But he wasn't. Something else was with him in his cell, and it wasn't human. At all.

*

Volk woke with a start. She had begun to shift in her sleep, spontaneously; it happened more and more frequently. She pretended to Pyotra that her early mornings were a matter of expediency. She hunted better in her lupine skin, and besides, it made her ready for the day's journey. But it wasn't that; it was the cub, nearing his frenzy. It was—Seryozha.

She had never heard Pyotra use the diminutive. Pyotra called her brother Sergei, always. Perhaps it was Boris's name for him. But somehow, Volk didn't think so.

No, someone was calling him Seryozha in her head, and her head was hijacked each and every night by the same recurrent dream: she was shut up in the dark, a dark so complete not even her were-eyes could penetrate it, but she scented plaster, concrete, steel, and urine. That last one came from a chamber pot under the bed. She knew, but she wasn't sure how she knew.

She threw back her head and howled. She tried to dig through the offensive, enclosing walls. She sank her fangs into anything soft she could find; she wanted Pyotra, she wanted Pyotra so badly.

But she didn't want her as Volk. She wanted her to hold her and call her Duck, to put her lips to the top of her head and whisper in her ears the old, familiar stories about Serafima, about Kolya, about Snegurochka and Ded Moroz.

Yes, especially that.

"Tell me about Snegurochka and Ded Moroz."

"It's just an old cartoon." Pyotra yawned, and Volk realised she must have spoken out loud. She wasn't quite wolf then, not yet, even if Pyotra drew her breath in as she focused her gaze on her. Her mate rallied quickly.

"The Snow Maiden and Grandfather Frost— although in the film he's her father. There are so many iterations of that story. But what made you think of it? Good morning, by the way." Pyotra smiled, her yellow hair kinky at her temples and neck. Volk wanted to stroke it, to bury her face in it.

"You used to tell me—him—about them."

Pyotra sat up, regarding her cautiously. "Volk—what—"

"When he was upset. Is that right? Why was he upset, Pyotra?"

"Sergei was—*is* afraid of the dark. Volk, why are you asking—"

She couldn't focus. The wolf was getting the better of her; she had quarry to catch, a sled to pull. A cub to rescue.

Dimly, she saw Pyotra resign herself to the inevitable; the human pulled her fleece top over her head, scooted down to the foot end, and opened the tent flap.

Volk yipped her gratitude and gave her mate a quick lick across the nose before she sprang outside.

*

In another night, the moon would be full. They would not reach him in time. Volk had known the chances were slim, but still it rankled. They had not even reached this fabled Naryan-Mar.

"Do I talk in my sleep?" Pyotra lay draped across her; she looked a touch pale as she raised her head to peer at Volk.

Volk was tempted to say yes. She knew why Pyotra was asking, and she didn't know how to explain what happened to her at night. It might just be nightmares, after all, and Volk wanted to spare Pyotra any unnecessary heartache.

But she could not lie to her mate.

"The cub is coming into his—his first frenzy, as Galina called it. Because I am...his maker, so to speak, we have a—a bond, of sorts."

"I understand."

Volk looked up in surprise. Pyotra's face was a calm, clean slate, so utterly out of character for her that Volk worried for a moment this too was a dream. "You do?"

"You knew something was wrong. I could tell. When we were in the taiga, I mean. I don't think you knew he'd been abducted though. You would have told me, wouldn't you?" Her voice wavered, and Volk saw that the calm surface was as brittle as spring ice.

"I would have told you," she affirmed, and Pyotra sank onto her chest with a sharp sigh of relief. "It took me a while to figure out what it was. Sergei is my first... I've never bitten anyone before, not like that."

Pyotra nodded, her cheek pressed to Volk's collarbone.

"He pulls energy from me, siphons it off; it's maddening. He doesn't know what he's doing, but I think that's why our pace—"

"Don't you dare blame him! He's just a child. He's been kidnapped; he's been bitten by a werewolf; he's—"

Volk caught Pyotra's fist in the air. Her lips twitched as she kept her eyes trained on that fist rather than Pyotra's face. This was the Pyotra Nikolayevna she knew.

"Of course he's not to blame." She drew the fist to her lips and kissed it until it opened, like the bud of a flower beneath the caressing sun. "Tell me—tell him—about Snegurochka. Let's try to give him a peaceful night."

Volk could feel Pyotra's tears pooling in the dip between her neck and her clavicles. She held her tighter, wishing for impossible things.

"Snegurochka lives in a tower on the tundra, in the land of eternal winter. When her grandfather calls her to him, she comes riding on a huge beast of a polar bear..." Pyotra's voice was as thin as a thread, but it held, seaming together the rifts of the long Siberian night.

Volk drifted off, drawn through the air by Ded Moroz's icy, ephemeral steeds, and for once, the cub's pain did not feel so urgent. The wolf in him wasn't clamouring to come out.

They had this in common, then, she and the cub: Pyotra Nikolayevna Kulakova. Soother of oboroten'. Tamer of wolves.

Chapter Twenty-Three

The boy was quiet this morning.

With rising elation, Oleg Vladimirovich had observed the fresh claw marks on the wall from day to day, the ruined bedsheets that spoke of the presence of that which he had only half dared hope for. And now—nothing. Only Seryozha, calm and composed, describing a night-time dream of his sister, who had held him and comforted him with bedtime stories more suited to a significantly younger child.

What fresh hell was this? On the eve of the full moon... But it was not possible, tonight was the night, everything had been prepared. He was ready. He had waited for this moment too long to be thwarted on the very brink of fulfilling his lifetime ambition.

The one thing he ever wanted. The only thing.

"She is coming for me. She is riding a big bear, like Snegurochka." Seryozha's eyes gleamed; he spoke with the single-minded conviction of a love-spoilt child.

Olezhka wanted to tear him to pieces. Foolish, ungrateful little imbecile. It was unfair; it was doubly, a hundred, a thousand times unfair that this doltish child should have been granted—when he, *he*—

"Are you not happy for me, Olezhka?" A shadow crossed the boy's face.

Oleg Vladimirovich fought to regain control of himself. "I am happy, Seryozha. But I am sad for myself. If your sister comes to take you away, I will be on my own again. I will lose my only friend."

"But Pyotra will set us both free!" Seryozha's face was aglow with vehemence. "She will find a way; I know she will. She went off to take down the wolf that attacked me single-handed. She will come here wearing its pelt. You'll see."

"Is your sister the Baba Yaga, by any chance?" Oleg smiled toothily. A witch in wolf's clothing, no less. But if this Pyotra Kulakova had survived, if she had managed to track the beast where Yegor had failed—

He must speak to Yegor. Oleg Vladimirovich rose from his seat.

The boy was sullenly silent.

"Come now, let us be friends again." Olezhka spread his arms. "It is only that I would hate to see you disappointed, Seryozha. I have come to care for you. I wish for nothing more than that we should both be free of...our troubles. But if you have such faith in your sister, then so must I."

"You must?" Seryozha eyed him suspiciously.

Oleg cursed himself. All of his careful measures to gain the boy's trust, and he could not keep a check on his mood swings on the very brink of the coveted event.

"I must," Olezhka averred, adding a heavy dose of saccharine to his tone. Miraculously, Seryozha relented and accepted his proffered embrace.

*

"Ask Yegor Mizulin to step into my office."

Oleg sat back from the intercom, not waiting to hear his secretary's timid assent. He didn't like the man, and he did not trust him. But he had been too preoccupied lately to oversee a change of staff. Klimov had come highly recommended, just at the opportune moment when Yelena Mizulina had breathed her last, and her son Yegor was many things, but a born administrator he was not.

No, Yegor Stepanovich Mizulin was something more akin to a first lieutenant, if Oleg Vladimirovich's mansion had been the Starship Enterprise, and Oleg was Captain Kirk.

He chuckled to himself. He watched too much foreign television; it was a guilty pleasure of his. A Russian had featured in the series too, a navigator: Pavel Chekov. But of course.

Oleg pressed his thumb to his forehead. A splitting headache threatened at the outskirts of his vision, along his jaw and zygomatic bones. A persistent tone rang in his ears—one his therapist had described as deferred anxiety.

Oleg had hated that woman with a vengeance, which was a breakthrough of sorts: his first clear and nonconflicted emotional response to another human being.

It had been a pleasure to—

Well, he had been very young.

The red light on his intercom blinked, indicating Klimov was calling to let him know Stepanovich had arrived.

Stepanovich. Yegor's patronymic had never sat quite right with him. The lad had been raised by a single mother. Yelenovich would have been more appropriate; as Oleg himself should have been Yekaterinovich. A frisson ran down his spine, gathering into a thumping sensation at his tail bone. It was as if he could hear Babushka's heavy tread down the corridor. Oleg bit his tongue until he tasted blood, and pressed the button to open the door.

The man who stepped into the room was nothing short of magnificent. Over two metres tall in his socks, broad enough across the chest to make Ludmila Andreyevna look positively dainty, with a thick, black beard disguising his features. He wore a military-green bomber jacket, perpetually hanging open; Oleg suspected it would tear at the seams if Yegor tried to zip it up. The edges of his black trousers were splattered with mud, and his coarse boots told of hundreds upon hundreds of miles travelled on foot, through every kind of terrain northern Siberia had to offer.

"Yegor." Oleg's mouth was dry. He took a sip of water from the crystal tumbler at his side.

The man tree nodded in mute acknowledgement.

He is like a separate species, Oleg thought, and not for the first time. A different breed of man altogether.

"Yegor, we have unfinished business to attend to. You know I am not at all pleased with the way you left things in the Nenets Autonomous Okrug."

The giant's proud shoulders fell.

"I need you to return and sort things out. I am not satisfied about the missing sister. She may be a threat to my interests."

Yegor beheld him imploringly. *He thinks I'm stark raving mad*, Oleg mused. And yet he would do his bidding. It was fascinating. Indulgently, he wondered what that long-gone therapist would have had to say about that.

"How could she be, gospodin? Their grandfather said she was dead. Our informant said—"

"Yes, well, he is a threat too, come to think of it. Never trust a man whose loyalty can be purchased for a few silver kopeks. You will go back and tie up loose ends." Oleg canted his head to the side. He ran the pad of his index finger around the rim of his glass. The sound it made was equal parts alluring and eerie. "Can you do that for me...Gosha?"

The big man's eyes flashed. His weatherworn temples reddened. He nodded curtly, and Oleg

Vladimirovich Gudkov pressed his button to let his favoured special-missions operative out of his office.

*

Olezhka had been Seryozha's age, give or take a year, when he had first come upon the stories of the *volkodlak*. They had captured his imagination, insinuated themselves into his heated dreams: powerful wizards who could take the form of a wolf; common people transformed into wolves by the spell of witchcraft. Werewolves who swallowed the moon or the sun during an eclipse; werewolves with wool growing under their tongues, with furry pelt on their infant heads; weres who were essentially vampires. He had treasured any snippets of lore he could come by, held it close, even as Babushka had tried to beat sense into him.

He had needed to believe, and so he had; like some clung to religion, Oleg Vladimirovich, little Olezhka, had clung to the wolf.

It had annoyed him unspeakably when reports on Mikhail Popkov, the prolific serial killer dubbed 'the Werewolf' by foreign press, had started to appear. Annoyed him, but also enticed him. Had Popkov indeed been a werewolf, he would never have allowed himself to get caught. And the sexual overtones of his crimes disgusted Oleg, debased everything that the name of volkodlak stood for.

Notwithstanding, Oleg had been desperate enough to test the thesis: Would mere bestiality bring out the

Beast? That had been in the Nenets Autonomous Okrug, too, a decade ago. It had done nothing for him, left him feeling nothing but tired and disillusioned. He loathed making a mess.

What *had* worked for him had been to linger and watch a pack of scavenging wolves feast on his spoils. He had longed to join them, to cover himself in the blood of his victim and let them have at him—have at him until they were one flesh.

But it wouldn't have worked; he had already tried it. One did not turn volkodlak from being mauled by just any flea-infested *Canis lupus*.

It would have been easy to give up, to begin to doubt himself, to fear he was turning into a don Quixote van Helsing. The children of the night, indeed.

That would have been tantamount to losing himself, however. To being nothing but poor Olezhka, under his grandmother's thumb.

More than life itself, he needed the werewolf to exist.

And here it was. The moment he heard about the boy, about the ravings of his blind dedushka, Oleg had known. This was it.

Tonight would be the final proof. Tonight, in his full-moon chamber, Oleg Vladimirovich Gudkov would finally see his dream come true, the dream that all the riches of Russia had not been able to procure for him.

The boy was the key.

Chapter Twenty-Four

It was an hour before nightfall, at the most. An hour before the full moon would shine forth in all its splendour, illuminating the Siberian plain.

The weather had been abysmal all day. Now, though, as if to highlight this night's importance, the sky had cleared, the wind had settled, the soughing of the pines had waned.

Pyotra was grateful they were surrounded by conifers on this stretch, on this night in particular. She was weary, so weary of the open fields, of nothingness stretching out before her, behind her, around her. Of having nothing to fasten her eyes upon but the shaggy back of her companion, straining under the weight of her and the sled. Volk's grey coat was mottled with snow, her loping stride powerful, her maw open to exhale her excess of body heat.

This morning, Volk had warned her she might not be able to shift into human skin tonight. Sergei's wolven self was calling out to her, baying for her. But he had slept well, she had confirmed with a relieved smile, and Pyotra had believed her.

She had to believe her. She had to believe that somewhere, for the time being, her brother was safe.

She pitched their tent in silence. Volk had run off the instant Pyotra removed the harness, a harried expression twisting her lupine features.

"Lyubov!" Pyotra had called after her, gutted by her desertion. She had to trust the wolf to return to her. There was little else she could do.

She cooked rice in a tin of condensed milk on her camping stove as virulent green tendrils played above her—like a clawing infection, Pyotra reflected, and frowned at the maudlin turn of her mind. But how could she not be maudlin? Here she was, alone in the middle of nowhere, while life as she knew it had been ripped into tiny pieces, scattered by the wind.

Was it only a month ago that wolves had been wolves and people people? That her sole concern when it came to Sergei had been his headstrongness, his tendency to do what he pleased, what he shouldn't? That he would get himself hurt, or worse—yes, but not that he would become...something not altogether human.

A mere month, a mere week ago, she had adored her grandfather. She supposed she still did, but it was a disillusioned, bitter kind of love, a Russian kind: love as a surfeit of pity. Wasn't that what Svetlana Alexeivich had postulated in that documentary film which the ever-diligent village teacher-cum-librarian-cum-administrator had screened down at the library a few years ago?

At the time, Pyotra had been raw with another kind of abandonment; Tatya had gone off to Petersburg a few months before, and Pyotra had thought that yes, that was probably how Tatyana Ivanovna had loved her, with pity for poor Pyotra, daughter of a dead drunkard and wolf-eaten Serafima, granddaughter of blind Boris, sister of an obstreperous little boy who could not share in his sister's fading recollections of their lost parents. *Poor lyubov.* A thin veneer of love, like gold plating over an untouched core.

And now, inexplicably, there was Volk. A *wolf*, a person, a soul who had broken effortlessly past Pyotra's carefully constructed defences, who had stripped her naked and shown her a pitiless, joyous breed of love, a love that traversed all boundaries.

If the wolf's teeth had not penetrated Sergei's skin, if her saliva hadn't mingled in his bloodstream, if— whichever way it worked—none of this had happened, what then?

I could smell you on him. If Sergei had not been his usual, disobedient self, but had stayed inside with his ded, and the wolf that passed in the night had not lingered...

Pyotra startled herself with the animal moan she emitted, as her eyes were momentarily blinded by the brilliant moon peeking out from behind a wisp of cloud. Her hands clutched at her cup of chay as she saw the outline of her duck in its dimples and seas, as her mind strained to encompass the unfathomable: that now, even now, those beloved, familiar limbs of his, those liminal, pre-teen limbs were changing, growing, contorting; distorting beneath the spell of Mat' Luna.

Just the day before yesterday, as she was resting in Volk's soft-pelted arms, Evane had taught her the word *po*—Nenets for "door," or the change from winter to summer, summer to winter. Even before she had turned vulpine, Evane's concept of time had been other. Pyotra wondered if she would ever know her lover's real age; the true origins of her seemed lost among the driving snow, the movement of nomadic tribes, reindeer herders bisecting the tundra.

Would Sergei, too, forget himself? Would she, Ded, their tiny no-place home fall from him like so much shedded fur?

But Sergei would not be a lone wolf. He would be part of a pack, guided by his alpha, his reluctant maker, *her* Volk. As sure as she knew anything, Pyotra knew this: Volk would never abandon Sergei to the wolves, so to speak.

She laughed drily.

The stickiness of the sweet rice that had been her solitary supper clung to the roof of her mouth. She ran her tongue over it, lost in desolate, disjointed reverie. Yuri Gagarin. Laika. The first wolf on the moon. Some lines of Anna Akhmatova. The aurora borealis danced en pointe over the frozen ground like so many prima ballerinas of the Bolshoi Theatre, and Pyotra hummed a tune to herself, somewhere between Tchaikovsky and Rimsky-Korsakov.

Oh, that this night would be over. That this anguish of unknowing would pass. That Volk would return to her and take her to Naryan-Mar, to Arkhangelsk, and into the very belly of the beast. That these same cold and distant stars that twinkled down on her with not a whit of compassion for her plight would also look upon her duck and Ded—yes, even her poor, misguided ded—and keep them safe.

"Evane," she whispered to herself as she rinsed her utensils in the snow, "Evane, Evane, Evane."

This resurrected name of Volk's seemed like a charm to her, an anchor by which she, Pyotra, could tether herself to reality, to the blind earth beneath the perpetual layers of ice and frozen remnants of the heavens' pitiful tears.

Pyotra crept inside the tent and burrowed down among Volk's pelts, her own sleeping bag. She would not sleep tonight, she knew; but she would rest.

Chapter Twenty-Five

The cub was calling her name, though he did not know it. She felt him inside her in so visceral a manner it was like she was about to give birth, like his wolf self was being physically wrested out of his lycanthropic progenitor. Oh, the pain.

Somehow, Volk had managed to suppress the memory of the inhuman pain of her first change. Galina had held her through it, as only another werewolf could. The heat of it was too much for the delicately human, though Pyotra had given it her best shot.

Pyotra always gave her best shot; Volk wheezed with a wolven approximation of unhinged laughter.

These frequent changes had fully healed her wounded shoulder. It made her question everything she had taken for granted about her own existence. Was it possible that this was how she was *meant* to live, whatever Galya's opinion had been? Galina had been adamant that they changed with the seasons; shifting between forms was not some kind of preternatural party trick. Volk didn't think Galina had wilfully lied to her. If Galya had been able to change at will, most likely she would have. Especially in the summer. Galya had hated those months of midnight sun, when she was shut off from the sluggish wolf within.

Poor Galya. She couldn't have known.

As she raced between the trees, Volk's train of thought was interrupted by a sharp stab that echoed through every bone in her body at once. With a yelp, she fell hard upon the snow, except—she was falling upon a stone floor; she was falling

falling

falling

into a wolf cub, not quite the size of a yearling, trembling from nose to tail. Pain was everywhere, in every fibre of their being, in the very air around and the surface underneath them, and the walls, the walls, the terrible walls that encroached upon them, that kept them from all that could have made this ordeal easier to bear: the fragrant pines, the scent of quarry, the tickle of earth and snow against the pads of their paws, so fresh and soft it was a crime in its own right to keep them from experiencing it, to keep them in these strange, unnatural surroundings, blinking beneath the orb of the moon.

The moon. It was directly overhead, framed by a round skylight, as though the space that contained them had been specifically constructed for a spot of moon-bathing. They yawned with pain. They blinked with pain. They howled with pain.

It was death all over again; death as they had known it, felt it, engulfing their little boy's body in the icy water. The kingdom of death, in the land of Ded Moroz. A pain that one drowned in. A freezing fire that ate up one's soul.

Their awareness shifted to within a pinprick of consciousness. They would die here, this night, at last, and Pyotra would never forgive them, would never know, perhaps, for sure what had befallen them.

And then. Nothing.

Tentatively, they lifted their head. The spectral half-light in the chamber would have scared them, just hours ago. But they could see now. The dark corners were of no consequence. They could hear the faint peep of some sort of rodent, coming from the farther wall, and it made them...hungry. Saliva pooled in their mouth, dripped onto their chin as they gasped. Oh, to sink one's teeth into living prey, even a morsel, a sweet mouthful of rat.

What were they thinking? But these were not thoughts, precisely. They were more akin to impressions: minute sounds, a thoroughly corporeal sense of their surroundings, and—the smells, the smells. One couldn't disentangle them one from the other; they filled up one's nose, tickled one's taste buds, and oh, it was marvellous. They wanted more of it. They wanted the world on their plate.

Gingerly, the two-souled wolf stood. Part of it was dazed, cowering; the other was crystal clear. The other knew all there was to know about being in this—state of being. One felt it instinctively, clung to it, fawned over it.

They tripped across the floor, half alarmed by the clicking of nails on stone. This was what one was, this monster-under-the-bed sprung to life.

One hung their head in utter desolation.

The other took the opportunity to sniff the ground like a connoisseur, investigating. The concrete filler wasn't all that old. There were mice here occasionally; they sneezed at the smell of their droppings.

One gagged.

The other admonished one not to be a baby.

They stilled, both of them, in this single body, as they caught the scent of human: a live, breathing, quaking human. Their ears twitched. Their hackles rose.

A low, aggressive growl rumbled in their throat. One started; the other soothed distractedly. Where was it, the human? They turned in a slow circle, nose in the air.

One knew this scent. It was a friendly scent, one tried to communicate. It was only Olezhka. Olezhka was one's friend.

The other snorted.

One cringed at the flash of anger that coursed through their limbs. Olezhka might have been one's friend before, but now? Besides, the other did not like this name, this scent. The other felt strongly about it, though one couldn't make sense of it. The wolf stepped back towards the middle of the room.

Something stirred in the shadows over by what appeared to be a door.

The other squinted their eyes, moved from paw to paw. One would have liked to pee. The other huffed, blowing hot air through their nostrils, forcing one to focus on what they were doing, what they were facing: the shape of a man, huddled and quivering, with a long stick in his hand.

He was afraid of them.

One whimpered, suffused by a sudden yearning to roll on the floor, to expose one's stomach, make oneself small. The other shook their head, cutting the whimper short.

The man moaned.

The air was pregnant with his bodily odours: fear-tinged sweat, alcohol-scented exhalations, a hint of urine drying in his shorts.

They barked, once, and the man scrabbled away from them, as though he could climb up the wall like a spider.

The other grinned. One whined desultorily.

"Ser...Seryozha." The man's voice was barely audible. The other froze.

Slowly, so slowly it almost didn't seem to happen at all, the man rose to his feet, bracing against the wall.

One made them sit back on their haunches.

The other swished their tail, baring their teeth in warning.

One pricked their ears and felt a rush of affection from the other, a warm, floaty feeling of approval. It was the way—the way Pyotra made them feel.

The other glowed.

One snapped their teeth, just for show.

"Seryozha." The man's volume had risen, approximating a squeak.

This was fun. Never in one's life had one inspired an adult man with trepidation. One tried out the growling thing.

"Seryozha!" The man backed up against the wall again, holding the stick out like a fencing foil. "Don't you know me?"

The other cocked their head. One was filled with the desire to play with Olezhka. They could tug at that stick and amaze Olezhka with their newfound strength, oh! Could they?

The other rumbled impatiently, and one felt the brush of the other's private thoughts: *Cubs! I should have known. First frenzy, my arse.*

It was a very rude thought.

One flattened their ears against their skull, more at the other than at Olezhka.

Even so, they heard the man gasp.

The other dithered. One grasped at the reins, pushing them forwards, tail wagging with excitement.

Olezhka groaned as though he had been physically hurt. He held out the stick to one, and the other seemed to start awake with recognition: *cattle prod!* But it was too late, they were within easy range already, and the electric shock buzzed into them, making every muscle in their body tense up.

One howled in terror.

Olezhka prodded them again. And again.

The other tried to regain control over their paws, but it was useless; the electricity kept them in near-constant spasms.

"Volkodlak," the human spoke, and there was awe in his tone, awe and wonder and a perverse desire, as he kept them dancing like a wind-up toy, a travesty of themselves. One and the other snarled in unison. "After all these years. How wondrous. How astounding."

With his free hand, the man—Olezhka—worked at the buttons of his shirt.

Disgust emanated from the other, and one could not disagree. Olezhka seemed a friend of theirs no longer. Maybe he never had been.

One was heavy with chagrin, torpid beneath the barrage of shocks.

Their heart would give out if the human kept this up.

The other strove to offer comfort, strength, but even she—yes, *she*—could ill sustain the onslaught.

Sima? one thought to themselves. *Are you my angel mother? Is this a dream?*

No, the other rebuffed. *I am...your wolf mother*.

Wolf mother.

Wolf mother.

The puzzle fell into place. Sergei had been maimed by a wolf, rejected by his grandfather, taken prisoner by— by a strange man with a beard, who was, more likely than not, in collusion with the demented Olezhka.

It had all started with the wolf.

I hate you, one thought. Then everything happened at once, explosively: Olezhka had bared his chest, taunting them, and one had no intention of being swayed by the other any more. He was surrounded by enemies, invaded by enemies, made enemy to himself; he needed to lash out, by fang and claw, and here was the only likely victim—a willing, panting victim—if he was not going to sink his teeth into his own tail. *His* tail. The other could go back to hell and stay there.

No, Sergei, please!

He went for that bared flesh, and it was easy, child's play, no match for a wolf. Blood filled their mouth with a heady, intoxicating aroma, spice and copper, and he wanted more, wanted the kill, the prize, the end scene of the hunt, but something stung at their neck and he was slipping into darkness, darkness he couldn't understand—

Chapter Twenty-Six

Yegor Stepanovich had not slept. He hadn't slept for what felt like days, weeks, though he knew that couldn't be right; he would have been dead by now if his body hadn't been asleep for that long. He might not be the most intricate Fabergé egg of the intelligentsia, but he knew that much.

Behind his pilot glasses, his eyes were runny and bloodshot. Secretly, he was relieved that Aleksey had insisted on manning the controls of the Kamov Ka-226. At their pit stop in Naryan-Mar, Yegor had staggered out of the pilot seat and wound his way to the closest bar like a drunken bumblebee. He wasn't drunk—not on alcohol, at least—nor had he sought out the bar in order to imbibe any of the drinks they had on offer, but when he got back, Aleksey had moved into the pilot's seat, his lips set, facial features impassive.

As he climbed in, Yegor had nodded his mute assent to the switch, feeling as though his face was melting from off his skull. The CNS stimulant he had injected in the grubby bathroom of На здоровье did little to lessen the effect. What he wanted was to crawl up in a deep, dark hole and sleep for months, until the white light of the polar day drew him out of his den.

Gudkov had no idea. The man was an honest-to-god sociopath, a narcissist without a shred of empathy, and Yegor should have known this, the way Yelena Mizulina had been besotted with the man. His late mother had her own set of issues, an unhealthy attraction to power-hungry personalities being foremost among them.

Yegor had more or less been brought up in the oligarch's secluded mansion. He had seen no other opportunities, no other prospects than seeking employment with Gudkov as soon as he was of age. At first, he had fooled himself into thinking it could be a stepping stone, something for his CV, a pathway to future connections. Once Oleg Vladimirovich had begun utilising him for his special missions, however, Yegor had realised he was in it for life—if he wanted to stay alive. Some days, like today, like the last few weeks, he wasn't all that sure it was worth it.

And they said serfdom was abolished in Russia in the 1860s.

Yegor grimaced. Aleksey had taken a sudden dip, causing Yegor's stomach to flop. He lowed like a forlorn cow.

His co-pilot had the gall to snigger at him.

Well, he knew Yegor. He knew him better than anyone, since Yelena had passed. Aleksey Khudi knew Yegor Stepanovich Mizulin's dark and dirty little secret:

the big man wouldn't hurt a fly if he could help it. He was the kind of man who plucked snails up off the road and carried them to safety after a heavy rainfall. He was the kind of man who went online to research fake sperm after his psychopath employer had asked him to ejaculate over his carefully selected, drugged-out samples of party girls.

Yegor knew it wouldn't make much of a difference, as he couldn't very well tell them about the double deceit. The whole point of the exercise was to make Oleg Gudkov come off as a garden-variety virile rapist, a prime example of ultra-masculine multibillionaire. What did it matter if a score or two of would-be prostitutes in Arkhangelsk were potentially scarred for life?

He had done what he could, Yegor had tried to convince himself; if it hadn't been him diffidently splashing those drowsing nubiles with methylcellulose, an actual sexual assault might have occurred.

It had made it possible for Yegor to live with himself, to sleep, intermittently. Until Gudkov had made him fetch the boy.

"Do you want to talk about it?" Alyosha wasn't looking at him. He kept his eyes on the flurry of snowflakes and night caught in their headlights, but there was no one else in the Kamov he could be addressing. It would only require the two of them to deal with the situation in the Nenets Autonomous Okrug, Gudkov had judged. His two most trusted men. The oligarch was nothing if not economical with his trust.

Oleg Vladimirovich Gudkov has no idea, Yegor repeated to himself.

Some people thought you couldn't pull the wool over a sociopath's eyes. They had obviously not lived their entire lives under his roof, in a country where, more often than not, the freely admitted love that dare not speak its name led to the inevitable gay-bashing. Or worse.

"There's no point." Yegor sighed as he reached over to squeeze Aleksey's knee. "You know it all, lyubov. I just wish—I wish we could get out. Alive, I mean. I wish we could get out of this alive."

*

When the two black-clad and vaguely military-looking men stepped into Mashka Leonova's shop in the godforsaken settlement Yegor had visited only once before, they were met by the muzzle end of a Kalashnikov, wielded by an irate elderly woman of subnormal stature— the owner herself, Yegor knew. He ducked back into an aisle of tinned sundries, as much as his own not inconsiderable height and girth allowed him to duck.

Aleksey—being himself—took a step closer to the counter, his eyes twinkling, palms held up in soothing supplication.

Leonova turned the automatic rifle on him, and Yegor stepped out in front of his partner, shielding him from the line of fire.

Alyosha shook his head, but brushed his fingertips up Yegor's back.

"My, my, Mariya Leonova! That's a pretty little piece you've got. I do believe it's the original 1949 make.

A collector's item if ever I saw one. How much do you want for it?"

The old woman's hold on the trigger faltered. The tradeswoman in her couldn't resist the siren call of a grand sell, it would appear.

"Well, I—" Her gaze swept between them, her head tilting this way and that like a small bird's. Her jaw tightened. "Don't distract me! I know who you are. I've been waiting for you. You are Oleg Gudkov's men. Boris told me all about you." She looked directly at Yegor. "You are the one who took little Sergei Nikolayevich away."

Yegor mirrored the slant of the crone's head. "Boris Kulakov is blind. How could you recognise me from his description?"

"Aha!" Leonova's finger was back on the trigger. Yegor had to admire the woman's ability to snap her trap shut. "I knew it! How many visitors of your ilk do you think we have around these parts?"

Alyosha sighed and elbowed his way past Yegor.

"Mariya Leonova, you had better put the gun down. It wouldn't be practical to shoot us, babka. How would you dispose of the bodies?"

A chill travelled the length of Yegor's spine as the steel-haired biddy beamed, a picture of grandmotherly magnanimity. "There are wolves in these woods." Her statement was blunt but effective.

"You shouldn't treat potential customers this way," Aleksey tutted, matching spunk with cheek. His amber complexion had paled though. Yegor hoped only he could tell. "That weapon could make you a rich woman. If you choose to use it against us, however, you will most assuredly bring the wolves to your door."

Yegor could almost hear the cogs turning in the canny woman's head. Finally, she grunted in defeat and lowered the Kalash. "What do you want? I swear, if you are here to touch a hair upon that blessed, unlucky man's head, I'll shoot you point-blank, consequences be damned. I should never have trusted that good-for-nothing nephew of mine to—"

"Dmitri, isn't it?" Aleksey was almost up at the counter now, and Yegor had followed suit. He marvelled at Alyosha. He was a true special-missions op, and no mistake. Not a gigantic fake like Yegor. Yet, for all that, underneath the rugged, seemingly impermeable exterior, Aleksey Khudi harboured a tender heart, large enough to contain even the likes of Yegor Stepanovich Mizulin.

They should have taken their chances and run away together, long before all of this.

"How do you know Dima?" Leonova's eyes narrowed, all but disappearing among the deep crow's feet, furrows and lines that made up her oval face. "What does Dima have to do with you?"

The shopkeeper's voice was laced with suspicion, bright and sharp as a stiletto knife. She was as quick as a field mouse, Yegor thought, a pesky, uncatchable little thing.

"We need to speak to Dmitri Leonov," Alyosha answered her, keeping his expression guarded. "A friendly chat, no harm done. Then we'll be back for the Kalash, Mariya Leonova. What do you say?"

The woman wavered. Oh, she was an inveterate saleswoman, all right. A bargain-striker to the core.

"Boris Ilyich?" she queried, her tone somewhere between querulous and tremulous. Yegor could have sworn he saw the whiskers on her upper lip twitch.

"We will leave him be." Aleksey flashed the stubborn matryoshka with the automatic an easy grin. "I have your word, Mashka Leonova, he will never breathe a word against our employer?"

"The devil take him." Mashka spat into the palm of her hand, extending it to Alyosha. Yegor winced in disgust, masking it as a sneezing fit after a reproving glance from his partner. "Shake my hand and be done with it, Gudkov bastard."

"It's a pleasure doing business with you." Aleksey grabbed the woman's hand in his without a moment's hesitation. "Where can we find your nephew?"

Leonova pursed her lips. "Dmitri's around the back, probably sleeping his vodka off. If he's the one who's brought all this trouble to Boris Ilyich's doorstep, he's no nephew of mine any more."

*

"What are we going to do?" Yegor asked as they stepped back out into the cold. He was rattled, to say the least. Rattled as no man in Oleg Gudkov's employ, and most especially not Yegor Mizulin, was expected to be.

It was different dealing with mafia bosses and their stony-faced henchmen, to being dropped out of the blue into a ramshackle shop at the edge of the world and greeted by a little old lady carrying an AK-47. Even in northern Siberia, that wasn't an everyday occurrence, was it?

Nothing seemed to be in the right place at the right time any more. He hated Oleg Vladimirovich Gudkov, it was true, but even by Gudkovian standards, the events of the last month, and his own missions in particular, were decidedly out of the common way.

Dmitri Leonov might very well be the ne'er-do-well his geriatric amazon of an aunt dismissed him as, but he wasn't—well, he wasn't an out and out crook, was he?

Disposing of the less-than-savoury members of the criminal classes who stood in Oleg Gudkov's way was one thing. It made his stomach turn, but it didn't cost Yegor his nightly rest. Not like with the women. Certainly not like the near-constant anguish he had lived with since he had brought the boy to Arkhangelsk.

The boy was an innocent. Dmitri Leonov had been the one who had set the wheels in motion for that particular snatch-and-deliver, yes—but he couldn't have known what the outré oligarch wanted the information for. Even Yegor hadn't known—still didn't fully apprehend—what was going on. The ravings of Boris Kulakov. The literal buying of the child like he was a piece of cattle. Oleg Vladimirovich's cool, off-hand assurance that the boy would come to no harm, no further explanation given. Yegor hadn't asked. He couldn't.

He had found himself wondering more than once if it would have been better for the boy—for everyone—if he had simply let go of the controls of the Kamov and allowed the two of them, boy and unhappy giant, to plummet to their end in the darkest corner of the taiga, rather than seeing his assignment through to its completion.

It was just that, if he had, he would have left Alyosha all on his own.

Aleksey put a calming hand on his shoulder.

"Those drugs you are taking are messing with your head, Gosha. Breathe, there's a good lad. Do you really imagine we are going in there"—Alyosha indicated the back door of what Yegor presumed were Mashka Leonova's living quarters with a nod—"to liquidate an unarmed civilian? Are you truly in the company of a monster, Yegor Stepanovich? Because I know I'm not."

Aleksey's soft black gaze held his. It didn't matter that the man barely reached the shoulder he was holding on to. He could have brought Yegor to his knees by merely tossing his head in that way of his—the way he had done the very first time he had asked his blushing-under-his-beard nineteen-year-old colleague over for a drink at his digs, after a particularly grim job on the outskirts of Kursk.

Was it already six, seven years ago? It felt like a night and a day.

"Sometimes I think we are all of us monsters. All of us and none of us," Yegor said, not knowing what he was saying. Alyosha's grip morphed seamlessly into a rub.

"You make it seem so easy, being human, Alyosha. In the midst of chaos. I don't know how you do it."

Aleksey frowned. "We need to talk, Gosha. You haven't been yourself for a while now. Maybe I shouldn't have— But this is not the time. Are you ready to go in? I don't trust Mashka Leonova not to have more firearms stashed away for her nephew's use, irrespective of her having taken her hand off him."

Yegor scratched his chin. There was an ache in his bones, a listless inertia spreading through his system. Tired didn't begin to describe his current mental and physical state. Dead man walking was more like it.

He reached inside his jacket and withdrew his handgun from its shoulder holster. "I thought you said he was an unarmed civilian?"

Aleksey brought out his own weapon and winked. His lasso hung from the belt that circled his narrow hips— a last remnant from his upbringing within the Khudi clan, right here in the Nenets Autonomous Okrug.

No wonder Aleksey felt at home flying across the taiga and tundra. He was.

"Potentially, hopefully, probably unarmed. But considering the shopkeepers around these parts, I'm not taking any chances." Alyosha grinned, simultaneously roguish and reassuring. One of his many peculiar knacks.

Yegor put his shoulder to the door, his hand around the handle, and Aleksey nodded his go-ahead.

*

The space they entered was teeming.

Staggering from the sheer surprise of it, Yegor put up his arm to protect his bleary eyes as a flock of green-and-yellow plumed birds—too many to count at a glance—swooped down from he knew not where, then scattered like unrealistically coloured leaves in an autumnal gale.

A din of chirping and fluting and screeching filled his ears, counterpointed—phantasmagorically—by a loud, clamorous choir of mewling.

Yegor stumbled over stinky, furry somethings that slithered around and away from his feet, and Alyosha caught his elbow to steady him, swearing under his breath. Notwithstanding, there was a hint of mirth in his partner's expletives.

Yegor pushed his way through the mad horde of ugly, alien-looking felines. One of the diminutive birds took the opportunity to land on his ear, nibbling at the cartilage with its beak. Yegor let out an ungodly howl.

"What's going on?" The startled words came from a room to his left.

Aleksey rolled his eyes and edged past Yegor, having closed the door behind them so as not to expose Mariya Leonova's private zoo to the lethal sub-zero climate of the northern Siberian outdoors.

Yegor batted the budgerigar away with a shudder and gripped his gun tighter. The little demons straight out of an ecstasy-fuelled rave-party version of Dante's *Inferno* remained unimpressed.

"*Tetya* Mashka? Is that you?"

Irrationally, Yegor was affronted. Surely his fluid baritone didn't even begin to approximate the piercing shrill of the off-her-rocker bird- and shopkeeper?

The unmistakable curling-upwards of Alyosha's lips told him he might have been a little off his ordinary scale.

An annoyed huff came from the room, followed by the clatter and banging of someone rising out of their seat in untidy surroundings. A particularly teddy-bearlike cat jumped onto the back of a badly scratched couch that stood along a side wall, and prowled towards the door, as though in mock mimicry of the two men with their guns.

Aleksey let go of Yegor's elbow and took aim with his pistol as the door swung open to reveal Dmitri Leonov, in star-patterned long johns and a gamer's headset, a three-o'clock shadow gracing his chin and cheeks. Big, bovine eyes blinked, once, twice, as they took in his would-be assassins embroiled in his aunt's menagerie.

Dima's jaw slackened. A wet spot formed at his crotch, and Aleksey lowered his weapon, nose scrunching up.

"Dmitri Leonov?" Yegor overdid it on the side of gruff and menacing as though he might still be mistaken for Auntie Mashka. "You may remember me from—"

"Please!" Dima squeaked, backing away from them. "I already spent the money, but please—for the love of God!"

He knocked over a battered balalaika, which fell to the floor with a twang. Alyosha tsked and signed to Yegor to put his gun away.

"We are not here to harm you unless you force us to, Leonov. We have come for a talk about your future. Now sit down in that expensive-looking desk chair of yours; there's a good boy. This might just be your lucky day."

Yegor narrowed his eyes, looking askance at his comrade. But as ever—or as he had done for the last six or seven years—he allowed the nimbler man to take the lead.

*

"We should have shot him," Yegor gritted through clenched teeth, holding a protective hand over his midsection.

He shouldn't have eaten that energy bar Alyosha had thrust upon him as they made their way back to the Kamov. He should have topped himself up on stimulants in Tetya Mashka's dingy little bathroom, consequences be damned. He felt worse than a twice-run-over dog.

Aleksey smiled brightly. "You didn't want to shoot him, Gosha. This is better. He won't cause any trouble from sunny Crimea. Chances are, he wouldn't have anyway. The man's as dense as a brick. Gudkov's being paranoid"—he held up his hand, causing the helicopter to swerve to his right and Yegor's stomach to flip—"more paranoid than usual, I mean. Why is he taking such a risk with this boy from the Nenets Autonomous Okrug? If he likes boys..."

Yegor dry-retched and wiped miserably at his mouth. "Would you please—"

Aleksey returned his hand to the steering rod, righting the aircraft and glancing over at Yegor. His lips pressed together. "You need to eat, lyubov. Eat and sleep and stop worrying so much."

Yegor coughed. "You weren't the one who brought the boy to him. We've—I've done some unsavoury work before, but this…"

Alyosha's expression softened. "I wish I had been with you. We could have—well, never mind. Tell me about the boy. What's so special about him?"

Yegor rubbed at his face, staring out across the snowy vista. It had a calming effect, despite everything. The blankness of it. "Nothing. I don't know. It's not a fetish I ever… He was assaulted by a wolf and survived. Gudkov had some—some form of advertisement on the darknet for survivors of wolf attacks, with a hefty finder's fee. That's all I know. I don't think it mentioned age or gender. I can't make sense of it. I mean, I've always known he's a mad bastard, but…"

"The boy was attacked by a wolf?" Aleksey frowned, his temples bulging slightly. "And we are pursuing a girl and—a wolf?"

Yegor tittered nonsensically. He was worn past the boundaries of reason.

They should have killed Dmitri Leonov. That had been their implicit instructions. Instead, they extracted the information they needed from him and left him with a ticket for a one-way trip to Crimea, at Alyosha's own expense, Yegor suspected.

How long had his partner been subverting their employer's orders? And why hadn't he told Yegor what he was doing? It stung.

"You are too transparent, Gosha. I love you, but there it is. I've needed time, years, to plan our defection. I don't think you could have lied to Gudkov with a straight face for that long. You're in direct contact with him. He likes you, after his own skewed fashion. Me, he barely registers."

"How did you know—"

Aleksey clicked his tongue. "Transparent," he repeated, shooting Yegor a sultry look.

Yegor considered that another man might have been irritated with the presumption of the Nenets tribesman turned hired gun. Another man, yes—but not he. "What are we going to do? The girl is the boy's sister, Leonov said. Will we—"

"We'll pick her up, of course." Aleksey chewed on his lip. "We may have to kill the wolf."

Chapter Twenty-Seven

The boy lay naked on the stone floor, covered by a thin wool blanket. It was one of Babushka's blankets, which Oleg Vladimirovich kept stowed away under his opulent bed, to be brought out on special occasions.

The boy. The boy lay on the floor. The boy who had been a wolf.

Olezhka hugged himself tight, quivering with exultation. It was all true, and better than true: real, tangible, loud, and pungent. The volkodlak had not been a half-formed creature, either. Oh no, it had been purely vulpine, a perfectly shaped thing, an approximation of the pre-teen as a wolf.

When Seryozha had changed—but this part vexed Olezhka. Despite his preparations, his foreknowledge, his wildest hopes and flights of fancy, when it came to it, seeing it, he had been so thunderstruck, so overwhelmed by what was happening, he could not fully describe it to himself, re-experience it the way he craved.

The grey pelt had erupted through smooth child skin like millions of tiny spikes. His mouth had elongated across his face like a wound. His clothes—in his inexperience, Oleg hadn't thought of the boy's clothes, which was why they now lay in a useless heap in the corner.

Wolf Seryozha had ripped them to tatters, as the seams burst from the strain of his shifting limbs.

Olezhka had fallen to his knees then, clutching his precautionary prod, tears streaming down his gaunt features. It was beautiful. It was more than beautiful. It was—divine.

And now the boy was a boy again. Innocuous, deceptively human, shivering in his induced sleep. The boy was a boy was a wolf.

Soon, the manboy Olezhka would be a wolf, too, and he would have no further use for the puny northern Siberian wolfling. It would be interesting, though—instructive in its own right—to find out what methods were required to rid oneself of a volkodlak. A stake through the heart? Silver implements left in festering wounds? A swift lopping-off of his head?

Oleg didn't know. He had always been at pains not to dirty his own hands. Once or twice, even three times, did not a habit make. But he favoured poison, for old time's sake.

He might be less diffident as a wolf.

Oleg Vladimirovich shook himself, his fingers flitting up to the dressing across his chest. Wolf Seryozha hadn't gone for his throat as he had expected, but had shot at him with an arrow's precision, intent on piercing his heart.

As a deadly attack, it had proved ineffective, but it carried a certain artistry with it. Also, it had made Olezhka shit himself. A scatological kind of art, if you will.

He had no trouble reliving that part. Absolute terror, as he had not experienced it since Babushka's days. How exquisite. What a triumph. How he longed for his own wolf to grow out of him to complete the picture.

Yes, his own power released at last, made flesh and tooth and claw.

Olezhka whimpered. He worried his wound anew, and his vision blackened with fresh, sharp, glorious pain.

He had waited so long for this day. Locked inside his minuscule childhood room, pressed against the floor under the bed, he had dreamt it, *willed* it into existence.

The wolf that would eat Babushka. The wolf that would set him free.

But for a little while yet, he must play his part as Uncle Olezhka. He was a careful man, the maker of a financial empire; Oleg Vladimirovich Gudkov knew when to be reckless, and when to hedge his bets.

Daintily, Olezhka wrapped the blanket more snugly around the sleeping boy and lifted him, his unconscious body awkward and uncooperative. Oleg bit the side of his tongue. If Seryozha remembered anything of the night's events, he would be profoundly distrustful of Olezhka on waking up. To sow the seed of uncertainty, however, Seryozha would wake in his own bed, and Olezhka would be all mildness and consideration, all ears to his infantile stories of Snegurochka riding her gargantuan beast.

Oleg would bring his cattle prod, though. Just in case.

"You were a gorgeous wolf, Sergei Nikolayevich," Olezhka pronounced, as he shouldered the door of his moon tower open and walked down the corridor, the boy a babe in his arms. "It's a pity we can't be friends. I would have liked to have a friend. But Babushka says all friends turn traitors, in the end."

*

"Gospodin Gudkov! What happened to you?" Ludmila Andreyevna clasped her hands together as he exposed the bandages under his shirt. He had done a neat job of it, he thought, not without pride.

"Nothing much," he said complacently, lying down on top of the table, hiding his wince as his own weight pushed against the wound.

He had dithered over whether to clean it or not, deciding against it, finally. If the bite of a volkodlak was comparable to being infected with some kind of virus, Oleg didn't want to risk diluting its potency. Better to endure any minor inflammations that might arise, he judged, even if his germophobic heart squirmed and riled at this decision.

For all her Olympian size, Ludmila Andreyevna looked pale and watchful. Oleg almost never came to any bodily harm; he rarely ventured outside his mansion. A homebody. He wheezed with held-back jocularity. "A hunting accident, Ludmila Andreyevna," he said, as soon as he could draw breath. "Do not be alarmed."

She was putting more lotion on her hands—a handy excuse for wringing them. Oh, he was giddy with good humour. He wanted to tell her. He wanted to tell the whole world what he had done, what he had accomplished—he, little Olezhka, like unto God.

He wanted to make them bow down before his might, like they had fallen at the feet of Stalin, teeth first into the ground. Who had Stalin been? Poor, Georgian Ioseb, son of a nobody. Who had Napoleon been? Why not Oleg Vladimirovich Gudkov, born an orphan, raised by his Siberian grandmother, an officer at a gulag?

"You hunt, gospodin? I wasn't aware." There was a blank smoothness to Andreyevna's tone of voice, a shielding off. She was clever that way, his masseuse. She knew when she didn't want to know. Was it women's intuition? Oleg had never believed in such a thing.

"Not very often, I grant you. But I have a feeling it will become more of a regular activity from now on."

"You've been bitten?" Ludmila bore down on his right thigh. "By the hunting bug?" She spoke lightly, innocently—metaphorically, Oleg realised, as the first rush of adrenaline settled. His butt cheeks had clenched under his scant covering, and he knew the bitch would have observed it.

All friends turn traitors...

"You could say that." He feigned a yawn.

Ludmila Andreyevna seemed to be holding her breath. He wondered if she, who knew his body inside and out, could feel the change in him. Could she feel his bones—his entire skeleton—becoming transmutable?

He would have to get rid of her also. Olezhka cringed. That, at least, Yegor could handle.

It would be a shame. His massage sessions were as good as religion with Oleg. He would be sorry to see them go.

Chapter Twenty-Eight

Volk limped out of the forest in the early hours of the morning. Pyotra would not have noticed her at all if her sweeping torch hadn't caught a glint of silver fur. Her heart swelled in her throat, prickling her eyes with tears as she shot up on wobbly, sleep-deprived legs and ran to meet the sorry excuse for a wolf.

"What happened?" Pyotra threw her arms around the beast, paying no heed to her instinctive growl. "Where have you been? What have you done? Oh, Volk, I've worried myself sick!"

The wolf moved and sighed into her ear. She couldn't answer such questions, not here, not like this, but Pyotra couldn't hold them back either. Her nocturnal agony spilled out of her mouth, all splinters and barbed edges, a verbal keening to match the ache inside.

"Poor volchonok." Pyotra ran her mittened hands down the wolf's flanks. Volk—her lover—seemed to have shrunk to the size of a worker ant within the wolf's consciousness. "You've been to the war, haven't you? Did you—do you know what's happening to Sergei? He is alive, isn't he? Tell me he is alive!"

The wolf's eyes met hers, filled with a dark hunger that should have—would have—frightened her, in another life.

Slowly, tortuously, Volk inclined her head.

Pyotra's hands balled into fists in the wolf's coat. "I have food and shelter. You need to rest."

*

They slept for most of that day, the day after the full moon; Pyotra and the wolf, entangled inside the tent. Volk's curving spine jutted into Pyotra's abdomen. Her white-ringed tail tickled Pyotra's face every so often, and it could have been annoying, but after her lonely, anxiety-ridden night, it was heaven. Heaven. A pulse beat in time with her own. A paw settled on her thigh, the pads warm and soft and comforting. The wolf's croup nudged her chin. Sleep came in undulating waves, from pure exhaustion; but it was fretful, flickering, all the same.

She dreamt of cubs.

She dreamt of running through the woods, and it was high summer; the obliterating white had receded for a month or two to reveal a fecund, mossy green. It called to her. It begged her to run barefoot across it, even as the spruce needles nipped at her soles, as she shivered, goosefleshed, with each garment removed and discarded.

Something was moving inside her body, under her skin. Her heart beat so loudly it resounded between the trunks of the trees, to the escalating rhythm of her breath, the call of *mate, mate* coursing through her.

She was neither startled nor surprised as the lithe, black-eyed wolf stepped into her path. She fell to her knees, her whole being palpitating with her need, a thick shimmer of lust coating the very air between them.

She pushed her tumbling hair to the side, exposing her neck, whispering, "Lyubov, lyubov." Then, with a throaty groan, "Take me!"

The wolf circled her. Pyotra quivered, then quaked in earnest as she was upon her, tipping her onto all fours, mounting her without effort, jaws attaching to her scruff—

Pyotra awoke to a hot, musky cunt in her face.

She woke up to Evane tonguing her, leisurely, mindlessly, and she was so wet she could feel it—her juices, Volk's saliva—running down the insides of her thighs.

She opened a little wider and her lover grunted her approval, gripping the backs of her legs hard as Pyotra herself set to work, enveloping Volk's engorged sex with eager lips.

It didn't take long for them to peak, but they kept at it, clinging together, half wrestling, half embracing, pushing each other towards that crest again, again.

At last, Pyotra tore her swollen mouth from her insatiable, superhuman partner and exclaimed, "Oh God! Oh, sweet virgin mother! I want you to fill me with your pups!"

In a moment, Volk spun around until they were face to face, mouth to mouth, her canines grazing Pyotra's tender lips, her arms folding around her.

Volk didn't say anything. Pyotra didn't expect her to; it had been a witless, idiotic desire to voice. She refused to take it back though. It was her deepest, instinctual yearning for oneness and multiplicity, turned into inadequate human language.

A rumbling came from deep within Evane's chest— Volk's chest—the wolf, the wolf, keen and ready to claim her.

Pyotra nibbled at her love's ear, trying to defuse the tension. "I'm sorry. I can be such a wolf-tease, can't I?"

Volk let out a shaky, husky laugh. "That you can, mate. You're—" She pushed Pyotra's tangled locks back, rubbing her thumb along her cheekbone. "You're perfect. If I had known before, I would have snatched you from your grandfather's house, like the stuff of legends and nightmares I am."

Pyotra shook her head, running a finger down Volk's short nose, tracing the outlines of her lips. "You wouldn't have. You would have run away from me, and I would have had to come after you, lasso in hand. Don't you go changing our story. I won't let you."

Volk smirked, rolling them over until Pyotra straddled her. "You're top wolf, are you?" Her dark eyes twinkled, and Pyotra felt that familiar heat on her skin, even as she leant down to whisper, gruff with emotion, "No, silly. Like you said. I'm your mate."

*

"You were...inside him?" Pyotra passed a hand over her eyes, struggling to accept what Volk was telling her.

The wolf was eager to be going, she knew. Already, Volk was undressing after their meal, preparing to change.

"I don't know how it happened." Volk's teeth gnashed together. She was plainly frustrated with her own lack of comprehension. "His pull is stronger than anything I have experienced, but as far as I know he is my first turn. Maybe it's always like this. Or maybe it's because he's a cub in distress, in dire need of me; I just don't know!"

Pyotra zipped up her anorak. "What do you mean 'as far as you know'?"

Volk grimaced. She was in the buff now, and it was distracting, but only mildly so. Pyotra ruefully acknowledged to herself that she was sated, and then some. Still, she couldn't take her eyes off the woman. It was a mystery to Pyotra how she had ever considered Evane anything less than completely captivating.

A complex set of emotions crossed Volk's face, contorting her features. She looked away, but not before Pyotra had observed the haunted expression in her eyes. "I've killed before. Humans, I mean. I should have told you, but..."

"You've *killed*?" Pyotra's voice seemed to crack into jagged shards in her throat. Her ears buzzed with the din of an approaching freight train as Serafima's image rose before her—her mother! Torn, devoured—how could she—it wasn't possible—

Hard, fuzzy-haired arms locked around her. A high-pitched sound rang through the air; it originated from out of herself, Pyotra perceived hazily—she was moaning, yowling, moments from passing out. But the werewolf was there, steadying her, despite—

"Not your mother," Volk mumbled into her hair, caressing the nape of her neck. "I promise you, lyubov. Not that."

Pyotra swallowed a hiccup. She was trembling all over, and she wanted to push the half shifted oboroten' away, but—but this was the same Volk she had professed her love to, mere hours ago.

"Who?" she breathed and allowed herself to relax, bit by bit, against Volk's sweltering frame.

"Hunters," Volk spoke softly but matter-of-factly. "The hunters who shot and eviscerated Galya. I…I was sick. I was out of my mind with grief. I don't think I left enough of them to make one viable wolf out of the lot. I really am a monster, Pyotra Nikolayevna."

A distant, logical part of Pyotra knew that one of those men could easily have been Kolya. Kolya, who had lost his wife to the wolves, who had every reason to wish to eradicate the species from the face of the earth. But no, Kolya had eradicated himself instead.

And Volk, like Kolya, had lost *her* wife.

So much senseless bloodshed. So much pain.

Belatedly, she noticed that Volk was no longer holding her. She turned to find herself face to face with the wolf. The wolf who had rescued Sergei. The wolf who had turned Sergei into one of her own. The wolf who had rescued her, time and again, in the taiga, out on the tundra. The wolf with whom she had forged a bond, which she was only beginning to learn the intricacies of. The wolf who had become her passionate lover, her otherworldly companion, her—*hers*. The wolf who was a slayer of men.

Pyotra breathed in, filling her lungs with cold, clear air. Volk bowed her head, pawing at the ground, displaying the infinite sorrow which only an animal can properly express.

Pyotra caught her snout and planted a chaste kiss on top of the beast's shaggy head. "You have made me believe in a thousand impossible things before breakfast, Volk. But I still don't believe in monsters. You are a person. Someone destroyed your world and you retaliated. You shouldn't have, but it would be hypocritical of me to judge you for it. Chances are I would burn down a village if they so much as touched a hair on your head. I'll try not to. Just promise me you will be careful with yourself, even in wolf form. I'm squeamish about killing people and animals both."

The wolf looked askance at her, rolling her right shoulder in an exaggerated fashion.

Pyotra bit her lip. "I wasn't shooting to kill! I was—upset, and given what you just told me—"

Volk laved her face. Then she scraped her teeth over Pyotra's neck, as she had in Pyotra's dream.

Pyotra inhaled sharply. "You were there?"

The wolf's black eyes glimmered. Heat spread from Pyotra's neck and up into her cheeks.

"So you know how it is with me," she said snappily. "Will you promise me?"

Volk made a series of cluck-like yips. She butted her head to Pyotra's and stroked against her, mingling their scents, Pyotra knew by now.

She should know by now.

"Let's get you into your harness, bitch," Pyotra muttered, fondling the wolf's ears, and Volk grinned her agreement, wagging her entire body. She trembled with pent-up energy, for all the world a happy, obedient specimen of *Canis lupus*.

Pyotra harrumphed and fastened the reins to her. She wasn't planning on using them—but then again, she might.

Chapter Twenty-Nine

Her mate was claiming her; offering herself up to her. Asking for her rightful place within the pack. It was a dream, but Volk felt the draw of her mate so strongly she knew it wasn't *just* a dream. It was Pyotra's dream. And she was there.

It was a vertiginous sensation, as mentally draining as it had been to be with the cub across space and time, and yet part of her was aware her body was lying snug against Pyotra's, in a tent on the snowy plain en route to Naryan-Mar. To Arkhangelsk. To Sergei, Volk's pack mate; Pyotra's duck.

The achingly beautiful vision of the naked woman on the mossy floor of the forest—*Volk's* forest—held her in thrall. Pyotra pulled her sunflower hair to the side, baring her neck.

Volk staggered under the compulsion to leap on her, to leave her indelible mark on her, to ravage her until they were one, one—a hopeless tangle of flesh and fur.

Pyotra wanted it. She wanted Volk more even than she wanted her own turning, her own becoming as a wolf.

The intensity of it made Volk's head spin. It was a dream. What harm could there be in finding release for this primal yearning here, where anything was possible and nothing was affected in the waking world?

But Volk couldn't be sure of that. She could not be sure of anything when it came to the oboroten' curse, the oboroten' blessing. Not any more. She had to wake them up—she had to—even as she felt her mate yield to her, her supple skin under her, her trembling bottom rising up to meet Volk's lupine sex, and it was too much, too good, it was—she couldn't—

*

A thunderbolt struck from out of the open sky. Volk's head shot up as Pyotra pulled on the reins, spasmodically.

It wasn't thunder.

It was a huge, airborne death machine; Volk yelped, thrashing against the harness. She was desperate to be free of it, desperate to be able to protect—

A rifle fell onto the snow beside her, and Pyotra bent over her, crooning, undoing the straps as the aerial behemoth descended on them in a barrage of noise unlike anything either Volk or Evane had heard before.

"—copter!" Pyotra shouted in her ear. "It might be Gudkov's men. As soon as I have you out of this, run for the trees. I'll cover you with my rifle. Go, go!"

Volk bared her canines. Her mate must have lost her mind. Volk was not about to run off and save her own hide. Not this time. No one, human, beast, or Coptic angel of vengeance, would be depriving Volk of her mate a second time.

"Bloody pig-headed—"

The thing had landed a hundred or so feet away. Its flank opened and two black-clad men emerged. Just men. Volk felt a surge of adrenaline, a wash of relief. She could do this. She stood a chance.

"Volk, for the love of—"

As the first shot rang out, Volk toppled Pyotra to the ground. She vaulted over her supine, swearing love; Pyotra was obviously fine, and speed was everything in a wolf versus men-with-guns encounter.

They were no hunters. Or rather, they weren't hunters as Volk knew them; they appeared unused to following and predicting the movements of animal prey, in spite of their adroitness with their chosen weapons. Handguns, Volk registered in amazement, charging towards them at an angle. No one in their right mind went wolf-hunting with a pistol; let alone werewolf-hunting.

She almost felt sorry for them.

But not sorry enough. She didn't think she would survive if they took Pyotra from her, not even for the cub's sake. A deadly rage flooded her. Volk snarled as she jumped the first man, the smaller one, catching him by the neck before he so much as had time to raise his weapon.

She bit deep, blood flowing into her mouth, tendons snapping and cartilage creaking.

"Alyosha!" The other man screamed, and there was so much pain—private, personal, palpitating—in that scream, even Volk in her frenzy was momentarily distracted.

Two shots were fired, one after the other.

Then everything was silent. Too silent. Someone was running towards her; the reverberations of their footfalls travelled through her paws and up her legs. Volk let go of the man called Alyosha. He sagged into a heap on the ground.

"Volk!" Pyotra threw herself at her, cheeks streaked with tears, her grip frantic. "I think I killed him! God forgive me, he was shooting at you, and I just... Can you help him, please? Can you—can you turn him, or something—oh God, Evane, I shot a man!"

Alyosha stirred. He was bleeding heavily, the snow blooming pink around him.

"Evane?" He spoke distantly, dreamily, as if through a veil. "You named your wolf...Evane?"

Pyotra glowered at him—she was Pyotra Nikolayevna, after all—and spat out, "I didn't name her."

She would have said more, no doubt, but Volk's mournful howl interrupted her. Yes, she was howling. Her soul was being rent asunder. She had sniffed the man haemorrhaging on the ground. The man—the boy— *Aleksey*—

"I had a cousin called Evane," he whispered, his eyes glazed, and it wasn't fair. None of it was. It was too much for a lone wolf.

Pyotra stared at the man, and Volk could see understanding dawning on her. She put her hand over her mouth, spoke through the wool of her glove. "What happened to her?"

"I don't... She was older than me. I was only eight years old when she...disappeared one night. Like that." He raised his hand, trying to snap his fingers.

Pyotra glanced over at Volk. Volk hung her head. *Do something*, her mate's eyes demanded. Volk bristled, annoyed and hurting, aching from a scar so old she had all but forgotten about it.

Little Aleksey. Who would have thought?

"Help him," Pyotra wheezed between clenched teeth, her panic over the man she had shot fading in the face of this new enormity. "I'll see to his comrade-in-arms. Bullet wounds have become something of a specialty of mine."

Volk snorted, but her mate was right. As Pyotra hurried away to their other assailant, Volk loped up to her long-lost, dying kinsman and proceeded to lick his wounds.

*

"You'll live." Volk let the man go. He smelled of both Aleksey and himself, but also of her mate who had tended to him, another impromptu operation in the snow before they brought their attackers turned patients back into the flutter beast.

Helicopter, Volk reminded herself.

The bearded man gazed up at her, his mouth agape in stunned speechlessness. Volk reckoned he wasn't used to being carried by anyone, let alone a female of the species. He was uncommonly large.

"Evane? Is it really you? Are we dead, then?"

She rolled her eyes before turning to face Aleksey. "Do you see any reindeers around? Surely, this isn't your idea of paradise, Khudi?"

Aleksey blinked and smiled beatifically; his eyes seemed to drink her in. Volk shifted uncomfortably.

"You don't look a day older," he observed.

Volk scoffed. "You do, I'm afraid. Look, Aleksey, I'm— I wish I had recognised you sooner. You shouldn't have borne down on us out of nowhere."

She couldn't offer more of an apology. Cousin or not, he and his partner had threatened her mate, herself. Shots had been fired. A tiny part of her still thought it would have been wiser to leave them for dead.

Pyotra gave her a lopsided smirk. She was applying iodine to the gashes on Aleksey's neck—unnecessarily, really. They were healing at a rate which could not be copied by man or machine, induced to close by oboroten' saliva.

Volk had turned him. With ninety-nine per cent certainty. Aleksey Khudi. Her cousin.

Her pack was growing out of control.

"We didn't mean to harm anyone. Except the wolf— Did I get it, Alyosha? The yellow-haired woman shot me, I—I don't recall—"

"If you had 'got it', I would have let you die," Pyotra answered the bearded man placidly. His eyes bulged.

Aleksey was scowling at Volk, brows furrowed so deeply it almost looked comical.

"You called the wolf Evane," he murmured, and it wasn't clear whether he was addressing Pyotra or her. "The wolf tried to eat me. It tickled."

Volk snorted in earnest at that. "Lesson number one, Aleksey. We do not eat human flesh."

Outside, the wind had picked up, blowing snow and hail against the sides of the helicopter.

"Turukhan?" Aleksey wasn't speaking Russian any longer. He directed himself to her, exclusively, in Nenets. "Tundra wolf? Wolf...heart?"

Volk sank to her knees. Pyotra extended her hand to her across Aleksey. She took it.

"Are you?" Aleksey repeated, and his features were twisted, in pain, in incredulity, in helpless—hurtful—disgust.

Volk bowed her head. She had no other option but to tell him. No other choice at all.

"I have the heart of the wolf," she confirmed. Something clouded her eyes. "We are one."

Her cousin reached inside his shirt; Volk saw it, obscured, as in a cracked mirror.

Pyotra saw it too. Her mate leant over Aleksey and cold terror seized Volk; she swept her aside, she—

A gun went off, the shot echoing within the metal chamber of the aircraft.

Volk sat back, the air knocked out of her. She heard Pyotra, aghast and furious, spouting accusations as quick as any stray bullets: "You shot her! You made her cry!"

Aleksey's throat gurgled incoherently. The big man gasped and swore.

Volk had to laugh.

Chapter Thirty

Alyosha had tried to shoot his cousin through the heart. The angle had been wrong, and the other woman, the boy's sister—Pyotra—had been half in the way; but Aleksey had taken the shot with his backup, a sleek, tiny Pistolet Makarova. He caught her in the shoulder.

Pandemonium ensued.

The yellow-haired fury knocked the weapon out of Alyosha's hand, shouting oaths that would have put the most foul-mouthed bartender in Arkhangelsk to shame.

Yegor began to rise, but one look from the wolf woman quelled him. She was laughing. Laughing! It was enough to make him soil himself.

Then, as if to drive home the lunacy of it all, Yellow-hair fell about wolf cousin's neck, shouting, "Lyubov! Lyubov!"

Yegor closed his eyes. He pinched himself. He wanted to wake up. He wanted to find that this palaver was an out-of-character hallucination. That he hadn't been felled like a deer, too preoccupied by the wolf mauling his partner to pay attention to the girl with the antiquated rifle. That Alyosha was hale and whole and—

"The other shoulder!" the madwoman hooted, and now Yellow-hair started to chuckle as well.

In the end, Yegor remembered his own pocket backup. He pulled it out with a sigh.

"Everybody calm down!" Yegor pointed the gun at the boy's sister. He had no intention of shooting her, but it seemed like the thing to do. "Alyosha, are you all right?"

His partner grunted. For now, Yegor would have to take that as a yes.

The women had stopped laughing. They were looking at him, quizzically, heads tilted like two demented hags.

Aleksey was right. Yegor needed to lay off the drugs.

"Please, explain yourselves," he commanded. Then he added beseechingly, "No one needs to get hurt."

*

"I'm not a wolf," Aleksey muttered for the seventh or eighth time since they had taken off, guiding the Kamov towards Naryan-Mar.

Yegor patted his knee. "I love you," he breathed, acutely aware of the two women in the seats behind them. Evane, in particular, seemed to hear and see everything.

She was taciturn, though, unless provoked. Another trait the two cousins had in common. Yegor's head hurt, trying to take it all in.

Turnskins. Clanspeople. Infectious bites. Lesbians. What next?

Aleksey addressed the women, not bothering to turn around. "You will have to make your own way from Naryan-Mar. It would be too risky for us to bring you all the way to Arkhangelsk. You understand?"

"We understand," Pyotra replied good-humouredly.

Alyosha's hands were shaking on the controls. Yegor wished there was something—anything—he could do.

The Nenets woman leant forward. She was short and unprepossessing, and yet, with one look she could make the bottom of Yegor's stomach drop out. She could literally pick him up and throw him about like a bowling ball. It shouldn't be physically possible.

Aleksey made a low, whining noise in his throat, and Evane put a hesitant hand on his shoulder. She mumbled something in their own language. Aleksey's lips thinned to a line, even as his dark eyes softened for a moment. He barked a monosyllabic answer and his cousin sat back again.

Yegor glanced over his shoulder. After Aleksey had shot his kinswoman, Pyotra had removed the bullet and bandaged the woman's shoulder. Evane seemed barely conscious of the wound. She had slung her arm around Pyotra, and Pyotra rested her head against it.

As he watched, Evane smiled knowingly at him. "You want me to bite you too."

It wasn't a question. Yegor's face heated up.

"Touch him and I swear I will find a way to kill you." Yegor hardly recognised Aleksey's voice.

"Don't worry, Aleks," Evane drawled. "You can turn him yourself when the time is ripe. He is your mate; is he not? He smells of you all over."

"Volk!" Pyotra elbowed the ungodly fiend of a woman in the ribs. Evane emitted a sound bizarrely akin to a yip. "How many times do I have to tell you that scenting people like that is rude?"

"I can't help it," Evane groused. "The man reeks."

"Enough!" Aleksey's fist thudded onto the dashboard. The Kamov wobbled. "If it weren't for Yegor—"

"I know," Evane said, in a soothing tone of voice which Yegor wouldn't have thought her capable of. He knew nothing, as usual; that much was clear. "Believe me, cousin. I know."

Silence descended upon them; as much silence as there could be in a flying helicopter. The whoosh and slash of the rotor blades easily filled up the space left by the lull in conversation.

They should have so much to talk about. They should be honing their plan of attack, picking through the details, sniffing out the blind spots. Hell, they should get to know each other. If they were really going to do this crazy thing together—

Yegor fidgeted at the stray wisps of beard on his neck. Snow was falling through the headlights. If it hadn't been for the green dot blinking on the navigation screen, he would be utterly lost.

"I'm sorry we had to leave your sled behind," he blurted at random.

Pyotra shrugged. "I hated it anyway," she mumbled, pressing her cheek to the back of Evane's hand. "I wish we could have burnt it."

"Don't be ridiculous, mate." Evane had shut her eyes, but Yegor didn't let that fool him. She knew he was observing them.

"I guess I can see that," Yegor mused. "I wouldn't like to put a harness on Aleksey either."

His co-pilot squeaked. The Kamov canted precariously. "Gosha, for the love of God!"

Yegor bit his lip.

But Pyotra beamed at him, and it was a start, wasn't it? It was something.

*

Alyosha had his arms around him, pulling him towards him from behind. It was so sweet, so longed-for, Yegor's throat tightened. His fists clenched and unclenched.

He turned in the embrace, the cheap hotel bed groaning underneath his weight. Aleksey's eyes were pitch-black and inscrutable. Just like Evane's, Yegor realised. He gulped, his Adam's apple bobbing nervously.

"You talk too much, Yegor Stepanovich."

"I do?" He allowed his index finger to trace the already-fading scars on Alyosha's neck. *They won't disappear completely*, the wolf woman had said. *They will show on his pelt.*

His pelt. Try as he might, Yegor could not envision it, his mind turning up empty whenever he strove to picture his lover as a...a wolf. "You're more of a fox to me."

Aleksey shook his head faintly. His hand had slipped under Yegor's shirt, caressing the line of hair that ran from his navel and down.

Yegor's breath hitched.

"And you are more of a bear." Alyosha's eyes were pools of liquid black now, ever shifting, beguiling in a way that made Yegor physically ache for him.

He always did. Even before he'd had any words for it, any way to define this need, this desire for skin-to-skin, it had been there: a dull, persistent throbbing, a churning in his chest, a response deep in his loins.

He grunted.

Aleksey dipped his hand inside his briefs, his face suffused with heat. "I love how you are always ready for me. Gods, Yegor, you're so big!"

He grasped him like he would the steering rod of the Kamov, swift and sure and on target.

Yegor's eyes closed. His hips jutted forwards.

Aleksey trailed a line of kisses down his neck. "I'm burning up for you, lyubov. I swear, since you talked about putting me in a harness—"

"Alyosha!" His eyes flew open. "I wouldn't, sweet saints, believe me—"

"Maybe you'll have to." Aleksey's onslaught was ferocious, merciless. Yegor couldn't think, couldn't string this and that together. He was going to peak, any minute, any second—and it wouldn't be the first time nor the last, and later Aleksey would—yes—and he would stiffen anew, like always, like forever, ready for the encore.

Hazily, he asked himself if it was like this for the women too. He would not have thought it possible. Not until he had met Pyotra Kulakova, a scant twenty-four hours ago, and he had seen that glow on her, and acknowledged that it was, indeed, the mirror image of his own.

She was the partner—the *mate*—of an oboroten'. And he? He was, or soon would be, one also.

"Bite me when you come," Aleksey whispered thickly.

Yegor didn't have to ask where or why. He wouldn't have been able to, at any rate. As a piercing ray of sun shot through and spilled out of him, he sank his teeth into Alyosha's neck, right across those shimmering, telltale scars.

Chapter Thirty-One

He came to.

He had dreamt—yes, he had dreamt something awful. But that was all; it was a bad dream. It had to have been. He curled in upon himself under the blanket and counted his own digits: two thumbs, two index fingers, two long fingers, and two ring fingers. Two trembling pinkies. His mouth tasted sour. Bile, Pyotra used to call it, and Ded would concur.

Bile seemed to have flooded him during the night.

He had no desire to peek outside his cover and see which reality he had woken up to. He had had enough, and too much, of reality. He didn't want to be a man any more. Dima Fyodorovich had never given him any advice pertinent to what he had—or hadn't—experienced tonight. Dima could go to the devil, as far as Sergei was concerned.

To the devil. A memory of Olezhka, his face screwed up with pain and rage—an all-devouring, unhinged type of rage that Seryozha had never witnessed before—flashed through his mind. His breathing quickened. He bit his pinkies to prevent himself from fainting with fear.

Olezhka, his friend. Olezhka, the devil. Seryozha, the boy. Seryozha, the...wolf. Wolf!

He pulled his knees flush to his stomach. It couldn't be. It had been a bad dream. A bad, bad dream.

People did not physically mutate into wolves. How could they? The bones, the skin, the nose and ears. It was too far apart, too fantastic, for a naked ape to morph into a four-footed, hairy beast. It was the stuff of fairy stories, but not the fairy stories he wanted. He wanted to be the knight, the prince, the clever farmer's boy. The wolf—the wolf always died in the end.

I am your wolf mother. He had fallen into the freezing water of the pond, and he had been stunned. It had been impossible to move. He had sunk like so much dead weight. And that was all—the only things he could remember—before waking up in his cot with a searing pain on his neck and a raging Pyotra.

Yes, his sister had been furious. But not like Olezhka. That was something else, something Sergei doubted his mind could have invented of its own accord.

So it must be true. He had to have seen it. It was too jarring, too incongruous not to be real.

One of them must be insane.

But then, Sergei was the one who thought he had been a tundra wolf.

"Time to wake up, *sonya*."

He clenched his teeth on his fingers, tasting iron. The blanket fluttered and flew away, and a man bent over him, with a kind, cheerful, non-threatening mien. The man's hairline had receded past his ears. He was old, Sergei realised, much older than Pyotra, though not as old as Ded. Could he be…Kolya's age?

"You have had a rough night, Seryozha," Olezhka observed in that strange, clipped voice of his. He was wearing a suit, as ever, in a shiny, indigo-hued material.

Since when did prisoners wear suits? Seryozha had been so stupid, so gullible. Well, not any longer. He was Sergei now.

"I hate you," he croaked, shocked by his own audacity. "You need to let me out of here, or else."

The man who called himself Olezhka laughed in his face. The hairs at the back of Sergei's neck rose. "Or else what?"

He was up close now, and he smelled—rank. Sergei had to fight back a sneeze. His nose was besieged by layers upon layers of scents and malodours—too much sensory information, all at once. Sergei sealed his lips, refusing to speak.

Olezhka leered at him. He revealed a metal stick from behind his back, held like a vicious extension of his right arm. "I've still got it."

Cattle prod. She had tried to warn him. He couldn't feel her any more, which was both a relief and a pity. She had been heavy on him, somehow, but she had helped. He could see that.

"I have a surprise for you, Seryozha. I'm taking you for a walk after breakfast. Would you like that?"

He wanted to tear the smug expression off the man's face. He wanted to rumple his fancy suit, slice through his skin, shred—*go in for the kill*.

Sergei nodded warily. He needed to get out of this room, this cell, if only to prove to himself there was something outside of this not-quite existence.

There's a good duck. He hung onto Pyotra, to the memory of her, the reality of her.

Whether or not she was coming for him.

"Good boy." Olezhka pointed the prod at the chair by the table, on which a tray was waiting for him. Sergei's nostrils twitched. Chay, strong and bitter, with not enough milk. Toast and butter and—orange marmalade.

Sergei sat up straighter, smoothing down his shirt. A treat. A treat from the man wielding a cattle prod like he was a dumb brute, an animal. It was impossible to figure out this odd species of grown-up.

What did he want from him? Why had he... Oh, but Sergei's head ached. His stomach grumbled. He would eat first.

*

Sergei could still taste the tangy sweetness of the marmalade as Olezhka led him up and down corridors. To the left, to the right, to the left? He would never be able to memorise their winding path; something he suspected Olezhka was well aware of.

At least the pretence had fallen away. He was the prisoner. Olezhka was the man with the prod.

But what else were they?

Sergei felt nauseous. All those days—weeks maybe—inside his cell, with little to no exercise. No wonder his mind had sunk into torpor. He was tripping over his own legs, time and again. It was as if he had forgotten the most efficient way to use them. One foot in front of the other, but just the two: one, two, one, two.

He missed his paws.

Sergei's heart skipped a beat. He held his head, emitting a low, guttural moan that made Olezhka's neck stiffen, a step or two ahead of him. That was his jailer's only response, however. He did not turn around to ask what was the matter. He did not so much as slacken his pace.

Sergei wanted to punch him. He wanted—he wanted to *pounce* on him, but there was the prod, carried like a jaunty walking stick, clicking every so often against the floor, keeping up the beat.

Sergei's moan sunk lower, rumbling in his chest in a way that surprised him into silence. This time, Olezhka half turned towards him.

Had he...had he just *growled*?

"No funny business. Remember who's in charge." Olezhka waved the prod at him. A bead of sweat trickled down the man's brow.

Sergei cocked his head. He was still holding it, his fingers curled in too-long tresses. No Pyotra here to cut it for him.

He is afraid. He stinks of it.

Sergei lowered his hands. He had to bite the inside of his cheek not to grin.

"The moon won't be up for another couple of hours."

Sergei didn't know what to say to that, but Olezhka didn't seem to expect a reply. He was talking to himself, apparently.

Crazy old geezer.

"Come on. It's not much further. Babushka's been looking forward to meeting you."

That made no sense, either. Surely, Olezhka was too old to have a living babushka? Maybe he called his wife that; old people had the weirdest habits.

Sergei was suddenly aware that apart from his hair being unkempt, he hadn't had a bath since he had come to this place. What kind of impression would he make? A woman...a woman might take pity on him.

"I need to pee."

Olezhka's eyebrows shot so far up his forehead they all but disappeared. "No, you don't."

"I do." He refused to be bullied. His wolf mother would approve, he thought. "I need a bathroom."

Olezhka rubbed a hand over his face. His trigger finger twitched on the prod.

"If you prod me, I'll pee myself," Sergei observed. "Babushka wouldn't like that, would she?"

Olezhka looked as if he'd been slapped. Oh, he was under her thumb, all right. If Sergei could make Babushka like him—

Olezhka sighed. "There is a bathroom in the hallway at Babushka's. I'm warning you, Seryozha. I have the tranquilliser gun with me. I won't hesitate to use it."

Sergei shrugged. His store of trepidation seemed to have been depleted for the moment. How could things possibly get worse?

"I need to pee," he repeated, simply.

Olezhka grabbed him with his free hand and hauled him along.

*

Something was off about the bathroom. Sergei couldn't put his finger on it, but it felt...out of place. Like it had been moved from its original location and dropped in this warren of endless, windowless corridors. How big was this place—whatever it was—anyhow? He didn't know. It wasn't a proper jail, he was fairly certain. It was more like—a memory palace.

Yes, that was it. Sergei was pleased with himself. His teacher had told them about memory palaces a few months ago. It was mnemonic device, a trick, really, not something tangible. But this was how Sergei had imagined it: an ever-expanding set of corridors. No beginning. No end.

The bathroom didn't fit. It had an old-timey atmosphere to it, and it smelled...of rust and mould and things he would rather not name. But there was a toilet, which he used, because why not? And there was a bathroom cabinet containing a disgusting glass with a set of false teeth in it that made him gag, a rose-scented soap, and—what he was looking for—a mirror.

Gingerly, Sergei lifted the dainty hand mirror by its silver handle. He was afraid now—senselessly—of gaining visual proof of the state he was in. He never used to care about his appearance. Back home, back in his *real life*, that had all been Pyotra's domain, Pyotra's fussing. For as long as he could remember, his sister had been there to wipe his face with fingers and spittle, check that his clothes matched, cut and comb his hair.

He missed her terribly. He was afraid of what she would think of him in this new, unprecedented state of being. The boy who growled. The boy who could barely walk upright, but who longed to run, run, forever, on four sturdy paws.

What would she think of his wolf mother? Had Pyotra not set out to kill her, after all?

What Ded thought had been all too evident. Ded thought him a monster. He had known, Sergei surmised. Somehow, Ded had known.

He had a keen nose, Sergei's grandfather. It was uncanny, the things he could smell.

"Do it! Just do it already," Sergei chided himself out loud, yet quietly enough he was sure Olezhka couldn't hear him from beyond the closed door. With a tremulous sigh, he flipped the mirror around and saw—

Himself. Sergei Nikolayevich Kulakov, a nearly twelve-year-old human boy, looking the worse for wear, yes, but... He touched his forehead. He touched his lips and his ears. Human. All human. It must all have been a dream, a surreal, crazy dream—oh!

Sergei dropped the mirror. It fell into the washbasin, clattering and cracking.

Olezhka pounded on the door, but Sergei didn't care, couldn't respond. He had opened his mouth to grin at himself and his incisors—his—his canines—

"Seryozha! Open this door immediately."

Sergei covered his face with his hands and he was whimpering, certainly, but also... That rumbling in his chest had started again, a low, lethal warning.

It calmed him. It strengthened him. It made him feel like...like the leader of the pack.

Ignoring the impotent yowlings of the curious little man outside, Sergei pushed back his shoulders, gathered up the pieces of the mirror, and shoved them back inside the cabinet. He picked up the soap and proceeded to lather himself up. He would smell like a posh flower garden, come what may, and his teeth—he would just have to keep his mouth shut. He could do that. Babushkas preferred quiet boys as a rule, didn't they?

He would bow his head and smile with his lips pressed together and— And if she didn't like the look of him, he would eat her.

Sergei's teeth tingled. He finished up his ablutions and snapped at the air.

One thing was crystal clear. However his sister might feel about it, Sergei wasn't a duck any more.

Chapter Thirty-Two

The boy had used Babushka's soap. The sacrilege of it confounded Olezhka; how many times had he wanted to—dreamed of—doing such a thing himself?

This isn't a soap for nasty little boys.

He flinched. Seryozha stood before him, calm as anything. The heavy scent wafted off him, teasing Olezhka's nostrils, tying his guts in a knot. The boy crossed his arms and slanted back against the door to Babushka's bathroom. He stared up at Olezhka with cool defiance.

"I'm ready," the boy muttered finally, impatiently. "Are we going to see Babushka or not?"

Oh, the cheek of him. Who had brought up this wild, uncouth child? No manners, no fear of God— Olezhka wanted to tear him apart. He wanted to rip him open and crawl inside his skin: to be, to become...

The boy flashed him a toothy grin.

Oleg's hand went to the wound on his chest—the imprint of those teeth on him. Little Seryozha was a nightmare come true. The contrast of his childish face with those lurid fangs was like something out of cinematic horror at its finest. Korean, or Japanese perhaps.

Oleg pointed at the farther door with his prod. "Through there."

Seryozha shuffled his feet towards Babushka's. It was as though he had turned adolescent overnight; as if the onset of lycanthropy had precipitated his human flesh into puberty. He moved, of a sudden, with a devil-may-care confidence. He held his chin high, in blatant disregard for old Olezhka and his cattle prod.

Oleg Vladimirovich bristled. Babushka would wipe that smug look off his mutt face. Oh yes, she would.

The boy halted in front of the closed door, peering in vain through the frosted glass. "It's all dark in there. Is she sleeping?"

His left eyelid had begun to twitch. Oleg slipped a hand into his pocket to bring out a handkerchief. "It's fine," he said, mopping at his face. "Go on through. She won't mind."

A hesitant look passed over the cocksure youth's features then, and Olezhka revelled in it.

"Don't be shy, Seryozha," he lilted. He was Uncle Olezhka once more, the sing-song tone of that fictional character of his own creation wrapping around his tongue like a gaudy veil.

Seryozha put a hand on the knob, licking his lips. It took all of Oleg Vladimirovich's not-inconsiderable store of self-restraint not to prod him.

Not so tough now, are you?

The boy had paled, shrunk back in upon himself.

Oh, Babushka. Even after all these years...

"She won't bite," Olezhka coaxed, tittering at his private joke. A burst of excitement, anticipation, dread—jumbled up—fizzed through his veins like a stiff shot of Stolichnaya.

His neck rigid, hitherto unseen muscles standing out in sharp relief, Seryozha turned the knob.

*

Oleg Vladimirovich was all but dissolving in the heat. His hand shook as he reached for his venik, lashing himself with savage abandon. The air he breathed scalded his throat. He wouldn't last much longer.

Oleg doubted he would ever be able to say precisely what had possessed him when he had brought the volkodlak mongrel into his shrine. No other living soul, not one, no one, had laid eyes on Yekaterina Gudkova since her grandson had had her embalmed and removed to her glass sarcophagus, deep within the secret recesses of his mansion in Arkhangelsk.

She was his, consummately his and his alone. So why...?

Sergei Nikolayevich had screamed when he saw her. He had screamed, a delicious, blood-curdling scream, like the scream of an old woman—*the* old woman—and Olezhka had been so giddy with it he had clapped his hands, his knees jerking as if to caper.

Yekaterina's mouth was perpetually open in just such a scream, though a silent one. The boy, thirty-odd years later, had elegantly voiced it for her, like a budding ventriloquist.

The spotlight overhead brought out the dull glow in the embossed buttons of her uniform.

It had been a moment to savour. A moment worth sharing. Perhaps the boy had earned his place next to Babushka? His originator and his stand-in—yes, Oleg Vladimirovich liked that tableau. As soon as he could be sure that the volkodlak's bite had taken, he would complete his *pièce de resistance*.

The best artworks remain hidden, sequestered in the private galleries of his cronies turned art collectors, open only to a select few. Of course, in Oleg's case he was the artist and the collector and the audience, wrapped into one.

Babushka had always called him a greedy, grasping egotist.

Olezhka leant back against the pinewood planks of his sauna, hoisting his elbows onto the seat behind him and stretching out his back. He had a foul taste in his mouth, a touch of heartburn. The last couple of days had been stressful.

The boy was trouble, pure and simple. He had gone down on all fours before Babushka, dirty dog that he was. It had taken Oleg a moment or two too long to grasp what was happening. When he did, Seryozha had already torn through his second set of clothes and come bounding at him at an alarming speed, fangs bared and ready to strike.

Apparently, being touched by moonlight wasn't necessary for transmutation. So much for Oleg's moon tower.

It had taken three shots of the tranquilliser gun before the wolf was down. Enough to bring down an elephant, or so he'd been told. Oleg Vladimirovich wasn't in the habit of sedating exotic beasts.

"How about a wolf?" he had asked his supplier.

The man had shaken his head and chuckled moronically. "You won't need that much for a wolf, gospodin."

Olezhka touched the grisly red welts on his bare chest and frowned. People knew nothing, less than nothing.

Well, he would show them. Soon enough, one way or the other, Oleg Gudkov would show them all.

Chapter Thirty-Three

The Epiphany Cathedral in Naryan-Mar was a towering wood-built church, with a golden onion cupola atop a pointy spire roof. Pyotra couldn't say how they had ended up there. Volk had needed a walk. She was fidgety, restless after the hours spent inside the whirring helicopter. Worried, endlessly, by something inside. Her wolf, she said, but Pyotra had a feeling it wasn't that, or not only that; it was her brother's wolf, more likely, calling out to Volk.

And now, Volk's cousin Aleksey's wolf too. Volk's— Evane's—cousin Aleksey, who was on Oleg Gudkov's payroll. Only in northern Siberia...

They had left their room at the hotel and wandered up and down the streets of Naryan-Mar, which wasn't much of a city, Pyotra knew, in comparison to the world's megalopolises. But the truth was neither she nor Evane had ever been to a place with so many people within just a few hectares of land.

They had clung to each other, cross-eyed with it all, and Pyotra had found herself thinking of Tatya in faraway

St Petersburg, in that other world, that other life—and she was glad, for so many reasons, that she had not pursued that path.

Somehow, they had ended up on Lenina Street, and there was the cathedral: lit up and as dazzling as an enchanted castle to their unschooled eyes.

"Church," Volk mumbled, turning to go in the other direction. Pyotra placed a hand on the wolf woman's arm and stopped her.

"Wait," she said. "Let's go inside. We might as well since we're here. I'm freezing."

Volk evaded her eyes, opening her fur coat to wrap it part way around Pyotra. "We should go back to the hotel thing. You need your sleep."

"As do you." Pyotra cocked an eyebrow. "But I want to go inside and light a votive. Please, Volk. Only for a minute or two."

"I...can't." Volk shook her head. "You go. I'll wait for you out here."

"But why?"

Volk met her gaze, at last. Her soulful eyes held such a pleading expression, Pyotra immediately backpedalled. "Of course you don't have to come, lyubov. I just don't understand."

"I am a werewolf. I am—" Volk flapped her hand in the direction of the cathedral "—unhallowed. I'm not allowed in."

"What? That's rubbish. Who told you that?"

Volk let out a long-suffering sigh. "I am a supernatural being, Pyotra Nikolayevna—"

"I know, I know, you're the big bad wolf that goes bump in the night. Spare me the marketing spiel." She stood with her arms akimbo.

"Why in God's name are we fighting about this?"

Pyotra's lips twitched. Volk looked nonplussed. Pyotra started to giggle. "Oh, love, you really are—" She broke off, deeming it wiser not to provoke the beast. "But seriously. You have such a tortuous set of ideas about yourself and the world. This is just a wooden hut. A rather grandiose one, I grant you, but I hate to see you cowering before it. If you have a theory that you will burst into flames the moment you cross the threshold— Fine, let's put it to the test. How about you stick your pinky in?"

Volk regarded her darkly. "Why must you always push me?"

Pyotra's face prickled. Volk was right, of course she was, and there was no reason in the world for them to step into the Epiphany Cathedral in Naryan-Mar, on this particular evening, in this particular life. But— "There are enough things out there to be afraid of. But not this. Not yourself."

"I'm not— Oh, very well." Volk threw her hands in the air and stalked towards her, and before Pyotra knew what had hit her, she had been whisked up the stairs and through the open doors.

Volk's face was scrunched up, her eyes squinting, her nostrils flaring with her rapid intake of breath—but as

Pyotra had predicted there was no instantaneous combustion, no promptly delivered smiting of the demon wolf.

Pyotra laid a hand on Volk's cheek. They were both of them quaking. "Okay, so you called my bluff. I really would have preferred it if you had started with a pinky. Dear God!"

Volk's face broke into a feral grin. "You can still call me Volk. I wasn't planning on taking up residence."

"Smart-arse."

"Pushy little minx."

"Hey, I'm taller than you!" Pyotra shoved at the impudent, extremely cocky turnskin.

"That's the part you take umbrage at? Plain pushy minx, then."

*

"You have the wrong end of the stick, you know."

They were back in bed, rolled up together like a pastry swirl, which was Volk's preferred mode of sleeping. She was uncomfortable with the bed; if it hadn't been for Pyotra insisting that was where one slept indoors, Pyotra suspected Volk would have rolled out their bedding in one of the grubby corners of the room. At this point, she comprehended how uneasy Volk had been in the cot at Ded's.

As it was, they had reached a compromise. They lay on their own bedding, surrounded by their mingled scents, on top of the bed. The bed in Volk's den had obviously been primarily for Galina's convenience.

Pyotra turned to peer at Volk's shadowed mien. "I do? What stick is that?"

Volk pulled her closer, running her calloused palm down Pyotra's belly. Pyotra hummed. "I don't...I have no problem being what I am. I had issues *not* being it. Before, I mean. As Evane."

Volk nipped at the sensitive spot behind her ear, and Pyotra shivered, sexual tension mounting within her despite her fatigue. "Do you mind when I call you Evane?"

Volk's roving hand found Pyotra's right breast, doing things to it that sent eddies of pleasure through her body. Her lips parted.

"Not you, no." There was a hint of surprise in Volk's voice. "I should have told you all of my names from the start. I am Volk. I am also Evane, of the Khudi clan. I honestly didn't think— I never expected to cross paths with any family members again. In deep wolf, I don't measure time very well. I thought they might all have crossed over by now."

Pyotra had a hard time keeping up. Volk's hands were playing her strings, as fluidly as a maestro gusli player giving an improvised concert. "I don't follow. You thought you were—what, like a hundred years old?"

She squirmed and wriggled her backside snug against Volk. A low rumble spilled from the were, resonating through Pyotra's limbs.

"My— Galya was turned in the nineteenth century. She was born in the 1870s."

"Holy saints!" Pyotra's exclamation was as much to do with Volk's mind-bending revelation as with the fact that her left hand had found its way between Pyotra's thighs, kneading her mound, teasing at her pubic hairs.

"I didn't want to shock you," Volk spoke against the back of her neck. Pyotra let out the ragged moan that had been building within her. "Turns out I'm not as old as all that, though."

Pyotra's head fell back. She had the urge to spin around and wrap her arms around the oboroten', but she was held in place, one hand firm over her breastbone while the other—

"Fuck, Volk, I couldn't— Oh, sweet mother of— Please, fuck me before I self-combust."

The beast had the audacity to snigger at her.

*

"Does it hurt?" Pyotra lay with her head on Volk's chest, her fingers tracing the fresh scar on her lover's shoulder. Her new bad shoulder. Where Volk's cousin, Aleksey Khudi, had shot her. Like Pyotra had shot her. And all, quintessentially, for being what she was.

"People shoot wolves." Volk ruffled her hair, responding to the unspoken implication of Pyotra's question. "It's instinct. I'll heal."

"But being shot by your relative, Volk. And—and your mate." She shuddered.

"It takes more than a stray bullet to kill a werewolf. You don't need silver, but you do need...persistence. The only way those hunters overpowered Galya, for example, was because they pumped her chock-full of lead, then cut her open before she had the time to heal."

Pyotra sat up. "You blame yourself for that, even though you have no reason to. But you let me and Aleksey get away with premeditated murder."

Volk scoffed. "It hardly counts as premeditated. I would have killed Aleksey if it weren't for you, Pyotra. And I turned the cub—Sergei—without his consent. I can't blame you, either of you, for acting out. Humans—act out."

"But you blame yourself for what happened to Galina."

Volk's mouth shut, her teeth clicking together. Pyotra leant down to kiss her troubled brow.

"Since I met you, yes." Volk spoke so low Pyotra wasn't sure she had heard her correctly.

"Since you met me?"

Volk pulled her back down, burrowing her nose in Pyotra's hair, rubbing her chin against her. "Since I met you...I can't wish the past undone. I can't...be sorry Galina died."

Pyotra's heart squeezed into a fist. "Oh, lyubov. But you wouldn't have met me."

"That's it. That's just it." Volk made a strangled noise and gathered her to her, and for the second time in a few precious hours Pyotra was too tightly held to turn and face her lupine love. But she felt tears dampening her scalp, slithering between the fine strands of her hair. Big wolf tears.

There was nothing to say. Pyotra couldn't be sorry either. And for that, like Volk, she was sorry. Existence was the damnedest thing, that way.

Chapter Thirty-Four

Do you mind when I call you Evane? Pyotra's question had caught her off guard. Volk's response to it was too complicated to articulate. The naming of things was a perilous business. Since her cousin had crashed back into her life, less than twenty-four hours ago, she had been emphatically Evane. The name, after all, was the magic word that had saved both of the men from death upon the plain. She could not retract it, like a recalcitrant child. Could she?

And she was not the only Volk any more.

Galya had enjoyed calling her Volk. She had enjoyed, Volk saw in hindsight, the complete obliteration of Evane's past that the rebuttal of her very name brought about. Volk had been Galina's creation, her pet project—literally.

Volk was Wolf. Evane was Orphan. And she had been both; her mother had died giving birth to her, refusing, even with her dying breath, to name her father.

Such was the power of names: to make known the unknown, to catch and cage chaos. To tame the beast.

She was comfortable with Pyotra calling her Evane. At first, her partner had latched onto the name as a handy splitting-off of the inextricable duality of her nature; but that had quickly fallen away. Now, Pyotra was just as likely to address the wolf as Evane as she was apt to use Volk for her non-lupine variation—and that, somehow, made all the difference. Volk's mate did not see her as either/or. She saw her as one and the same: all of her aspects loved and cherished.

The orphan wolf had found a home, and it wasn't a place so much as a scent, a feeling, an indelible bond—two lanky human arms wrapping around her, sunflower hair tickling her muzzle.

Volk sighed in contentment. If only it weren't for—everything—her life could not have been more perfect.

It had been cleansing, acknowledging the guilt she felt over Galya, seeing it for the holding on to grief that it was. Galina would not have wanted that from her. More than anything, Galya had been a free spirit, to the core.

But there was—everything—to deal with still.

Volk scratched her ear as she raised her fist to knock on the men's door. She needed to speak to Aleksey. She owed it to him. The debt was long overdue.

No one came to answer the door. Volk huffed. She deserved this, and more, but that didn't make it any less frustrating. She put her mouth to the keyhole, hissing, "I can smell you're in there, Aleks. The both of you. Send Yegor down to Pyotra. We need to talk."

Yegor wouldn't hear her. But Aleksey, she suspected, already did. It had been that way for her, being bitten as an adult. The auditory sense was the first to change.

As for what the cub's experience had been... Volk's chest rumbled. She should have been with him. She should have been with him long before now.

The door was wrenched open, all but toppling her into her cousin's scrawny arms.

He glowered at her, belligerent. "Quit growling at my door."

Volk righted herself. She had come to talk, to help, she reminded herself, but her hackles rose at the challenge. She stared hard into little Alyosha's eyes, until he lowered his gaze in deference. To his pack leader or his older cousin?

"I was thinking about the cub," she explained, and bit back a smile as Aleksey's answering growl erupted, startling him and eliciting a surprised squeak from the big man over by the bed, who was dressing himself in a hurry.

His pack leader, then. Volk relaxed, shifting her gaze onto Yegor. "Pyotra is feeding—is having breakfast. Downstairs."

Yegor peered furtively over at his mate.

Aleksey sighed, standing aside to let Volk saunter into the room. "It's okay, Gosha. My— She's right. We need to talk."

Yegor did not appear convinced, but with a final shrug to get his shirt in place, he made his exit. Volk looked on in silence.

"You've trained him well," she remarked, as the door clicked shut.

Aleksey growled anew. His hands went to his scalp, pulling hard at his short-cropped hair. "I—I—"

"You will learn to control it. Mostly." Her nose twitched at the stark scents permeating the room. "You've spent yourself. Good. That helps too."

Aleksey's mien darkened, wrath and humiliation vying for eminence.

"I didn't come here to fight you, Aleks. Stand down."

"Bitch."

Before he had time to react with more than a slack-jawed "Oh," Volk had him by the scruff, pushing her thumb into his scars. *Her* scars. Her maker's mark on him, which hummed to her touch.

Aleksey yelped, sagging in her grip.

"You're freakishly strong," he gasped in grudging awe. "It's not right, Evane. You're possessed, you're—"

"I went to church last night." She dropped him onto the floor and crouched beside him. The room held one chair over by the window, but she failed to see the point of them. "Nothing happened." She couldn't quite keep the relief out of her voice. "A priest even spoke a blessing over me, before we left. I touched his kaftan."

Aleksey groaned, his face against the floorboards. Volk blew out her breath and pulled him into a seated position.

"How's Syvne?" She sat back on her haunches, allowing herself the luxury of studying the man in front of her. His face had been perfectly round the last time she had seen him. The memories were sluggish, unwilling to surface after all this time. A chubby little boy, swathed in pelts from top to toe. One might have mistaken him for a bear cub at a distance. He had used to hug her. He had used to look up to her. He had used to call her "Ev'ne," conflating her name with that of his mother's. Her aunt's.

"She's dead," Aleksey replied flatly. "She felt so responsible when you disappeared. It aged her twenty years overnight. Did you ever stop to consider that? What it would do to her? What it would do to us?"

Volk's eyebrows rose. Aleksey squirmed and looked away. "She had cancer of the guts. She crossed over ten years ago."

"I'm sorry to hear that." She was. Syvne had been kind to her, even if she'd had six children of her own to care for. But Volk refused to accept any more blame for people having died while she was still alive. Not today. "Was that why you left the tribe?"

Aleksey bowed his head. "There was nothing there for me. I was—restless. I figured there was more than reindeers in the world, you know? Turns out I was right. There are monsters too."

Volk clicked her tongue.

Aleksey gave her a faint smirk. "I meant Gudkov, actually."

"How did you end up in his employ?"

"There aren't that many employment opportunities for runaway teens with a sketchy education. I made it to Arkhangelsk, and from there I had my sights set on Moscow, but...I didn't make it that far. I had no money. Gudkov offered a fair wage for menial jobs, and by the time I had advanced to special-ops..."

"No way out." Volk stroked her chin. "You'd have been better off as an oboroten'."

Aleksey's eyes narrowed. "No way out of that either, is there?"

Volk tilted her head to one side. "Would you have preferred to die, Aleks?"

"Yes!" He bit his lip, blew out air through his nose. "Well, I—"

"I could say I was sorry, but you meant to kill me, didn't you?"

"The wolf!" Aleksey spluttered. "We only meant to incapacitate the wolf and bring Pyotra along."

She had nothing to say to that. His eyes were riveted on her, daring her to speak; then he paled, the colour draining from his face the way the night sky was bled by the bite of the morning sun.

"I would never have known." His voice was small and cowed. And there he was, at last: little bear cub Aleksey, her next-to-youngest cousin and her favourite, by far.

"What's done is done." Volk shook her head wearily. "Being turned is supposed to be a boon, an honour. I never had a wish to form a pack. But now that it's done… I can't tell you… It's like a gift from the universe, Aleks. That it's you."

Aleksey's chest rumbled again, and this time, he let it. Diffidently but deliberately, he sank his head onto his cousin's, his pack leader's, *her* shoulder. "We need to bring Sergei home."

Volk concurred, nipping his ear tenderly in response.

*

"Did you sleep well?" Pyotra gazed at him across the table, stirring raspberry jam into her chay. The white of her eyes had a faintly blue tone, Yegor noted. He had noticed that about her brother, as well. It was as though their eyes were not content to have those disconcerting, fiercely grey-blue irises—oh no, the eye in its entirety had to be blue on the Nikolayeviches.

A tear leaked out of his own right eye, trailing down to the tip of his nose. Pyotra placed her hand on top of his, with a soft cooing sound he hadn't heard since Yelena Mizulina was alive.

"You're too nice to me. I don't deserve it."

Her right eyebrow arched. "I shot you, Yegor Mizulin. I am the direct cause of your pain. It's a bad habit of mine, really. But you *were* threatening my mate."

"Is she— Did she— Was she the wolf who…?"

Pyotra nodded dismissively. "It was an accident. She saved Sergei's life and broke his skin in the process. It's all—all of this—one brief unfortunate incident that has spiralled out of control. She should have... It should have been me, you know?"

Yegor peered down at his plate of bread and eggs. Two floors above, he had left Alyosha alone with a werewolf. His hands shook, and he wasn't sure if it was from withdrawal or the preposterous notion of werewolves roaming the Russian wilderness. "I deserved every last bullet in your rifle. I was the one who brought your brother to Arkhangelsk. My instructions were— I was to bring him at any cost."

Her knuckles had whitened, gripping the table.

He closed his eyes in remorse. "I should have killed myself a long time ago."

"Nonsense!" Her brusque response made his eyes open wide. "If you had, Gudkov would have found someone else to do his dirty work. Who knows what kind of person your replacement would have been? All things considered, I'm grateful it was you, Yegor. We will sort this out. We have to try. And you— Gudkov trusts you. You have a vital role to play in this."

Despite himself, he nodded and took a bite of his bread. Pyotra's words did not magically dispel the suffocating gloom that had lodged in him like a resistant strain of bacteria, but they did offer a sense of purpose. A frail, erratic twinkling of hope. "She won't hurt him, will she?"

She had no trouble following his abrupt change of topic. Snorting in derision, she glanced up at the ceiling. "Don't you worry about that." She lifted her cup to her lips. "My wolf is a big softie at heart. Same as yours, I'll wager. They are related after all."

Chapter Thirty-Five

He lay flat on his back, staring into darkness, the second time his wolf mother came to him. He wasn't even a wolf; he brought his front paws up to his sweat-slick face and felt fingers. Bare human flesh. Briefly, splendidly, he had been wolven again, fully fledged, fear-triggered rage spearing through him and making him break out in fur. It had been... He had stood in front of a corpse in a glass coffin, and it had been neither Lenin nor Snow White, but—Babushka. Olezhka's babushka, preserved like a costly relic, a ghastly, mummified howl on the pasty, brittle-looking face.

It had made him lose his skin.

Where were you? Sergei nudged the presence within him, winding his own consciousness around it, as though he could hold it fast. *I needed you.*

His lungs deflated in a sigh. *I'm sorry, volchonok. Please keep your strength up. We are coming for you.*

Sergei relaxed into the thin mattress, his spine straightening one vertebra at a time. His hand came up to stroke his head. His nostrils widened in examination of his own scent.

You are exceptionally brave. Pyotra wants you to know that she is very proud of you.

Pyotra is there? You're with her? Let me speak to her!

Sergei, this isn't—

He pushed through. He didn't know how or what he had done, but suddenly his big sister was right in front of him, gazing at him with a slight frown. She looked worried. She looked—wonderful.

"Volk? What's the matter?"

So she knew—she knew what he had become. He threw his arms around her neck and started blubbering, as though a terrific dam inside him had crumbled. "Pyotra! *Sestra*! Please, don't hate me, please. I won't ever bite you, I promise!"

She felt different in his arms, slenderer, smaller. His arms had grown ridiculously large. And strong, so strong he felt as though he could lift her up and throw her twenty metres into the air, no bother.

Pyotra plaited her fingers through his hair. She wiped at his tear-streaked face, petting him gently.

"Volk?" she said again, confusion edging her voice.

"I'm still your duck," he bawled, not caring if he came off as five years old. "Please, Pyotra. Tell me I'm still your duck!"

"Sergei?" She looked spooked, and his heart shrunk and shrivelled. Vertigo blurred his vision as, from one breath to the next, his wolf mother grabbed him by the skin of his neck.

Bad cub. You could have given your sister a heart attack.

He fought to shake her off, worming away from the grey mist she was dragging him towards.

"Pyotra! I love you so much!"

Her face floated above him, and then he felt her soft lips on his forehead.

"I love you too," she said calmly. "I love you both. Never doubt that."

Wolf mother thrilled at his sister's words, a shudder running down her shaggy flanks. She slackened her hold on him, and Sergei spun around, staring into eyes as black as the taiga in winter.

He had seen those eyes before, in a frozen dream, in a fever rush. He had seen them and not credited his own faculties. He rolled and tossed, and he wasn't sure if there were sheets or snow-covered ground beneath him. He nipped at the adult wolf's shin. *Where are we?*

She rubbed her muzzle over his head, down his neck. *I don't really know. Nowhere. Somewhere. In-between. Halfway between Naryan-Mar and Arkhangelsk maybe, or just—somewhere on the tundra of my mind. I wasn't prepared for you to push inside my consciousness, cub. Are you always this unruly?*

He went for her left front leg, but she eluded him easily, dancing out of reach before spinning back and bearing down on him. He yipped and flattened his ears.

I take that as a yes. She sounded—felt—amused. *I guess I should have known. You are the brother of Pyotra Kulakova.*

Take me back to her!

The black eyes darkened, deepened. He would not have deemed it possible. *I don't think that is a good idea. I'm exhausted from keeping up this link already. I don't— I don't know how it works. I don't want you stuck inside me, for your sake as much as for mine.*

His hackles rose. *She's mine—my sister. It's not fair; why should I be left to rot away in a stinking prison, while you—*

She ran her teeth down his neck, quieting and subduing him. He felt the warmth of her tenderness, like a quickening spring.

You're right, Sergei. It isn't fair.

He whimpered, touching her chest with the pads of his paws. *Are you really coming for me? It's true, then? You are Snegurochka's bear?*

Wolf mother licked at his ear. Laughter bubbled up inside him, against all reason. A tendril of hope looped through him, making him lighter, airier. The adult wolf nudged him to his feet and along the plain.

We will come for you, volchonok. You are pack.

*

He gasped as he woke up the second time, his tongue curling in upon itself. His eyes were filled with muck, his limbs heavy and useless. He felt as though he had travelled a long, long way, all through the night. *From Naryan-Mar to Arkhangelsk.*

With effort, he touched his lips. He was Sergei again, and it relieved him and saddened him unspeakably.

He was Sergei. But he was also—Volk. Pyotra had called him that. He realised now that she had been speaking to *her*—but it fit. *She* could not monopolise it. He had been transformed in a way his mind could not encompass or contain; he, too, was Volk.

Pyotra had said she loved them; she loved them both. In spite of Sima, of Kolya, of everything. It was...

He didn't know what it was. He didn't much like the idea of sharing his sister with anyone, let alone a—this Volk. What if she bit her too?

A growl rose within him. It was a complex, confused growl. He couldn't imagine what the future would be like if they came out of this alive. Would they return home? Would Ded share his cabin with a—with wolves?

And what would happen to Olezhka? Would he let them go? Somehow, Sergei doubted it.

He would not tell Olezhka about his dream—or whatever it was. Not this time. Whether or not Pyotra and Volk were on their way, Olezhka didn't need to know.

Chapter Thirty-Six

"Good luck!" Pyotra waved to the men as they readied for take-off. She could just make them out through the windscreen of the helicopter. Yegor didn't hear her over the chopping of the rotor blades, but Aleksey turned to glance at them, inclining his head. He had been different since Volk had gone to talk with him. Resigned to his fate, if still chafing at it. Pyotra chafed at it as well. Volk seemed to bite everyone but her.

You know that's not true. You agreed to wait, for Boris's sake. She huffed. Threading her arm through Volk's, Pyotra and the wolf woman began to walk back towards the building that served as a combined arrivals and departure hall for the diminutive airport. Their flight wasn't scheduled to leave for hours yet. It gave Yegor and Aleksey time to implement the first stages of their plan: a repurposed part of Aleksey's own scheme to bring about an escape for him and Yegor from the clutches of the oligarch.

Yegor had been as taken aback as themselves when Aleks had divulged the extent of his preparations. Pyotra suspected there was more, some final destination he had had in mind. But that had become impossible now, null and void, since Aleksey could not leave Volk.

Yes, Pyotra could see why it chafed him. She asked herself if the time would come when Aleksey, like Sergei, could push his consciousness into her lover's body. It was a disturbing idea.

But Pyotra also shared a psychic bond with Volk. Volk had been in her dream; a dream which, Pyotra acknowledged, would have undone all their waking decisions. She was convinced that if Volk had not woken them, she, Pyotra Nikolayevna Kulakova, would have been oboroten' by now.

A frisson ran through her. Volk glanced at her as they entered the building through the revolving doors—a set of three to keep the bite of the Siberian freeze at bay.

"It's nothing. I just... Nothing."

Volk canted her head, and it was such a picture-perfect likeness of the wolf—*her* wolf, the very first time she laid eyes on her—Pyotra could have wept. She ached for the freedom they'd had, all of the tundra at their disposal, if only...

"I wish I could be with you like the others are with you," Pyotra admitted. "I suppose I am jealous. And a tad apprehensive... I mean, I don't want you to turn into my brother when we— You know?"

Volk brushed her palm down Pyotra's back, indicating for her to take a seat on the garish contraption of orange plastic to their left. Resting her hands on Pyotra's knees, Volk crouched before her. "Sergei will not challenge me like that once we are home. And I don't think— I think I am learning to shield myself. He took me unawares."

Pyotra wove her fingers through Volk's mane, massaging her scalp with firm circular motions. The wolf rumbled. Several heads turned to look at them. Pyotra reddened and let her hands fall to her sides. "Maybe you need to learn to shield yourself from me too."

Volk caught her right hand, and before Pyotra knew what she meant to do, she had run the tip of her tongue along her palm to her pulse point. Pyotra sucked in her breath between her teeth.

"It would take more than superhuman strength to do that, mate." The werewolf held her lips still against the delicate skin of Pyotra's wrist, the bluish veins throbbing as she teased at them.

Pyotra could see the glint of Volk's fangs, sharp and carnivorous, and it made her hot, so hot. It was as if they were no longer in a forlorn Siberian airport but in a tropical clime, surrounded by sand, sea, palm trees. Things that were more fantastical, more theoretical to her these days than a human wolf. A wolf human. A fable made flesh.

"Do it," she murmured, as Volk's warm breath moistened her exposed wrist. "Just do it. Screw Boris. Screw it all."

There was no white left in Volk's eyes. They were as black as an overcast night on the tundra.

Pyotra whimpered. Her hand shook in the predator's grip.

"You don't mean that, Pyotra Nikolayevna," Volk said at length, her voice so tinged with wolf it was barely recognisable as human speech.

Pyotra closed her eyes and saw Ded in his chair at the table in front of her, head bent, the bones of his shoulders as fragile as bird's wings under her hands. A broken man, blind and abandoned, confronted by Yegor the giant, the tower piece in Oleg Gudkov's elaborate game of chess. Ded, with his uncanny ability to sniff out wolves. Ded, with his old man's grudge. Ded, who had given them his all.

She exhaled through her nose.

"Fuck." She released her hand from Volk's grip, wrapping it around the back of the turnskin's head, gazing into those fathomless eyes. "How do you know me so well? How do you know—when I don't even know myself?"

Volk's cheekbones shifted beneath her skin. There was red on her bottom lip, Pyotra saw, from where she had bitten herself.

"I smell it," she breathed. "But, Pyotra, I—Evane— can't keep the wolf in check forever. I *will* claim you. You know that, don't you?"

She couldn't speak. She clasped the oboroten' to her, letting Volk burrow her nose into her midsection, not giving a damn about the handful of other travellers in the waiting hall. *Lesbiyanki*. They didn't know the half of it.

*

The plane was much larger and quieter than the helicopter, even if Pyotra could tell from Volk's pained facial expression it was noisy enough. Volk was on edge, twisting and turning in her seat. There had been a cacophony of human scents at the hotel, sure; but it was off season. Apart from themselves, Aleksey, and Yegor, the hotel had had only a handful of guests. On the plane there were twenty or more active scents to keep track of, and the wolf was freaking out.

"*Kofe*, chay?" The perambulating flight attendant's eyes widened as Volk let out a warning growl.

Pyotra dug her nails into the turnskin's thigh, earning her a dirty look before Volk lowered her head in submission. "My friend is afraid of flying. First time, more or less. Do you have anything stronger?"

Pyotra bit her cheek. The situation would have been absurd, if she hadn't felt how Volk's entire body trembled.

The stewardess reached into the lower compartment of her trolley and brought out a bottle of *Russkij Standart*, like a magician pulling a rabbit out of her hat. Her fake smile showed off her teeth—not the best way to assuage a beast of the wild.

Pyotra leant into Volk, drawing the werewolf's head onto her shoulder and shushing her, as much to calm her mate's frayed nerves as to keep her from attacking the oblivious woman pouring out vodka in a small plastic cup.

"Here we are." The flight attendant set the cup on the fold-out table in front of Volk. "Anything for you, madame?"

"Just chay, please."

"Spasiba," Volk muttered as the stewardess continued down the aisle. She sniffed the contents of her cup with suspicion. "This...smells like poison."

Pyotra's lip quirked. "It sort of is. It's the stuff that killed my father. But in small doses, it relaxes you. Blunts your senses. Give it a try."

"Why would you want to do that?" Volk looked incredulous. Then her gaze strayed to the view through the cubbyhole window where the ground rushed away beneath them, and she knocked back the alcohol in one big gulp.

"Disgusting!" Volk gagged, falling forward across the table, which groaned underneath the unanticipated load. It reminded Pyotra of Sergei, when prompted to eat cabbage soup. The man in the seat in front of them turned, indignant, but one look into the oboroten's eyes was enough to make him swerve back, his huff morphing into something reminiscent of the frightened squeal of a dachshund.

Volk eyed Pyotra balefully. Pyotra sucked in her lips. "It can be a bit strong the first time you try it. I was going to suggest you take it in sips."

"Pyotrushka Niko—" Volk's eyes crossed. "Oh, I don't—feel so good."

Pyotra stroked Volk's rumpled hair out of her face. "That was fast. I suppose... Come to think of it, I think I read somewhere that wo—that, uh, people like you have a higher than average metabolic rate."

Heat rushed to her temples. This might not have been her most brilliant idea. She was fairly certain Dachshund Man was still paying them too close attention.

"Mmm, metabolism." Volk hiccupped. "You use such pretty words. Met-aah-beau-lism." She stretched and put an arm around Pyotra. An alarmingly warm arm.

"Vol—Evane!" Pyotra grabbed her chin. Volk's face was slicked with sweat, a soft fuzz visible across her T-zone. This was going from bad to disastrous. Talk about a drink to put hair on one's chest. "Evane!" Pyotra forced her tone of voice down to an agitated wheeze. "Listen to me, lyubov. You—cannot—change."

Volk yawned, a huge, vodka-scented grimace that showed off an impressive set of vulpine incisors and canines. Pyotra put her hands over the werewolf's mouth.

"Shit. Shit. Shit." Why hadn't she stopped to consider this? Why had they not made a contingency plan for the very real possibility that Volk might be tipped into a shift mid-air, from—from panic at the whole abnormal situation or, just maybe, from her mate's sheer stupidity in persuading her to imbibe a heretofore untried substance?

"Oh, love, please. Now is not the time." Pyotra's mind raced as Volk leant into her, nuzzling her neck with her furry face. She was burning up. "I think you need to sh—" Her eyes flitted to the flight attendant who had finished her round and was making her way back down the aisle. "The bathroom! That's it. Planes have bathrooms. When you've got to go, you've got to go."

Volk tittered. Pyotra thought that was what she was doing. It sounded more like mewling.

"I'm just going to—there." Pyotra pulled the hood of Volk's coat up over her head, concealing her features as best she could. She stood, easing the drunken were to her feet beside her. "Nature calls."

Volk leered at her. She pawed at Pyotra's shirt front. "Too much—" She broke off with a belch. "—clothes."

"Uh-huh." Pyotra licked her lips and dragged Volk's head back onto her shoulder, pushing her out into the aisle. There was a bathroom at the back as well as up front. At least, she fervently hoped there was. "That's it, one leg in front of the other. Good job."

"Is everything all right, madame?"

Pyotra closed her eyes briefly. The stewardess had caught up with them, because of course she had. It was practically part of her job description. Holding Volk's hood firmly in place and praying the officious woman couldn't see the angry red blooming on her own neck where Volk's skin came into contact with hers, Pyotra mustered her best apologetic smile. "A bout of motion sickness. Nothing we can't handle. There's a bathroom this way, isn't there?"

"There is." The woman's expression was one of breezy concern, mingled with a touch of distaste. She adjusted the cuffs of her burgundy blazer. "Do you require any assistance?"

Pyotra shook her head frantically as Volk began turning towards the woman. "We'll be fine. Evane, just relax against me, and we'll be there in no time."

Volk growled. A happy, contented growl, but Pyotra didn't think the stewardess spoke wolf fluently enough to make the distinction.

"Noisy stomach!" Pyotra gave a woefully insincere, high-pitched laugh. "We better get a move on."

She turned from the woman who was blinking her eyes as though someone had thrown a bag of salt into her face and half ran, half stumbled between the seats, Volk either as loose as an overcooked plate of noodles or as stiff and unyielding as a brick wall at her side.

Volk stopped to run her hand over a woman's fur hat. She snapped her teeth in the direction of a man with an uncommonly impressive set of whiskers. Inexplicably, miraculously, no one seemed to twig what was going on.

No one will look me in the face any more, Pyotra recalled Kolya complaining when he was in the late stages of his disease. That must be what was at work; people saw what they expected to see. A common drunk rather than a werewolf mid-shift.

Volk gave Pyotra's ear an affectionate lick.

"Focus, Evane." Pyotra kept her voice even, her eyes square on the prize. "Only a little further. We're almost there."

And they were. Without knowing how, Pyotra managed to work the finicky handle and open the door. She pushed the now jabbering Volk inside and snuck in after her, locking up.

Volk slid to the floor. She peered blearily at Pyotra.

"Oh, lyubov, I'm so sorry. What a mess!" Pyotra sunk to her knees in despair.

Volk angled her head. She barely understood her, Pyotra realised. She had to get her out of her clothes.

Volk was going to shift. As Pyotra undressed her on the floor of the airborne bathroom, a mile or more above ground, she tried to mentally adjust to this being a fact, not a mere possibility. Would the wolf be inebriated too? How on earth was she going to restrain her?

"You must be very quiet, Volk. I'm Pyotra, your mate, remember? You have to trust me."

Volk panted and squirmed. She was unclothed by now, but the angles and planes of her were all wrong. Her shape made no kind of sense. What if the vodka had somehow damaged her system? What if she would be stuck like this forever?

"Shift, love. You can do it. Show me my beautiful wolf."

Volk grunted in pain. But her ink-puddle eyes gleamed in response to Pyotra's call. With a last, prolonged animal moan, her skin rolled back like singed paper, and the wolf, the wonderful, perfect tundra wolf with that distinctive ring around her tail, spilled out and into Pyotra's waiting arms.

Part Three

Chapter Thirty-Seven

Ludmila Andreyevna stood before the solid sweep of the White Sea. Still frozen-over, yes, and her cheeks were stinging from the cold. Her breath was made visible, tangible almost, in the form of little puffs, miniature clouds drifting leisurely away from her. She hugged herself. Her shoulders ached; one of those ironic occupational hazards of being a professional massage therapist. When she had been part of a team, working with the Olympians, this hadn't been an issue. They had taken turns, being sure to treat each other as well as the sports stars. It was after she came back to Arkhangelsk that she had let herself go.

She kicked at one of the glistening pebbles that lay strewn about her on the small stone beach. It was unnaturally pristine, this stretch of land—the private property of Oleg Vladimirovich Gudkov. Trespassers were prosecuted. But Ludmila Andreyevna was part of the household.

Casting a last glance out across the ice, she turned to make her way back to Gudkov's mansion. Ice had always attracted her. Even as a child, she had marvelled at this ability of water to change from one state to the other. Liquid, solid, gas. All of it water; water adapting to and changing with the environmental conditions. It seemed like an appropriate simile for something she couldn't quite express: something about the variability of being in the world. Her mind strained and reached for it, but her words fell flat as blinis. She was better with her hands.

As she plodded through the knee-deep snow, following the tracks she had made on coming out, Andreyevna's ears caught the rumble of the Kamov returning. Khudi and Mizulin would be back then. Good. She had missed their presence, missed the feeling of having allies at her place of work.

Her place of everything. When Gudkov had offered her an izba at the edge of his estate, it had sounded like a generous—more than generous—deal. She had relatives in Arkhangelsk whom she could have taken up residence with, but it had felt like an overlong commute. Besides, the oligarch paid her enough that she didn't need any additional work. Her plan had been to do this for a while until she had saved up enough to retire. Ten years ago, that had been.

Now she would be grateful if she made it out of here alive.

Liquid, solid, gas. Ludmila Andreyevna could not name the exact day, the hour she had become cognisant of being trapped, of her entire existence having become something that hinged on a megalomaniac despot's whim or pleasure. When she had, she had been ready to throttle the man. She was, after all, one of the few who could. One of the few who had access to his corporeal limbs, in all their bare-naked vulnerability. It made her lips curl in distaste.

Ludmila had never been the squeamish sort. As she had gone into her line of trade, she had known her clients would come in every shape, shade, form, and texture. It didn't bother her, nor did it entice her: when a person laid themself out on the table before her, they became all body parts to Ludmila Andreyevna. She didn't belong to the holistic phalange of alternative medicine; she offered no Jungian insights as part of a myofascial release. There might well be psychological reasons behind any number of muscle knots and tensions she had treated over the years, but that was frankly none of her business. She wasn't interested.

What she wanted was her own *dacha*, somewhere where there were seasons, real seasons, not just darkness and light. She wanted thaw. She wanted the sound of water dripping from her roof. She wanted two or three cats and a bookshelf stuffed with her favourite poetry collections.

Gudkov had seemed like the once-in-a-lifetime shot for a massage therapist to make enough money for these dreams to come true. She had liked that he was a recluse; she had assumed his reasons were similar to hers. How laughably, horrendously mistaken she had been.

Ludmila did not hate people, and she did not fear them. There had even been a skater, once— But no. She had wanted him as she wanted those cats for her dacha, as platonic companions, and she didn't know how to broach such an out-of-the-common-fold request. She had enjoyed watching him, enjoyed his perfect spins and combination jumps, and when he had defected to the USA, she had been sorry.

Ludmila dreamt of a dacha outside Moscow, not a cottage in the Nevada desert. Were there even cottages in the Nevada desert? She didn't know.

Life never turned out as you expected it to; she had known that, incorporated it into herself, from an early age. But this.

Exhaling, she swiped her access card at the side door that led onto Oleg Gudkov's private banya with his sauna and pool complex. Her treatment room was tucked away behind it, within easy reach of his changing room. She had a closet-cum-office-space where she usually passed her days at her master's beck and call. It would have suited her fine—would have been ideal—if her niggling doubt hadn't grown into an all-consuming certainty that Oleg Vladimirovich Gudkov was a Bad Man.

She could leave, but she wouldn't get far. She was just another oblivious fly who had happened to become entangled in the spider's web. And then Aleksey Khudi had approached her.

Aleksey Khudi, with his fool's gold and madman's hope.

Ludmila's lips twitched as she opened the door and slipped into her workspace, unbuttoning and unzipping her layers of outer garments, revealing her plain, white uniform underneath. She was glad the boys were back, her comrades-in-misery. They were lovers, she was certain, but it didn't trouble her. Why should it? Each to their own.

Andreyevna checked her plaited hair in the mirror, smoothed her palms over the crown of her head. She sported a few grey strands among the sorrel brown.

So be it. She was ripe and ready to give her life chasing the men's impossible dream of liberty. Or, if they succeeded, to wither away in a state prison. At least there was some honesty in that.

*

"Yegor Stepanovich!" Ludmila peered over at the man from the towels she had been folding, surprised in spite of herself. She had had few dealings with the Mizulin boy during her decade at the mansion, even though he had come of age under her very nose. It was odd. Every time he came before her, she had to do a mental double take, reminding herself that the burly giant was the gangly sixteen-year-old she had first met all those years ago.

Yegor shifted his weight from his left foot to his right. "Ludmila Andreyevna..." He wet his lips, hesitating. He had a recent wound above his chest, left-hand side. She could tell from the way he moved, the way he held himself. Gunfight? Mob dealings gone awry? The less she knew the better.

Up to a point.

She carried the stack of newly laundered and folded towels over to him. "Top shelf, if you please."

As suspected, he accepted the load and carried out the task with his right hand. Which would have been perfectly natural if Ludmila Andreyevna had not known that Yegor Stepanovich Mizulin's dominant side was his left.

She cocked her head. Yegor's complexion went ruddy.

"Do you want me to have a look at it?"

The young man shook his head brusquely. "No, no, you're all right. It's—nothing. Ludmila—"

"—Andreyevna. Yes, that's me. You said that already." She spun on her heel and went back to the hamper with the remaining towels from the tumble-dryer. "Did Aleksey send you? Is he okay?"

She glanced back over her shoulder, her eyes scanning his face, looking for any minute signs of worry. But then, Yegor Mizulin had always been a worrier.

He had good reason to be, she supposed.

"Alyosha is fine, he's...tired. Ludmila... Mila, it's time."

"Time?" She didn't have to ask, not really. Khudi regularly called her Mila, but Yegor—never. Even dropping her patronymic had been a stretch. "When?"

Of his own accord, Mizulin moved forward to pick up the new pile of folded towels. She hadn't even noticed her hands had kept busy.

"Tomorrow." The answer came on an exhalation.

Ludmila Andreyevna inclined her head.

Chapter Thirty-Eight

It had begun to snow. Right after they landed in Arkhangelsk, by which time Volk was thankfully clothed in human garb once more. Ragged flakes fell out of a lowering sky, looking like nothing so much as paper tissues filled with crystallised tears.

They walked in silence to the hostel where Aleksey had booked one of only two private rooms for them. Pyotra felt a pang of gratitude as they were once more able to shut and lock a door behind themselves. On the plane, she had spent three-quarters of an hour with the wolf in the bathroom, using her scent, her physical presence as much as her voice, to control the tipsy, amorous beast.

After she had sobered up and changed back, Volk would scarcely look at her. Fortunately, Pyotra knew her well enough by now to recognise that she was embarrassed rather than angered.

Almost the moment they stepped into their room, the phone on the bedside table rang. Volk jumped. Pyotra touched the back of the were's neck for comfort and lifted the receiver.

"Let me speak to Evane."

Her gaze slipped to Volk, who nodded. She had heard, of course, and could probably tell it was Aleks too. Pyotra handed over the receiver and moved away. "I'm going to take a shower. I'll be just down the hall." She mouthed the words; Volk squeezed her fingers in response.

Pyotra managed a weak smile and left their temporary sanctuary. There were shared shower rooms at the end of each corridor, the receptionist had assured them. Volk had given him a blank look, but Pyotra had been overcome with longing at the mere mention of it. A shower! She couldn't even remember the last time she'd had one. It might not be what one generally did to prepare for a face-off with one's baby brother's billionaire kidnapper, but to hell with it. For once, Pyotra Nikolayevna Kulakova was going to be squeaky clean.

As she stepped into the tiled room, she virtually purred. The moisture in the air was high enough for her to surmise it had been vacated only recently. Sighing in anticipation, she peeled off her grubby layers and grabbed a towel and robe.

The water was scalding. She didn't care. As her skin turned a lobster shade of red, Pyotra stood rooted under the driving spray, letting herself relax, tendon by tendon. She lathered up the soap, which had a sharp, institutional smell, but it was heaven, pure heaven to rinse weeks' worth of filth from her thick, troublesome hair.

Sima's hair, Kolya had observed, more than once. Pyotra knew it was true. She remembered—she treasured the memory of—her mother's hair. It had pained her father, no doubt: this constant living reminder of his dead wife in the form of his daughter.

Pyotra frowned and tugged at a particularly stubborn knot.

"I love your hair."

Startled, Pyotra swung around and Volk was there: a feral sheen to her eyes as she discarded her pelts and skins in an untidy pile.

She stood brazenly nude before her, a line of fur down her sternum, trailing down her middle and becoming lost among her pubic hair, a fair portion of which was silver-tipped too.

Pyotra put a hand against the slippery tiles of the shower cubicle. "You— You're—"

Volk came into the stall, and Pyotra didn't need Boris's nose to catch the musky, all-pervading scent of wolf. Her lower abdomen throbbed in acknowledgement.

"It's not just the alcohol," Volk murmured, pulling her to her, rubbing her cheek against Pyotra's. "It's— everything. I need you, mate. What with your brother…Aleksey… I can barely keep from shifting—"

"Hush." Pyotra sank to her knees on the tiles. The warm shower still pelted them, but she registered it only vaguely, at the outskirts of her perceptions. Her focus was fixed on the wolf woman before her, the soft, damp fur that she traced with her tongue and fingers, eliciting a groan that turned into a throaty growl.

Her own skin tightened with lust as she dipped between her lover's thighs and administered to her, unquestioningly, the taste of wolf exploding in her mouth.

*

Volk had ripped the door to the shower room off its hinges. Funny how a wide-open door could be as much of a deterrent to an unwelcome audience as a locked and bolted one. Pyotra had smoothed it over with the owners, greasing their palms with Boris's silver. With Gudkov's gold.

Volk supposed she should be bothered by her own erratic behaviour, but the wolf was too close to the surface, claiming too much of her attention. Roaring for blood.

She needed a kill.

In the early hours of the morning, in compact darkness, Evane slipped from Pyotra's embrace and snuck out, shifting from one breath to the next. Volk took off at a running canter, a shadow slinking behind the human-made buildings and out into the snowy wilderness. The stars gazed down on her, pricking her eyes, fixtures in the changing landscape from tundra to taiga to town. To the lip of the sea: an endless expanse of salty water roaring beneath its crust of ice, the way her growl thrummed against her breastbone.

The wolf halted in her tracks. She had never seen it before, this hearsay sea. It turned her world topsy-turvy, threw her off-kilter. She wished for Pyotra.

She wished for the white wolf that flitted through her, before her mind's eye, whenever she beheld her mate. They should have been here together. They should have experienced this flank to flank, muzzle to muzzle.

Turning away with a snort, Volk caught the scent of a hare and lost herself to the thrill of the hunt.

*

When Volk returned, Pyotra was ready for her. She had packed a change of clothes in her rucksack, as well as the last spare cartridges for her father's rifle.

The wolf's coat was flecked with blood, but Pyotra took it in her stride, stroking the top of Volk's head, placing a kiss on the tip of her nose. They had a ways to go, the snow bearing down on them. Even had Evane been in her non-wolf skin, they couldn't have shown up at the oligarch's doorstep by public transport. It was better like this.

Pyotra gave Volk a final pat and hoisted the gun onto her shoulder. "Let's go get Sergei," she said, and the wolf took off, gambolling around her, as excited as the snowflakes being tossed and twirled by the wind from the northeast.

Chapter Thirty-Nine

A strange woman stood by his bed when he awoke. She peered down at him with intention, yet calm emanated from her, as though her presence meant nothing really bad could happen.

This was an illusion, he knew. Not even had it been his mother's ghost come to comfort him would Sergei have been able to believe with that certainty reserved for the childlike mind that everything would be all right.

For all he knew, this might be some new terror, a new wolf in sheep's clothing. He smiled faintly at this thought: the irony of it, Pyotra would have pointed out.

The woman did not smile back. She was a large, towering presence; she looked as though she could snap his back in two, just like that, with a quick flick of her wrists.

Still, he was not afraid of her. He couldn't explain it, even to himself.

Slowly, she sank into a crouch, her brows knitted. "You are Sergei," she told him. It wasn't a question, but he nodded anyway. She hadn't called him Seryozha. That must be a good sign. "I'm Ludmila. I'm not very good with children, I'm afraid. But trust me, Sergei, if I had known..." She shrugged impotently. Now that she was closer, he saw there were lines along the sides of her eyes, creases surrounding her thin, pale lips. She looked tired. Kind.

"Did Olezhka send you?" His voice sounded foreign to him. He hadn't spoken out loud to anyone other than Olezhka for so long he felt stupidly shy about it.

"Olezh— Oh, you mean Gudkov." The woman looked vaguely amused. "Is that what he calls himself these days?" Ludmila did not seem to require an answer. "Has he been hurting you, Sergei? Has he—"

"He prodded me with his stick."

Ludmila looked aghast.

Sergei sat up, feeling awkward about lying down. He tried to remember the term his—*Volk*—had used. "Cattle prod. Like with a current running through it. But I'm not a scaredy-cat"—except when he was, but Ludmila didn't need to know that—"I bit him back. I bit him real good."

"I see." Ludmila still didn't smile. Sergei was starting to wonder if she ever did; but her eyes had softened. Her hand was warm and steady as she placed it on his shoulder. "You're a fighter. I'm glad to hear it. But you shouldn't have had to be. This should never have been allowed to happen to you. I am so very sorry, and Yegor— Yegor is even sorrier, I think. We will do our best to put things right."

Her fingers had moved up to the back of his neck, kneading at it in a manner that made Sergei as limp as a rag doll. An appreciative rumble escaped him.

Ludmila started.

"I won't bite you," Sergei hastened to assure her. He didn't want her to stop. It felt so good, being touched by well-meaning hands after all this time. Being made to feel safe, contained, at rest, for a fleeting moment. "He showed me his babushka, you know."

Her face melted with concern. He liked her, he decided; he liked her carefully plaited hair, even if it wasn't as pretty as Pyotra's. Another soft growl slipped out of him.

Ludmila's eyes grew. "So it's true," she whispered. Her digits did not waver in their work. "I thought they had gone mad, as mad as him. But here you are, and you are…"

"Volk," he supplied helpfully. "I am Volk. But please don't be afraid of me, Ludmila—Ludmila—"

"Andreyevna." The corners of her mouth twitched, at last. Her fingers moved to rub behind his ears. "Who could be afraid of such a polite volchonok?"

Of a sudden, tears brimmed in his eyes. Ludmila Andreyevna clicked her tongue, and then she was sitting on the bed with him, patting his back as he cried and cried in her arms.

"Are you a mirage, Ludmila Andreyevna?" he asked, when the last tears had been wrung from him, and he felt as sad and used-up as the old tea towel in Boris Ilyich's kitchen nook.

"Not at all," she replied, wiping his wet cheeks with her crisp, white sleeve. "I'm a massage therapist."

*

Aleksey Khudi felt ill. He wasn't used to it. He had always had a healthy, tenacious constitution, been at home in his own skin. He had watched others at odds with their physical being: the cancer consuming his beloved parent, the struggle with addiction that ravaged the robust frame of Yegor Stepanovich, his Gosha— But even as he had empathised, even as he had been deeply concerned and filled with futile rage at their afflictions, it hadn't been enough, not by a long shot, to prepare him for this.

Things crawled, just beneath his epidermis. His muscles felt too loose or too tight—never right, never as though they could be trusted to support him. His bones— Oh, his skeleton! This was the one pain he could name; during his childhood on the tundra he had yowled like a drowning kitten through the night, and Syvne had comforted him with cooing solicitations and a salve that burned but also distracted him. *Growing pains*. That was what he felt.

"Your wolf wants out," Evane had told him, over the phone. "It's too soon, but it's the pull of our cub in distress, I think. I'm only just managing to keep my skin myself and I'm...more experienced. Ask your mate to soothe you. It will all be over soon enough, one way or the other. Is everything ready for tomorrow?"

He had answered in the affirmative and they had hung up. It wasn't until he sat there, staring at the blank screen of his mobile phone, that he realised how the pain had subsided from merely hearing his cousin's voice.

Evane's voice. Brought back from the dead; except she never had been dead. He couldn't even begin to imagine what Syvne would have made of it all.

In all likelihood, she would have been as fuming as Ludmila Andreyevna, who turned up at his lodgings in the evening, red blotches on her cheeks and neck. Her usually serene face was contorted into a tragicomic mask.

"The pair of you!" She thumped Yegor in the chest as Aleksey rose from his reclining position. "I can't believe you. An innocent little boy, left to fend for himself against this—this manbeast."

Yegor crumpled. Aleksey went to touch a burning hand to his partner's cowering back. There was nothing he could say to justify either of them. "You found him, then?"

He should have known she would. No one could have shadowed Gudkov as effectively as Mila Andreyevna. Despite her height and width, she was the quietest human being he had ever met. *Wolf-like*. The thought scintillated through him before he could interrupt it.

Ludmila slumped onto a chair. "I had to leave him there. It was the hardest thing I have ever done. I—I'm sorry, Yegor, Aleks. How you can bear it—"

"We can't," Yegor mumbled wetly.

"How was he?" Aleksey felt as though his skin was about to tear from his bones.

Ludmila looked up and blanched. "He's one brave little wolf. Sweet saints, everything you said was true."

"You—you could tell?" Yegor took a step towards her but stopped. A threatening growl had risen from Aleksey.

"Sergei's rumble is sweeter," Ludmila remarked, as an avid protectiveness stole across her features. "Of course I could tell. I'm a massage therapist, aren't I?"

Chapter Forty

Someone was tailing him. They were good—oh, they were more than good—but Oleg Vladimirovich Gudkov had a sixth sense about these things. Perhaps it was a newly awakened volkodlak sense. Perhaps it was starting to manifest in him, at last.

What a triumph it would be to meet the boy's sister in the shape of a wolf. Because he knew she was coming. She was a pertinacious little bitch. His two best men had been unable to track her down and bring her to him, although they had made short work of her milksop dedushka and Oleg's informant, whatever his name had been. Everything was coming together.

Except now, someone was following him. In his own house, into his secret passageways. It should not be possible; no one should have the gall. But the hairs at the back of his neck refused to settle, the creeping sensation up his back made his movements jerky.

It could only be one person.

Olezhka swerved around and glared down the length of the corridor. The strip lights buzzed overhead, and the echo of his own footsteps subsided. There was nowhere to hide.

He gripped his cattle prod tighter.

He had no intention of visiting Seryozha. The truth was his interest in the boy was waning fast. He had interrogated him endlessly on what he did to shift from one state to the other, but Seryozha offered only abstracted, nonsensical answers. Oleg had presumed moonlight would do the trick. That first fabulous change in his moon tower had seemed to corroborate his assumption. But then the boy had shifted in front of Babushka.

Oleg had been so unprepared it had nearly been the end of him. A shock to the system. A heightened emotional state. Oleg Vladimirovich had to figure it out, and soon.

Stealthily, he opened the two sets of doors and slipped into Babushka's boudoir. It gave him a delicious sense of transgression, even after all these years, a sick feeling of anxiety-riddled yearning, twisting through his hollow core.

He wasn't allowed.

He wasn't allowed in here, but here he was.

Olezhka knelt before the glass sarcophagus, putting his face flush against its side.

The corpse of his grandmother kept mum. She always did.

"I wish you could beat me like you used to, Babka. If anyone could coax out the wolf in me, it would be you." He choked on his words, his breath clouding the glass, obscuring her features, or what was left of them.

Olezhka knew she was dead. He wasn't crazy, whatever that blasted therapist had implied. The one who had disappeared. He couldn't remember; something inside him put up a blank wall, a resistance, a clouding over as effective as his breath over the previously clear pane.

He didn't do his own dirty work.

Except—*except when he did.*

The woman in the forest of nowhere, in the Nenets Autonomous Okrug, way back when. All in the name of science. Collateral damage to his quest. Volkodlaks were supposed to be killers, weren't they? A baptism in blood, to crown the god of wolves.

Something stirred in him. A quickening, a new understanding—yes, *yes.* Of course. It hadn't worked all those years ago because he hadn't been bitten. But now—

Now it would.

The conviction came over him like a new religion, a zealous, impassioned species of clarity. His secretary. His *new* secretary, as he still thought of him; that loathsome, snivelling weasel of a man. He was the one. Olezhka had always known, always thought he could not be trusted.

The man would rue the day he took it upon himself— Well, not for long. Oleg Vladimirovich would let him have the final privilege, the honour of being the key to his lock.

*

"Gospodin Gudkov!" He jumped as the door sprang open; his attention had been occupied by the papers in front of him. Ilya Mikhailovich Klimov pushed his reading spectacles up his forehead and rubbed at his eyes.

His employer had an unhinged look about him. He usually did, but Ilya didn't care, didn't mind—loved him the better for it. It wasn't something he could explain. Oleg Gudkov was simply the kind of man who stirred that fanatic devotion in him, of the sort that had landed him in less-than-appealing situations since boyhood. But he was safe here. Gudkov wasn't the ordinary bully.

"Who sent you?"

He stopped what he was doing, his hand coming away from his eyes. "Who—what?"

He shifted in his seat, crossing his legs. He should stand up to show his deference, his respect for the great man, but—he couldn't. It would be too humiliating.

Gudkov moved like a Siberian tiger, eating up the distance from the door to Ilya's desk.

Ilya swallowed audibly. He folded his hands together, bowing his head low. "I don't understand, gospodin. I was going through your recent correspondence concerning your shares in Gazprom. I have not taken the liberty, I assure you, of sending anything off without your prior consent."

"Oh, you've been awaiting my consent, have you, Ilya Mikhailovich?"

His insides quaked. Gudkov had fixed him with those gimlet eyes, and he felt fairly run through. He pinched himself. The great man's cufflinks twinkled in the light from his office lamp, as he extended his arms to grasp Ilya by the shoulders.

"I don't think you have, Ilya Mikhailovich. I think all this subservience of yours is little more than an act. Tell me; come, it will be better for you. You are a government agent, are you not?"

The grip on his shoulders was vice-like. Flummoxed, he blurted out, "You're stronger than you look, Gospodin Gudkov." He clapped his hands over his mouth.

Oleg Gudkov's eyes glimmered dangerously. "You have no idea, little Ilya. But I will show you. I will make an example of you. You have earned it."

"Gospodin, I—" What had he said just now? "—I am no spy. I couldn't be. I am a lowly secretary, but..." He didn't finish his sentence. He could think of no acceptable way of doing so. The mere physical proximity of his—his master, his idol!—made him weak at the knees.

Gudkov hoisted him to his feet. Ilya squirmed and almost reached for the panic button. But what would calling security avail him, when Gudkov himself— Besides, they had the day off. Everyone did. Khudi had come in to tell him, seeming displeased when Ilya had refused to budge.

He didn't care if he wasn't paid to be at the mansion today. There was nowhere else he would rather be.

"You've found nothing to report, I gather?" Gudkov's voice had taken on a conversational tone. He had slung his arm around Ilya's shoulders and pressed him close to his side, leading him out of the office.

Ilya stumbled over the threshold.

"You can't have." Oleg Vladimirovich smiled, a thin, mirthless expression. "Everything you have had access to has been strictly within the confines of the law. Frustrating, isn't it, Ilya Mikhailovich? Did you really think my trust was that easily won? Do you think I would be where I am today if I put my faith in any *bomzh* who turns up at my doorstep waving a handful of worthless state university certificates around?"

"I—" He seemed to float at the tiger's side. Gudkov was accusing him of something. He was a ruthless man; everyone said so; but Ilya Mikhailovich Klimov could not take this in. This was all a misunderstanding. Maybe it was some sort of test.

If it was, he was determined to pass it. He would go wherever Gudkov wanted him to go, do whatever he wanted him to do. Even—yes. No, he was too unworthy. But a man could dream, could he not?

"I wasn't sent out by the government." His voice held only the fleetingest of tremors. "I will do whatever you need me to do to prove it, gospodin. You have my unswerving loyalty." A trickle of perspiration ran down the length of his spine.

Oleg Vladimirovich laughed. It was the most unprecedented of sounds, a piping, boyish peal, as though the laughter, unlike Gudkov himself, had never gone through the voice change of puberty.

The tips of Ilya's ears warmed.

"I almost wish it were so, Ilya Mikhailovich. You are quite pliant, aren't you? Ready to turn your cape with the wind? I should have known. I, on the other hand, am not so flexible. It is a weakness I cannot afford to indulge in. Here, just to our left."

A faintness had come over Ilya Mikhailovich. The oligarch was speaking in riddles, which was as it should be, but Ilya couldn't begin to unpack them, could not wrap his mind around anything but that Oleg Gudkov was leading him into the private part of his sprawling mansion, and there was no one, not a soul... And maybe, just maybe, this had been Gudkov's intention all along, the reason he had dismissed his staff for the day, so that he—so that *they*— He, Ilya Klimov—

"My bedroom is soundproofed," Gudkov offered as he opened the forbidding door and pushed Ilya before him. "No one will hear you scream."

*

He had been lying in wait for her. Well, not for her, but for anyone, everyone: the next person to stroll down the forest path. He was pleased it was a woman, not from any perverse preference but because she was smaller, easier to overpower. A child would have been ideal, but he had been young and inexperienced, tempestuous; he had been too consumed by the possibility that his experiment might work to wait for another prey.

It was something he had read, but it might be an old wives' tale; scientific insights on werewolves were hard to come by.

But Oleg Vladimirovich Gudkov knew they existed. He knew it, because he needed them to; it was his life goal, his life's meaning, the only thing that mattered, the only thing that would prove Babushka wrong.

He had seen one once. Back in the gulag, as a boy: a woman who had vanished around the corner of a building, and in her place, when Olezhka had followed, a vicious-looking, foul-smelling tundra wolf.

If only he had stayed to let her bite him. If only he hadn't been the little good-for-nothing coward Yekaterina Gudkova always called him out as and run away.

His story about the she-wolf at supper had earned him nothing but a thrashing.

Despite this, it had turned into a lifelong obsession, a fixation, which took him deep into the taiga of Nenets Autonomous Okrug, looking for a victim that would bring out his claws. *Behave like a beast and you will become one.* It had sounded like a promise to Olezhka's unschooled ears.

Afterwards, he had left the woman on the forest path to the wolves. He could not remember much about her at all, but her hair had been yellow; he recalled this detail distinctly: such a strange shade of yellow. Like orange juice, like rapeseed blossoms. Like the petals of sunflowers.

If he had not been so thoroughly disappointed by the outcome, or the lack thereof, he would have been tempted to cut off a lock of it as a keepsake. A trophy.

Oleg Vladimirovich sighed. He sighed as he plunged the serrated blade of his hunting knife into the stomach of his secretary and spilled the man's guts over his king-sized bed. He sighed as Ilya's screams turned into a blood-filled gurgle, as he sagged in his arms, the light in his eyes fading much too soon. Just as with the woman.

He wanted to howl. He wanted to break into pelt. He wanted this to work already.

Oleg lifted a section of Ilya Mikhailovich's large intestine from off the soaking sheets and sniffed it. No part of him wanted what he did next, but he had to try. He put the body-temperature piece of offal in his mouth and chewed.

The door slammed open.

Olezhka didn't understand what he was seeing. He looked on it as on a vivid dream: the woman, the yellow-haired woman who had been dead, ripped to pieces, mangled, for well-nigh a decade, stepped into his lair, snowflakes dotting her anorak, and—*oh, Babushka!*—at her side was a silver-grey wolf with eyes as dark as Lucifer's soul.

He stood up, the mess of Ilya Mikhailovich all over his tailored suit. He hadn't shifted. He hadn't even begun to shift. The boy's bite was a dud.

Oleg Vladimirovich took a step towards the black-eyed wolf, and the woman raised an ancient-looking rifle. She pointed it straight at his chest, right where his useless volkodlak wound was, and fired.

Epilogue

Some nights, when she woke up in a sweat, her heart beating furiously, the worn sheets clinging to her skin, Pyotra Nikolayevna Kulakova could have sworn she smelled the fire. The smoke seemed to push into her lungs, replacing much-needed oxygen, even though they had all been well out of that house of horrors when Yegor Mizulin had lit the fuse.

Such a disparate assortment of characters, they had been: a massage therapist, a hired gun turned werewolf, herself, and Volk in lupine form. And—and Sergei, her beloved duck, who had caught one whiff of Volk and promptly shifted. Although Pyotra had watched it happen to her lover countless times since that first, memorable shift out on the tundra, she still cried out; she still would have fallen to the floor in a faint if Ludmila Andreyevna hadn't caught her. Volk had growled, torn between her mate and her cub.

Because he was her cub. With a big, wolfish grin, Sergei had jumped at Volk, yipping happily, toppling her to the floor and nipping at her ears. Volk had huffed and caught him by the gullet.

Pyotra had gone to her knees then and run trembling fingers through thick, baby-soft fur, as the big blue eyes of her brother turned to her, finally, from out of the face of a wolf.

Not twenty minutes before, she had shot a man. She had shot and killed; it didn't matter that this man, this deranged individual, had been in the act of committing a bloody piece of butchery himself, that he'd spirited Sergei away from her, that he had caused unspeakable pain to an untold number of people—it still woke her up at night.

At the wolf hour.

She would rise and go over to the kitchen sink and wash her face and torso with a damp cloth, counting Boris Ilyich's snores.

If she saw a light on, which was more often than not, she would brave the dark and cold and cross the few hundred metres over to the outhouse converted into temporary living quarters, where Yegor Stepanovich would, unfailingly, open his door to her, his samovar ready with enough chay to see them through the remaining hours of the night.

They had spoken, in the beginning. Yegor had shown her Ludmila's letters, tentative at first, then more and more confident in her unanticipated happiness: her dacha, her cats, her poetry. She never failed to inquire after Sergei, which warmed Pyotra and made her ready to weep.

Later, Yegor showed her other letters, from women back in Arkhangelsk, whom he had done things to in Gudkov's name. Pyotra could never grasp what it was he had done, exactly; but he had needed to tell them, he said, even if it was risky.

The investigation into the spectacular case of arson at the oligarch's mansion had been farcical. Not one of the staff came forward to say that there had been anything out of the ordinary about them all being told to take the day off.

The authorities were none too keen to keep the inquiries going. The government was the main benefactor from Oleg Vladimirovich Gudkov's untimely demise.

What had surprised Pyotra and Yegor was the finding of a third set of remains among the ashes, not belonging to either Gudkov or Klimov. They had deferred speculating over it, chay in hand. They had looked at each other, and that had been all that was necessary: they would know with the coming of spring.

When their wolves returned. When Pyotra would have managed to persuade Ded to pick up on Mashka's offer to move in with her, after her nephew had unexpectedly gone off and settled himself in Crimea.

When they would both be claimed.

*

Yegor had seen Alyosha shift into a wolf before his very eyes. Up until that point, he realised, there had still been a holding back in him, a measure of subconscious disbelief. In theory, he had accepted that Alyosha's strange cousin Evane and Pyotra's even stranger Volk were one and the same, but his mind had balked, to the very last, despite all the signs, despite Aleksey's apparent infirmity, at the idea of—this.

The brutal transformation had nearly torn Yegor's heart from his body. To stand there and watch, powerless of offering any relief, any succour. On the contrary, if the other wolves had not been present—the wolves he was told were Evane and Sergei—Yegor wasn't confident Alyosha wouldn't have upped and attacked him.

He almost wished he had. Instead, the sinewy russet wolf had pointed his ears backwards and barked at Yegor, telling him in no uncertain terms to stay back. Then he had obeyed the siren call of the others—his pack mates—who were already at the edge of the taiga, raring to go.

And off they went, the trio of oboroten', two of them young and eager and quickly forgetful of their humanity and the third...

The third had looked back at the two of them, Yegor and Pyotra, that eerie but steadfast gaze skimming over him and latching onto Pyotra. She had lifted up her paw, and Pyotra had reached out her hand towards her.

The wolf threw back her head and howled.

Names and Terms

Names and Diminutives

Pyotra Nikolayevna Kulakova—Pyotrushka

Sergei Nikolayevich Kulakov—Duck, Seryozha

Boris Ilyich Kulakov—Ded, Dedushka

Serafima Anatoliyevna Kulakova—Sima

Nikolay Borisovich Kulakov—Kolya

Mariya Petrovna Leonova—Mashka

Dmitri Fyodorovich Leonov—Dima

Tatyana Ivanovna—Tatya

Evane Khudi—Volk

Galina—Galya

Oleg Vladimirovich Gudkov—Olezhka

Ludmila Andreyevna—Mila

Yegor Stepanovich Mizulin—Gosha

Ilya Mikhailovich Klimov

Aleksey Khudi—Alyosha, Aleks

Yekaterina Gudkova—Babushka, Babka

Syvne Khudi

Glossary

BABA YAGA—a witch-like, supernatural being in Russian fairy tales

BABKA—old wife, old woman, grandmother

BABUSHKA—grandmother

BARANKA—bagel-shaped bread

BOMZH—(lit.) bum, homeless person; a common slur

BYLINA—a traditional East Slavic epic poem

CHAY—tea

DACHA—a seasonal home or cottage

DED, DEDUSHKA—grandfather, granddad

FORTOCHKA—a small ventilation window, uniquely Russian

GOSPODIN—Mister, Sir

GULAG—Soviet forced-labour camp

GUSLI—an East Slavic multi-string plucked instrument

НА ЗДОРОВЬЕ—To health (toast); here, the name of a bar

IOSEB—Stalin Joseph Stalin

IZBA—cabin, log housesamovar a metal container traditionally used to boil water for tea

KALASHNIKOV, KALASH, AK-47—automatic rifle

KAMOV KA-226—a small, twin-engine Russian utility helicopter

KOFE—coffee

KOPEK—1/100 of a Russian rouble

LESBIYANKI—lesbians

LYUBOV—love

МАГАЗИН, MAGAZIN—shop

MAT' LUNA—Mother Moon

MATRYOSHKA—(lit.) little matron; typically the Russian stacking dolls (also known as babushka dolls)

OBOROTEN'—turnskin, shape-shifter, werewolf

PREKRASNYY—beautiful

RUSSKIJ STANDART—Russian Standard, a vodka brand

SESTRA—sister

SMETANA—a type of sour cream

SONYA—sleepyhead

SPASIBA—thank you

STOLICHNAYA—a vodka brand

TETYA—aunt

VENIK—bath broom

VOLCHONOK—little wolf, wolf cub, wolfling

VOLK, ВОЛК—wolf

VOLKODLAK—a wizard taking wolf shape, or a regular man turned into a wolf by wizardry

YA TEBYA KHOCHU—I want you

Acknowledgements

I owe a big thank you to my editor for her patience, zest, and unrelenting support—and for never being flummoxed when I skip between genres at the drop of an ushanka.

The idea for this twisted tale sprang, in part, from Sergei Prokofiev's 1936 symphonic fairy story *Peter and the Wolf.*

No cats or budgerigars were harmed in the making of this book.

About Elna Holst

Often quirky, always queer, Elna Holst is an unapologetic genre-bender who writes anything from stories of sapphic lust and love to the odd existentialist horror piece, reads Tolstoy, and plays contract bridge. Find her on Instagram or Goodreads.

Email
elna.holst@egj.name

Website
www.elnaholst.com

Instagram
@elnaholstwrites

Other NineStar books by this author

Lucas
In the Palm

Tinsel and Spruce Needle Romances
Candlelight Kisses
Little x
Wild Bells
And Then They Were Four

Also from NineStar Press

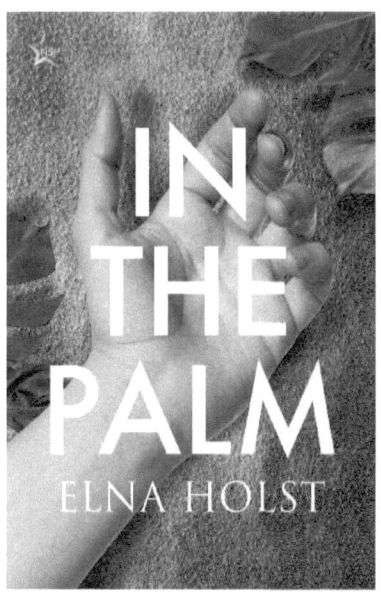

In the Palm by Elna Holst

Stranded on a tropical island, Dr No-Name has no mobile phone, no wallet, no keys, no passport. No left hand, no shoes and no memory. What she does have is a blister pack of nicotine gums, two minibar-sized bottles of whisky (consumed), and what appears to be an endless supply of coconuts. She can't possibly get into any worse trouble, can she?

Lucas by Elna Holst

I thought ease would come, here, tucked away in the safe uneventfulness of Hunsford. It would seem I was mistaken.

In 1813, upon her marriage to Mr Collins, the rector of Hunsford Parsonage, Charlotte Collins *née* Lucas left her childhood home in Hertfordshire for Kent, where she is set to live out her life as the parson's wife, in an endless procession of dinners at Rosings Park, household chores, correspondence, and minding her poultry. But Mrs Collins carries with her a secret, a peculiar preference, which is destined to turn all her carefully laid plans on their head.

Lucas is a queer romance, a mock-epistolary novel, and a retelling and continuation of Jane Austen's *Pride and Prejudice*, teeming with Regency references and Sturm und Drang. It is an homage to English literature—and a brazen, revisionist fan fiction. But, first and foremost, it is a love story. Read it as you will.

Liquid Courage by Stephanie Shea

Alexandria Van Kirk has always been a slave to her romantic nature. When a night of liquid courage lands her in bed with one of her best friends, Alex is confronted by a host of feelings that terrify her. Feelings about her friend and, unexpectedly, a barista from her favorite café.

It's a tug of war between heart and body. Desire against all her daydreams of someone to share silence, sunsets, and coffee with.

But Alex's past is also about to catch up with her. Tortured memories and the girl they're all about. It's like fighting the pull of a whirlwind. A surefire losing battle. But embracing a newfound romance amid the return of an old flame is a precarious balance, one not even Alex herself is sure she can manage.

How the hell does she choose between the girl she loves and the one she could never confess loving to begin with?

Connect with NineStar Press

www.ninestarpress.com

www.facebook.com/ninestarpress

www.facebook.com/groups/NineStarNiche

www.twitter.com/ninestarpress

www.instagram.com/ninestarpress